KNOWING ELLIE

Nick Gilbrook

1

For Edward and Cynthia Nelson married life had two distinct phases: with Ellie, and without Ellie. Phase One had abruptly come to an end on 25th May, 1985, when Ellie, their only child, went out for the evening and never came home again. The problem was nobody knew where she had been going that night. She was twenty-three years old and living with her parents, but having already been away to university, and now being in that awkward post-graduation stage with no job and no money, she was obliged to live at home for the time being. However, desperate to hold on to the independence she had gained, it was not unusual for her not to share her plans with her parents. So Phase Two began for Edward and Cynthia that night. Anxiety had given way to fear as her absence became more prolonged, and despite the best efforts of the police, no leads were ever established to offer any explanation for her failure to return, nor even where she had gone.

Life effectively ended for Edward and Cynthia that night. Ellie had been their life; Ellie was gone; life was over. They had continued to breathe in and out, to put food in their mouths, and muddle on from day to day, but once hope had faded that Ellie would ever again walk through the door, banging it behind her with her customary unnecessary vigour and pounding up the stairs with a force incompatible with her size, it became nigh on impossible to derive any pleasure from any of this new life's activities.

In many ways Edward had seemed harder hit. He was a man of almost autistic insularity, with few friends and few words, for whom Ellie had been everything. Although Cynthia was more outgoing and sociable, with a circle of friends with whom she could share her grief and from whom she could draw some comfort, it would be a misinterpretation to read her apparent resilience as evidence that her grief and sense of loss were any less raw than Edward's.

In the more than thirty years since that awful time, the dreadful burden both parents bore had taken a toll on their health. Now, unable really to look after herself, and knowing that Edward was ill-equipped to care for her - or indeed for himself given his failing eyesight - Cynthia, at eighty, had decided they would both be better off in a care home. In order to facilitate this move, the Nelsons had put their house, in a leafy street in South London, on the market, and had been surprised when the first couple to view it had offered the asking price. Suddenly, what had been an abstract if genuine desire to sell, had become a scary reality, and Cynthia knew she would have to make a decision very quickly on which of the care homes she had checked out was to be their new residence.

Having settled on Meadow View, being quite close and reasonably fragrant when visited - although no meadow was apparent from any window Cynthia had looked through - and having fixed a date for the move, Edward and Cynthia had to set about sorting out their possessions and furniture; getting rid, by sale or gift, of the bulk of what they owned. This of course meant they had had to tackle Ellie's bedroom, which till then had effectively remained as left in May, 1985. How could they have done anything else? To have even crossed the threshold would seem a betrayal, let alone to have disturbed anything; although of course the police had done so in their quest for clues.

A friend of Cynthia's had got her son to make an inventory of saleable items and advertise them online. He had then enlisted the help of his two sons to move all sizeable pieces into the Nelsons' front room, from where prospective purchasers could view and remove them. Then it was just a matter of waiting for bites.

Within a couple of days, they had shifted several pieces

of furniture, and gradually the front room had started to become as bare as the rest of the house. Today, however, was different. Cynthia had held back from allowing any items from Ellie's room to be advertised, but eventually she had relented and, once emptied, Ellie's wardrobe, bed and chest of drawers were added to the sale. One piece of furniture in Ellie's room had seemed more sacrosanct than the others though. It was an escritoire that, unlike the rest of her furniture, was her own purchase. She had found it herself and taken it with her to university. All her subsequent essays and assignments had been written on its desk. It seemed, for Cynthia, to retain something of Ellie. Finally, realising there was no way they could take it with them, Cynthia had allowed the escritoire to be advertised, and the previous night they had had a call from a woman who felt, from its description, that it was just what she had been looking for.

When the doorbell rang, Cynthia felt a momentary panic and looked across at Edward, reading his paper through a magnifying glass at the small kitchen table, one of the only remaining pieces of furniture. Cynthia was frustrated he could no longer catch her eye and take his cue, but when she spoke his name, he raised himself slowly and shuffled off into the hall. He opened the front door to a middle-aged woman, similar in age in fact to what Ellie would now have been, who stood smiling outside.

'Mr Nelson?'

'Yes.'

'Excellent. I'm Rosemary. Rosemary Hart.'

When they seemed not to be making further progress, after a pause, Rosemary continued.

'I spoke to your wife last night. About the escritoire?'

'Oh, yes?'

Edward stood peering at the woman. Cynthia, who had managed to get herself to her feet and, with the aid of a Zimmer frame, to the door, took control.

'Let her in then, Ted. Don't leave the poor woman out there.'

Edward opened the door wider, while Cynthia allowed Rosemary space to enter.

'Come through, my dear. ' Cynthia indicated the front room and Rosemary made her way into it.

'Thank you, Mrs Nelson.'

As soon as she entered the front room, Rosemary knew she had found what she was looking for.

'Yes! That's it. How wonderful.' She actually clapped her hands together with glee.

'You've seen one of these before?' Cynthia asked.

'Oh, yes. I had one. I believe there were only a few made. A company in Romania. Mine got destroyed in a fire.'

'Oh dear. I hope no-one was hurt.' Cynthia put her hand on Rosemary's arm in sympathy.

Rosemary reassured her. 'Oh no. Just furniture - and everything else I owned at the time. My first flat. Dodgy landlord and dodgy electrics. But I was at work. Fortunately.' She shuddered at what might have been. 'I've been trying to find a replacement one of these ever since. I loved it so much. So, as you can imagine, this is a happy, happy day. Oh, perhaps I shouldn't be too keen. You might put the price up.' She laughed nervously.

'Not at all.' Cynthia didn't want to see it go, but she wasn't going to play that game.

Pulling down the desk, Rosemary started opening drawers and generally inspecting the escritoire. 'It's in excellent condition.'

Cynthia said, 'It's not been used for a long time', and left it at that.

'They were so well made. But still affordable for me at the time. I love this bit...' Rosemary put her hand around the back of the escritoire, and as she did so Cynthia saw a slim drawer pop out where no drawer appeared to be beforehand.

'Goodness me.' Cynthia was taken by surprise. 'Did you see that, Ted? A secret drawer.'

Edward shuffled closer to try to see.

'There's a button at the back,' Rosemary explained. 'Not at all obvious either. Just looks like part of the structure. Press it, and out pops this drawer. It's spring-loaded'.

'Well I never', Cynthia exclaimed. She moved closer and peered into the drawer, then suddenly let out a little yelp. There was something in the drawer. A book. It had a flowery cover and a little brass effect lock on it. A diary.

Edward was alarmed. 'What is it, dear?'

Cynthia's voice shook, 'It looks like a diary, Ted.'

'A diary?' Edward, too, was now struck by the significance of the discovery.

They both knew that the police had gone through everything that was in this desk, and found no clues to Ellie's disappearance. But had they found this? Given that it was in a secret drawer in an unfamiliar, limited production piece, probably not, they suspected.

Cynthia found that her hand was shaking as she reached to pick up the diary. The little lock appeared not to work and she was able to open the book and flick through it. Rosemary and Edward looked on, Rosemary awkwardly and Edward transfixed, as Cynthia read to herself from the pages. Tears started to roll down her face hearing her long-lost daughter's private thoughts. She felt compelled to read, but nevertheless guilty that she was doing so. Suddenly struck by a thought, Cynthia started flicking forward through the pages until the curly letters no longer filled them. She started reading the final entry, until suddenly, with a sharp intake of breath, she lost her power to stand, and as she buckled, Rosemary, and to a lesser extent Edward, had to support her weight and get her over to one of the remaining chairs to sit her down.

'Are you okay?' Rosemary asked once she was settled.

'I think so. It's just... I think we will know now.'

Rosemary didn't understand what she meant by this. Already feeling she was intruding on the private matters of strangers, she looked to Edward. He had taken the diary from Cynthia's hand, and, through the magnifying glass that he kept on a cord round his neck, was now staring at the last entry. When he then raised his head and turned towards Cynthia, she might have thought he'd seen a ghost. He just stared at her for what seemed an eternity, his eyes flickering as though reviewing vast screeds of information.

Cynthia broke the silence. 'Who's Marcus?'

2

Stepping from the tube station, Kai Holding looked up and down the busy street. He was a young man in an unfamiliar part of South London, and, as was the norm for him, he was wary being in new surroundings. Kai had a white mum and a black dad, and had become used to the fact that, when it came to how people perceived him, his dad's contribution to his skin tone seemed to take precedence over his mum's. Noting that the area appeared to have a cosmopolitan demographic, like most of London, he relaxed, satisfied he didn't stick out from the crowd.

Pulling his mobile from his pocket, he checked it for his given destination. He had no idea where it was and was well aware he could find out easily enough with the phone, but he was running late - getting away from work was a real problem sometimes - and he felt confident and flush enough to jump into the nearest taxi and let its driver do the work. Anyway, it was a warm July evening and he had no wish to arrive hot and sweaty from pounding the streets.

As he got into the back of the first cab on the rank, a private minicab, and caught sight of the driver's eyes in the rear-view mirror, his instinct was to jump straight out again. The only reason he didn't was because he was transfixed by the menace in the dark eyes that perused him, and froze as though confronted by a wild animal he didn't wish to anger. The driver's voice was no less chilling as it boomed with deep, fruity resonance, "Whither?" At first still frozen, when Kai saw a dark eyebrow rise above one of the dark eyes, and realised he'd been issued a question not an instruction, though not entirely convinced he was providing the required information, he supplied the address he'd been given.

'The Sack of Balls', he said dubiously, unsure if a terrible trick was being played on him.

'Ah, the Sack of Balls?', roared the driver. 'A fine hostelry, with handsome wenches aplenty. Good choice. I will convey you post-haste, if you can assure me you are furnished with adequate funds.'

This driver seemed unusual, Kai was thinking. Not your standard London cabbie. He assured him he had enough money, though he wondered if all passengers received this enquiry, and sat back hoping he would arrive at his destination in one piece. Looking out of the window, he familiarised himself with the lie of the land, before realising the scenery was not moving, as indeed the car was not. He looked back towards the driver, and was startled to find both fearsome eyes now directly on him, the predator having turned his head the better to scrutinize his prey. This inevitably increased Kai's alarm. The face was grizzled with thick greying stubble, puffy eyes and a sallow complexion, and the large head made much larger by a riot of tangled curls which had almost completely failed to resist the greying process.

'Is something wrong?', Kai dared to ask.

'Indeed not. Just checking you're safely buckled in. It's a jungle out there.'

For a moment Kai thought, here we go, the racist onslaught begins, but when nothing further followed, and the driver started the car and moved off, he hoped he had misinterpreted.

As they drove, the image of the driver's face, burned as it was on Kai's brain, underwent the processing that brain's give new information.

'Don't I know you?' Kai found himself involuntarily blurting out.

'Know me?' bellowed the reply. 'Isn't that my job?' Then in a cockney accent, so different from his own, 'Do you know who I've had in the back of my cab...?'

'Yes. I suppose so.' Kai attempted a laugh, which came out

more of a squeak. Drops of perspiration oozed from his forehead.

'How old are you?' the driver then barked.

'Twenty-five.'

'Twenty-five? Oh, I doubt it very much. One so recently off the dug is most unlikely to have had the pleasure of an acquaintance with this monstrous mush. Not that it was always thus. Time was when knickers slid down unaided under the weight of expectation when I merely raised an eyebrow.'

Kai thought, I'll take your word for that, but still he couldn't shake the feeling that, at some time in his life, this face had featured.

'Have you always driven taxis?' he found himself asking, unsure of the wisdom of engaging this dinosaur in further conversation.

'Ah. Indeed not. Life has a way of dealing bitter blows that bruise the soul and deplete the bank balance. Like Sir Andrew, I was adored once. Not just for my beauty, but also for a modicum of talent.'

'Were you an actor?'

'How painful that past tense is. Such pathos in failure. Indeed, I once bestrode the theatrical world like a colossus. Well, perhaps in that there is a little hyperbole, but to many lost souls I provided some distraction from their daily drudgery by presenting them with a finely-honed and meticulously researched facsimile, on one of the nation's most-viewed televisual outlets, of one of those undervalued yet invaluable healthcare professionals, the dispensing chemist. More often styled latterly, a pharmacist."

Kai considered this information. '*Primary Care*. Of course.' He was delighted he had the man pinned down, despite what the intervening years had inflicted on his features. 'You were... What were you called?'

'Matthew Hope. Alas, I am now without Hope, in all conceivable ways.'

'That's it. My Mum used to watch that. All set in a health

centre, wasn't it? You got off with that nurse, didn't you?'

'Also in all conceivable ways. On screen and in cold reality. Extremely cold, it transpired.'

'I'm sorry to hear that.'

'As was I to experience it. Still, out of that frozen swamp of a woman was born a creature of divine beauty, whom I have ever after delighted to hear call me Daddy. In many ways my raison d'être.'

'That's good.' Kai didn't know where to go from here, although he felt chuffed that he had met a celebrity, albeit one who'd fallen from the firmament. He was also pleased he was now able to contextualise the strange delivery and vocabulary, which in turn eased his concerns for his safety. Actors. They're all barking aren't they, but usually harmless.

He was trying to dredge up further childhood memories of the primetime *Primary Care*, when his chauffeur announced, 'The estimable Sack of Balls, sir. Please alight, but not before unloading the spondoolies.'

Kai looked out at the pub. Its sign had a picture of a large netting sack filled with many black and white footballs. 'Ah, great. What's the damage?'

'Shall we call it a fiver for cash.'

'Do you take cards?'

'Alas, no.'

'A fiver it is then.' Kai fished one from his wallet and handed it over. The driver looked at it suspiciously, then held it up to the windscreen. Someone had written the number 63 on it, but otherwise it seemed to be okay. He put it into his wallet. Opening the car door, Kai stepped on to the pavement.

The driver lowered his window and bellowed, 'Enjoy those wenches! That's what you've come here for, I take it?'

'Well, sort of. A date.'

'First?'

'Yeah.'

'Ah. Found on your phone, no doubt?'

'Yeah.' Kai looked at his reflection in the car window to check he was presentable, and was about to enter the pub, when he turned to his theatrical driver, who was still eyeing him quizzically. 'By the way, what are you really called? It won't come to me.'

The once household name swallowed his hurt pride, and announced with what self-respect he could muster, 'Marcus Thorn, sir. Marcus Thorn.'

3

After their dramatic discovery, Edward and Cynthia Nelson asked Rosemary Hart if she would be kind enough to leave the escritoire with them for now, in case the police wanted to inspect it further, and assured her that, as soon as they had finished with it, she could come back and complete her purchase. Rosemary was a little alarmed that this find should necessitate the involvement of the police, but she realised this was a personal and clearly significant matter, and graciously retreated.

As soon as she had closed the door to the departing Rosemary, Cynthia was all for phoning the police at once, but Edward quickly intervened. He had to read the whole diary first. It was Ellie's private thoughts, and, if strangers were going to have to pore over it, it was only right her parents did so first.

'I suppose so. Yes.' Cynthia could see Edward's point. 'Let's go back into the kitchen then. I'll put the kettle on and we can go through it together. What's the matter?'

Edward was gripping the diary to his chest, and tears were now running down his cheeks.

'Oh, Ted. I know. I know.' She transferred her weight from her Zimmer to his shoulders, then gave her husband a tight hug, their daughter's words between them.

It wasn't until a couple of hours later that Cynthia picked up the phone and dialled 999. There was a time when they had the number to take them directly to the investigating officer's desk, but that was long ago, and Cynthia assumed it would no longer work, even if she could find it. When she had been put through to the police call handler and had answered all the questions asked of her, Cynthia was told someone would be back in touch with her later, and to wait to hear from them.

'Wait to hear? Ha!' she said as she put down the phone. 'We know all about waiting, don't we?'

Edward was still sitting flicking through the pages of the diary. 'We do,' he said almost under his breath. 'Why did she tell us nothing about this Marcus? She seems to have been besotted with him.'

'Doesn't she. I wonder who he was. Where she met him. She doesn't go into much detail considering how highly she seems to regard him. Where does it say she's going to meet him?'

Edward shuddered, 'The bog. Sounds awful.'

Cynthia agreed. 'Let's hope the police can make some sense of it.'

It was after 3pm when the doorbell rang, and Edward answered the door to two police officers in plain clothes; a middle-aged man and a woman in her early thirties. The woman spoke first.

'Mr Nelson? I'm Sergeant Stephanie Moore, and this is Inspector Richard Hutchinson. May we come in?'

Sergeant Moore was holding out her warrant card. Edward lifted his magnifying glass and peered at it, then raised the lens to her face. Satisfied with her bona fides, he stepped back and let them in.

'Please do.'

Cynthia now arrived with her Zimmer in time to direct the two officers into the front room, to see the source of the new evidence. 'Thank you for coming. The escritoire is in here.'

Now Inspector Hutchinson spoke. 'Mrs Nelson. Hello. Richard Hutchinson. Remember me? An Inspector now, but a Constable in 1985.'

Cynthia stared at this grey-haired, well-built policeman, and tried to picture him so much younger.

'I was the one who always made the tea,' he offered.

'That's right. Tall beanpole, weren't you?'

'Tall barrel now.'

'What a coincidence you got this case again,' Edward said, his surprise obvious.

'Not really,' the Inspector admitted. 'Your daughter's disappearance was the first intriguing case I was part of - if you'll forgive me putting it like that. I've always hoped to uncover what happened to her and put your minds at rest. So, as I'm now running Missing Persons in this area, when your call was brought to my attention, I made sure I assigned myself to your case again.'

'I see.'

'I'm nearing retirement, and to put this one to bed would close the circle, so to speak.'

Edward wasn't entirely sure what closing the circle meant and contented himself with closing the door, an act he understood and successfully accomplished, with a clunk.

The Inspector was now looking at the escritoire and shaking his head, the secret drawer sticking out like a mocking tongue. 'How did we miss that? Unbelievable. I am so sorry. We let you down badly there.'

'Not at all,' Cynthia soothed. 'It's impossible to see when it's closed. Look.' She pushed it in till it clicked.

'I see what you mean.'

They all spent the next five or ten minutes trying to find the button to open it again, which they eventually managed, after which any desire not to forgive anyone else, or themselves, had been thoroughly banished.

'Okay then. So that's the hiding place,' carried on Inspector Hutchinson, 'but where is the diary itself?'

'In the kitchen, sir,' Cynthia informed him. 'Shall we go through? *I'll* make *you* both a cup of tea this time.'

'That would be most welcome, Mrs Nelson', said the Inspector.

Cynthia had lifted her Zimmer to step forward, when she lowered it again and craned her neck to look up at the towering policeman. 'Oh, by the way, would you both mind grabbing a chair from in here and bringing them with you? We're down to these few now and there are only two in the kitchen. We're selling up, you see.'

'So I understand. That's no problem at all. Steph?' Hutchinson indicated for the Sergeant to choose first, then picked one up himself, and the whole convoy set off towards the kitchen, via the hall, at the glacial pace set by Cynthia in the vanguard. Along the way, Inspector Hutchinson felt obliged to keep up the conversation. 'What a shock this must all be for both of you? Out of the blue like that.'

'Well yes,' Cynthia agreed, 'but I really hope it gives you what you need to finally get to the bottom of it all. It's been too long. It really has.' She had to stop for a breather. Speaking and walking was asking too much of herself.

Inspector Hutchinson was paying enough attention to avoid bringing down his size eleven on Cynthia's slippered heel, and brought it gently down beside its counterpart instead. 'I know, Mrs Nelson. Believe me, I will not rest till every last clue in that diary has been thoroughly explored. We just had nothing to go on last time. We have all the CCTV and phone records and the like to help us now. Back then things were very different. We relied on witnesses, and, as you know, none came forward. Despite an extensive media campaign.'

Edward, bringing up the rear, begged to differ. 'Extensive? Is that how you remember it?'

'Pretty extensive, I'd say. You know, TV, radio, posters.'

'Didn't seem to last long though.'

'Well we were very much in the hands of the media there. There were no details. No clues, remember. Nothing to fire the imagination and sell papers. Had someone come forward saying they'd seen someone hanging around the house, or, of course, if we had found her diary then, things would have been very different.'

The convoy rolled into the kitchen and the two police officers positioned their chairs around the small kitchen table, on which the precious diary lay. Cynthia parked her walking frame by the end of the kitchen units and used the work surface to support her progress to the kettle and the sink, where she set about making a large pot of tea.

Edward settled himself in his usual seat and laid a hand reverentially on the floral cover of the diary, after which, first Inspector Hutchinson, then Sergeant Moore, felt able to sit too. Edward then gently picked up the diary.

'Please be very careful with this. Having only just found it, the last thing I want is to part with it, but I realise I must.'

Inspector Hutchinson held out a hand and Edward reluctantly placed the diary in it. 'Of course we'll look after it, Mr Nelson. You have my word.' Then carefully opening the book, as one might an ancient manuscript, the Inspector started to read, while Cynthia went about her preparations and the kettle started to make itself heard.

Sergeant Moore leant a little towards her senior officer and did her best to read what she could, and Edward watched them both, trying to gauge the impact his daughter's words were having on them. This tableau maintained itself till the kettle had boiled, the teapot had been filled, and until Cynthia announced, 'Would one of you mind carrying this tray over to the table?'

Sergeant Moore jumped up and hurried over to take the tray. As she did so, Cynthia placed a packet of biscuits on it. 'Hope you'll excuse the lack of ceremony,' she said, and conveyed herself, with a little support from Edward's shoulders, to her seat, where she set about the duties of the hostess.

When everyone had a steaming cup in front of them, Inspector Hutchinson held the diary clear of any risk of spillages, and started to gently seek clarification on some of the things he was reading. 'So. This Marcus. Neither of you were aware of him?'

Both parents shook their heads.

'Never heard of him,' Cynthia assured the Inspector.

'And you have no idea what bog she may have been referring to?'

The Nelsons looked uncomfortable. They really hoped this was not as it sounded. They shook their heads and turned their attention to their tea.

Inspector Hutchinson steeled himself, then continued, 'And

your daughter, Ellie, can you remind me? Was she in the habit of going off to meet men?'

Edward immediately bristled. 'What are you suggesting?'

'Nothing, I assure you, Mr Nelson. It's just that we will go through this diary extremely thoroughly, and it would help us read between the lines if we had a fuller understanding of your daughter's character and motivations. That's all.'

'My daughter was a bright, sweet girl with a great future ahead of her, until...' Edward knew he was losing control of his emotions and shut up.

Cynthia took over. 'She was very independent. She didn't always tell us everything. Well, having read this diary, I realise she told us very little of what she was really thinking. I'm sure there were boys. She'd been away at university. Who knows what she got up to? Not really our business, was it?'

Sergeant Moore looked towards the Inspector to judge whether she might contribute, then asked, 'What did Ellie study at University, Mrs Nelson?'

'That's all in the file, Stephanie,' the Inspector interjected.

'Yes, but...'

'English and Drama, dear. Probably why she hadn't found a job.'

Sergeant Moore glanced at Hutchinson and continued, 'And do you think this Marcus could be a boy from her university?'

'Possibly. But she did tell us quite a lot about her time at university. You know, in the holidays and once she'd finished, and that name never came up. I'd have remembered. I once knew a Marcus myself.' Despite herself, she blushed.

Edward, who'd been chewing on a biscuit and staring into his tea while he regained his composure, was suddenly re-engaged. He looked towards his wife; an eyebrow involuntarily raised.

'When I was a child,' Cynthia quickly added.

Inspector Hutchinson had been flicking back through the pages. 'I think this is the first mention of this Marcus. She says "Went to the Bullpit again last night. Marcus was magnificent. Got to meet that man." Mean anything?'

'No. We were wondering ourselves. Weren't we, Ted?'

'Yes, we were. I've been mulling that over all day,' Edward admitted. 'Identify whatever the Bullpit is and I reckon you'll have your man.'

'I shall do that very thing,' Inspector Hutchinson assured Edward. 'In fact, I have taken enough of your time and hospitality already, and the sooner I get this diary back to the station and set about deciphering it, the better.' He pushed back his chair and stood. Sergeant Moore followed suit. 'You two stay where you are. We'll see ourselves out. And put these chairs back.'

'Oh, okay,' Cynthia said. 'If you don't mind?'

The two police officers took their chairs back through to the front room. Inspector Hutchinson took another look at the escritoire. Then he came out into the hall and poked his head into the kitchen again. Two faces were looking at him. 'I need to get that desk thoroughly examined, but rather than sending someone over to get under your feet, I was thinking I could get it collected, if that's okay? Just in case there are any other drawers. Don't want to repeat the mistakes of the past, do we?'

'No,' Edward said, perhaps a little firmly.

'No,' Inspector Hutchinson agreed.

'Yes, that's fine,' Cynthia assured him. 'Any time.'

'Thank you, Mrs Nelson. Well goodbye. We'll be in touch soon'. He smiled, nodded reassuringly and retreated to join his Sergeant in the hall.

Hearing the front door shut, Edward and Cynthia looked at each other. Cynthia put her hands over her husband's, gripped together in front of him on the table.

'It's alright, Ted. It's nearly over now. I feel sure.'

Edward looked down. 'Yes. Maybe. Maybe.' He was struggling with something. After a pause he looked up again and, searching his wife's eyes, said, 'She was a good girl? Wasn't she, Cynth?'

4

Kai Holding leaned on the door of the Sack of Balls and pushed it open, then peered into the murky interior. As a rule, he didn't lack confidence, but he sensed many eyes swivel in his direction and felt his self-possession dissipating. He knew among the eyes fixed on him would be those of his date, so he affected an air of charm and sang-froid he was not feeling and searched among the faces for the one that had so memorably popped up on his dating app. When at last he saw it, and the gorgeous dark eyes met his, he produced his most winning grin and bounded over to her.

'Imogen.'

'Kai.'

She was sitting on a stool at the bar, and looking over her shoulder at him in a delightfully coquettish manner, her long dark hair cascading down her back.

'Yes. Hello. Lovely to meet you at last. What are you drink...? Oh, a pint?'

'I'm thirsty. Want one?'

Kai smiled and tapped a finger on a lager pump. 'A pint of this would be most acceptable, thank you.'

Imogen seemed to have the full attention of the landlord, a tall, heavily-built, middle-aged man with a shiny, hairless head and ruddy cheeks, who immediately started to pour a pint of the chosen lubricant as soon as she turned and smiled at him.

'You have them well-trained, I see.' Kai beamed, then caught the landlord's unsmiling eyes on him, and felt his smile tighten.

'Colin is looking out for me. Making sure I'm not meeting a weirdo,' Imogen explained. 'Are you a weirdo?'

'Absolutely not.' Kai picked up the pint Colin placed in front of him. 'Thank you. Cheers.' He took a sip. 'So...' He could feel Colin's eyes burning into him, studying his every move. He looked round, then back at Imogen. 'Shall we move over there?'

'Not comfortable here?'

'Well...'

'Colin? I am going to move over there with this possible weirdo. Keep an eye on us, would you?

'Sure, Immy.'

Imogen slid off her stool, which brought her close to Kai. He grinned again. She lowered her eyes and turned away from him and set off towards the empty table by the far wall. Kai watched her go. Was that her natural walk? Wow. He glanced at Colin, who pointed two fingers at his own eyes, then jabbed them in Kai's direction. He repeated the move to make sure the message had been received. It had. Kai sloped off after his date.

Imogen sat down facing the bar on a banquette. Kai considered sitting beside her, but decided not to be too forward and sat down across the table from her with his back to Colin. He could still feel his eyes though, but it was preferable to seeing them.

'Do you come here often?' Kai asked.

Imogen raised an eyebrow. Kai realised the line, but he'd asked it genuinely, given the evident relationship she had with the landlord.

'A girl needs to be careful. It's a big, bad world. So yes. I do.'

'Your local?'

'Sort of.'

Kai knew already he really liked this girl. This made him lose some of his self-assurance. He smiled rather more shyly and found himself looking down at his drink.

'Something wrong?' Imogen asked.

Kai quickly sought to reassure her. 'No. Absolutely not.'

'Thought you were finding your pint more interesting than me.'

Time to find a line now. Save the situation. 'There is nothing in this pub more interesting than you.'

Imogen guffawed. A full-on belly laugh. While some men might, indeed while *he* might usually, be a little miffed to be laughed at, especially so enthusiastically, Kai found himself laughing too.

'Fair enough. Crap line,' he conceded. 'True though,' he added as endearingly as he could.

Imogen studied him, weighing up if this boy was worth her time. She liked the look of him; she had as soon as he popped up on her app, obviously. Then he sounded nice when they had their little introductory chat on the phone. Now he was here, with his warm, brown skin and hint of an afro and, yes, a very nice smile, well, she guessed he was worth this evening anyway. She decided she would review the situation later, in the light of any further gaucherie.

'What is it you do again?' Time to grill him, she thought.

'Oh. Advertising. I'm... I work for an advertising agency. Account manager.'

'So you manage accounts?'

'Basically.'

'So you're an accountant.'

He laughed. 'No. Definitely not.'

'So you're no good with money?'

'No. I mean yes, I mean... I'm fine with money. I just don't deal with it as a job. I manage clients. Tend to their needs and stuff.'

'Sounds a bit dodge.'

'Keep them happy.'

'As I said, dodge.'

'I think you know what I mean.'

'Oh, you know me already? Presumptuous.' But she was smiling, so Kai just grinned and held her gaze. Oh yes, he definitely liked her. Other parts of his anatomy were beginning to show their appreciation too. He pulled his chair further under the table. He didn't want Colin getting a glimpse of his enthusiasm.

'And you?' His turn. 'What do you do?'

'Ah. Well...' Her phone started ringing in her bag beside her. She looked to see who it was. 'My dad. Do you mind?'

'Of course not.' Her dad? Isn't Colin enough?

Kai then listened to this gorgeous girl having a conversation with this man he couldn't see, but whom he started to consider, potentially, if things worked out, his future father-in-law, and tried to get some sense of the man from the one side of the exchange he could hear.

'What's up? ... The Sack. ... No. ... Might have. ... Would that be a problem? ... So why do you ask? ... I see. ... ' She glanced at Kai. '...Yes. ... I don't know. Not yet. ... I will. ... Bye.' She hung up.

'Checking up on you too?'

'I guess. Nice really.'

'Absolutely. Does he worry a lot?'

'Suppose so. That's just our relationship. Since Mum went.'

Kai was momentarily taken aback. Went? Did she mean died? 'You lost your mum?'

'Sort of. She took off. When I was little. Never saw her again.'

'That's awful. Your mum? Why?'

Imogen shrugged. 'Who knows? Couldn't hack motherhood, I guess. Or Dad.'

'Is he difficult?'

'What do *you* think?'

'What do you mean?'

'How did you find your taxi driver?'

'Tonight?'

'Yes.'

'Bit odd. Possibly racist. Why?'

'That's him.'

'That was your dad?' Kai felt a cloud descending on his future happiness.

"Fraid so. He's not that bad. Did he put on a show for you?'

'Yeah. He did. He's Marcus Thorn. The actor. Right?'

'Yes, and he loves an audience.'

'Imogen *Thorn*. Of course.'

'Immy. If you like.'

'Immy.'

He took another draught of her eyes. She wasn't guarded at

all, this girl. He felt a real connection, despite having only just met her. Well, he wasn't going to let any doubts about her father spoil tonight. Anyway, why was he jumping ahead like that? It's a first date. What was the matter with him? He was usually much cooler than this. He gave her a smile of reassurance and received one back that started an unfamiliar fluttering in his chest. What was happening to him? He was in trouble here. He wanted to leap across the table and take her in his arms and... well, he wasn't sure he had any control over what he would do then, but, as if pre-empting him, suddenly he was aware of Colin at his shoulder.

'Everything okay, Immy?'

'Yes thank you, Colin?'

'Another drink?'

'I'm okay. Kai?'

Kai knew it was his shout, but he also knew he couldn't leave the table to go to the bar, not yet, even though Colin's presence was quite a dampener. He needed to play for time. Or was he taking their order at the table? Actually, he seemed to be, didn't he?

'I'll take another of these. If that's okay.'

Colin stared at Kai, expressionless.

'Stick it on my tab, Col, and we'll fight over it later,' Imogen said.

Colin's stare had done the trick. Kai pushed back his chair and started to stand. 'I'll come and get it.'

Imogen exchanged a look with Colin, who put his hand on Kai's shoulder and pushed him back onto his chair.

'You're alright. Happy to oblige for this one,' he said, and set off back to the bar, with a backwards look to Kai which left him in no doubt he was still on probation.

Kai turned back to Imogen. A much better view. Where now? he thought. He had so many questions for her. He wanted to know everything about her, but he needed so much for her to like him. To want to see him again. He'd been on a few of these dates, and nothing had ever really led to anything. In most cases, he was fine with that. He wasn't ready to get serious. And in those cases when he did mind, it was more because his date had clearly not been interested in him. Pride. He had had 'successful' dates. Girls who let him take them to bed, or who took him to bed, but with whom one or other party, or both, wasn't interested in repeating the experience. There was one girl with whom an encore did occur the following week, but that had ended when she took out a riding crop and asked him to hurt her. Not his thing at all.

These experiences had led him to review this dating game. This way of finding a partner. In theory, you only dated 'compatible' people, but human beings are more nuanced than the bare likes and dislikes on these profiles, although it would have been helpful if Miss Whiplash had been a little more forthcoming on hers. You can't know how a person moves or smells. What happens when your eyes meet. So Kai was coming to the end of his online dating journey anyway. But now, tonight, he wanted it to have all been worth it. This was what he had been hoping for, he realised. Meeting someone who matched their profile, of course, but with whom, as they put it in all the best romantic fiction, it just clicked. For him at least the click had been deafening. Had she heard it too?

He suddenly realised he hadn't said anything for a while and Imogen was looking at him quizzically.

'You okay with black people then?' he blurted out. Shit. Why had he said that?

'We're having this date, aren't we?'

Of course they were. What was the matter with him? Don't fuck this up.

'Yes. Thank you.' Thank you? Was he grateful? Well, yes, he was, because she was magnificent, but...

'You're welcome. Are you alright? You've gone a bit-'

'I'm fine. Sorry. Was I...? Ah, Colin. Great. Thanks.'

Colin placed a pint of lager in front of Kai, picked up his empty, exchanged another look with Imogen, then headed back to the bar. Kai took a deep quaff. When he had put down the glass, he looked up to see Imogen smiling gently at him.

'I get it,' she said. 'If it's any comfort, I'm not entirely a whitey myself.'

'You're not?'

'Only recently found out. I did one of those DNA tests. I'm eleven percent African-Caribbean, apparently. If you can believe it.'

'Blimey.' Maybe that's it, Kai thought. This immediate connection. 'Do you know where it comes from?'

'Mum or Dad, you mean?'

'Yeah. Of course, I've seen your mum. Wasn't she in that *Primary Care* with your dad? As a nurse?'

'He told you that too?'

'He did. If I remember right - I was very young - she was pale and blonde. Blue eyes, I suppose.'

'Yes. Whereas Dad... But he's having none of it.'

'Well what about his parents?'

'I never knew them, and he only knew his mum. I've seen pictures, and she's pretty white, I'd say.'

'What happened to her?'

Imogen shrugged.' Died, I think. Before I was born. He doesn't really talk about her. Don't think he got on with her. That's the impression I got, anyway.'

'Why don't you get *him* to do a DNA test?'

'Funny you should say that. I did. Actually, the results should arrive soon, I think.'

'How do you think he'll handle it if it turns out it came through him?'

'I look forward to finding out.'

Kai grinned. He rather wanted to see it himself. 'So, you live with him, do you?'

'I do. For now. I can't afford anywhere else.'

Kai understood perfectly well. He was paying a fortune for a room in a shared house himself. The problem was, that was the other side of London. Taking things on to the next stage was not going to be straightforward. But then, the success of this night was not going to be measured by their sleeping arrangements. It was dependent merely on her desire to see him again. So that must be his focus.

'Getting ridiculous, isn't it? So you and your dad live nearby?'

'Might do. Why do you ask?' She was playing with him again.

'Just wondering. Making conversation.' Not the question to ask. Focus, Kai. Do not put her off. 'Did you tell me what you do?'

'Weren't you listening?'

God, did she say? 'Yes. Every word, but-'

She must stop teasing him, but she was enjoying herself. And he was actually quite cute when he was flustered. 'And there was I opening up to you.'

What did she say? What did she say? He tried to replay the evening thus far.

She took pity on him. 'I didn't say. You asked and my Dad rang.'

Phew. 'And?'

Imogen hesitated. She considered making something up, but she was realising she didn't want to set off on the wrong foot; that, if he played his cards right, this may not be their last date, and telling him porkies might prove unhelpful. So she steeled herself, knowing that, if he was not the sort of man she hoped he was, he might be intimidated. Then again, if he wasn't, why was she worrying.

'I'm a doctor.'

'Really? Medical?

'Medical. An F1. So pretty recently qualified. Still training really.'

If her beauty weren't intimidating enough, he now had her brains to contend with. But contend he would. He was a man of ambition. 'Cool.'

'Cool?'

'Yeah. Pretty cool.' He considered making some joke about her bedside manner, but stopped himself. Don't mention beds tonight. Remember the long game. 'Do you work long hours then?'

'Quite long.'

'Tiring, I'd say.'

'I'd have to agree.'

'Looking good on it.'

'Why, thank you.'

As Kai took another gulp of his nearly empty second pint and saw his date was still nursing her half-filled first, he realised this newly-received information should give him pause. She was probably weighing up his drink habit. He didn't want her to take him for an alky. He left a little in the bottom of his glass.

'Fancy a walk? It's still light. Maybe get something to eat.'

Imogen looked at him for a moment, weighing up this question, it's potential implications and the risk she might be taking if she accepted the invitation. She glanced across at Colin behind the bar. She inhaled deeply. 'Okay.' She surprised herself. To trust so soon.

'Cool.'

They got up from the table and headed towards the door. As they passed the bar and Colin realised what was happening, a look of alarm crossed his face. Kai took out his wallet and slapped a twenty pound note on the bar, then hurried to get to the door before Imogen and pull it open for her. She let him do so and crossed in front of him and out into the still mild, summer evening. Kai looked back towards Colin, smiled, winked and exited, letting the door close behind him.

5

Marcus Thorn watched his fare disappear into his favourite pub, raised his window, indicated and pulled away from the kerb. Nice enough lad, he thought. He didn't really mind people of colour, as he believed he should call them, but there were rather a lot of them in London. In many colours. He'd worked with several. Some had talent. But he'd never really got close to one. Different cultures, he thought. He wondered what brought this one to the Sack. Didn't appear to be from round here. Something was niggling at him. He came to a T-junction, indicated left, and was about to head back towards the underground station for another customer, when he changed his mind and turned right instead, causing a car to break hard to avoid hitting him. Its driver leant on the horn. Ignoring them, Marcus accelerated homeward.

The flat he shared with his daughter was the entire first floor above a takeaway, the moderately amusingly titled Ken Tucker's Fried Chicken. Whether this gentleman was anything other than the laboured imagining of a desperate entrepreneur, or indeed a flesh and blood businessman who saw an unchallengeable opportunity to ride on a big boy's coattails, Marcus didn't know. All he did know was that the place emitted noxious vapours, and living above it was at times nauseating. He pined for the days when it was an odourless bookshop, as it had been when he and Fleur had bought the flat.

Fleur Hardy was Imogen's mother. She had joined the cast of *Primary Care* a couple of years after Marcus, when he was a well-established and much-loved regular. She was the new practice nurse, Millie Moffat, and her resemblance to the similarly initialled Marilyn Monroe had fired the producers' and script writers' imaginations. While Millie sent the nation into a frenzy of lust and envy, Fleur sent Marcus bonkers with desire, and, though she played it cool for a while, he had the advantage that the script writers allowed Matthew Hope to make love to Millie Moffat, and Matthew Hope had to use Marcus Thorn's lips. It wasn't long before Marcus had got to a more advanced base than Matthew had. They became the nation's favourite couple for a while - followed by paparazzi, always in the tabloids - and they revelled in their success. After a few years, a few pay rises, a few pantomimes and a few magazine features, they were well able to buy a home in London, and settled on the flat Marcus still owned, in large part because it seemed so romantic to live above a bookshop.

As Marcus pulled up in the precious parking space behind the shop that had come with the flat, he looked up to see if there was any sign of life upstairs. It was still daylight, so he couldn't look for lights, but he hoped there might be a window open to indicate Imogen's presence. There wasn't. He climbed the outside stairs that led to the flat and let himself in.

'Imogen?' Nothing. He looked into the lounge. Not there. He knocked on her bedroom door. No answer. No-one in the bathroom either; the door was open. He sighed. He didn't like it when she went out without telling him. He knew she was quite old enough to do as she pleased, and she was only living with him out of necessity until her new career started to pay at a level which afforded independence in London. But he was only human. And lonely.

He went into the lounge and flopped down on the settee. Picking up the remote control from the coffee table, he switched on the television. News. He hadn't listened to the overfed, chinless Government minister long before he wanted to put his foot through the screen.

'Cunt!' Marcus used this word often. Amongst the acting fraternity its shock value was small. In more polite company, he often offended. Now, alone, only he heard it and, as always, enjoyed its sharp, Germanic appositeness. He muted the sound, took out his mobile and called Imogen. She answered fairly quickly and he relaxed.

'Where are you? ... On your own? ... You have a date? ... Is he black? ... No. ... I may have dropped him off. ... Is Colin there? ... Good. Do you want me to come and get you? ... Let me know. ... See you later. ... ' He ended the call. Shit. As he feared. What was he going to do now?

The lardy face had given way to a glamorous, bespectacled, female newsreader, with plump, glossy lips, making love to the camera. Hardly Kenneth Kendall, he thought. Although, maybe the man would have liked a little gloss on his lips. You never know.

Suddenly the screen was filled with another face. A young woman in a dated hairstyle, wearing a graduation gown and mortar board, squinting into the sun. She seemed familiar. Must have been in the eighties he guessed, judging by the hair. And the shoulder pads, which were evident even under the gown. Who was she? He put the volume up.

'...has come to light after more than thirty years. Rosemary Hart, a librarian from Tooting, was witness to the discovery of a diary at the home of Ellie's parents, Edward and Cynthia Nelson. At first unaware of the significance, but intrigued when the Nelsons made clear the police would need to be involved, she undertook an online search, and came across the 1985 disappearance. She remembered that the Nelsons had found a man's name in the diary. A man they didn't know. Police are angry that this information has been made public. They believe it may jeopardise their investigation, but they want to make clear that they have identified this man and will be speaking with him shortly.'

Poor bugger, Marcus thought. They've got your number. He was staring at the photo, still on the screen. Why was she familiar?

'If anyone watching this has any information which might help the police,' the newsreader continued, 'please come forward. Ellie's parents have waited a long time to find out what happened to their daughter.' The picture then disappeared and the newsreader moved on to another item. Marcus turned the sound off again. He needed to think.

Ellie? Didn't he know an Ellie once? His brain was dancing around something, but he couldn't get to it. What was it? That mousey brown hair. The strong chin. The large nose. Ellie? Suddenly it was as if he had been kicked in the stomach, and the features he had just seen on the screen became features he had seen in life, now dredged from his memory. In context. In his history. Ellie. That was the name of that girl who kept turning up at his shows. Who was always in the bar afterwards. At the Bullpit Theatre. His Mercutio. When was that? Must have been around that time. He'd need to check. God. Didn't they...? He used to drink quite heavily then. He couldn't be sure, but hadn't she come back to his one night? Had he...? Icy footsteps scampered up his spine. This wasn't good.

He stood up and started pacing the room, trying to see what else he could remember. Vague recollections of an encounter. Of her lying in his bed. Was there a... What do you call those things? A chain round her middle. Like a necklace, but round the waist. Was that her? It was all such a blur. Why did he think that was her?

Then another memory slapped him. Wasn't she the one who sent him all those postcards? From her holiday. Incessantly. Every day. What if it was? Doesn't mean he'd be any help to the police. He certainly didn't know anything about her disappearance. God. A one-night stand. That's all. There wasn't even any memory of pleasure associated with it. Just a drunken fuck. He didn't even know why. He didn't fancy her. That much was confirmed by that picture on the telly. Nothing to look at. He hadn't given her another thought since. Well, maybe if he ever received a postcard, but only the memory of how annoying it was. Had he led her on? To expect more from him? He had no idea. All far too long ago and ethanol-suppressed.

He didn't feel good though. It had brought to mind a time

when his career was growing, but probably he was a bit of a twat. Certainly a pisshead. There were too many drunken encounters, and no desire to be tied down by any of them. No. He was going places. He needed his freedom. Being pursued by fans was inevitable. He was a hunk. Especially then, in his pirate phase. A time when his dark eyes and curly locks and tanned skin fitted perfectly with the fashion. Think Adam Ant meets David Essex, only swarthier. Yes, the look suited him. Billowing white shirts with puffy sleeves, open to the diaphragm. Leather trousers. Waistcoats. Long coats. He loved it. Then. Looking back though... yes, a bit of a twat.

So, this girl, this Ellie, had disappeared? He had no recollection of it. Surely it would have been on the news? He would have known, wouldn't he? Why didn't he? He needed more information. When exactly did this happen? He took out his phone and googled 'Ellie 1985 disappearance'. Up popped several links. Picking one at random he got the date - 25th May. What was he doing on 25th May, 1985? Fuck knows. How could he find out? Well, what jobs did he do that year? That would be a good place to start. His CV. Did he still have one? Must have somewhere.

He went across to a large oak cupboard at one end of the room. Opening the full-length doors, he revealed an array of inner cupboards and drawers, and started opening the cupboards and pulling out the drawers trying to find the relevant paperwork. Eventually an old CV was located. He surveyed the long list of jobs he had done to that point. Well, the ones he was prepared to put on his CV. He hadn't specified years on it, but they seemed to be in roughly chronological order, so he looked back near the beginning. Yes, there was the *Romeo and Juliet* at the Bullpit, when he first seems to have drawn this Ellie's attentions. The next job listed was... Of course! His Heathcliff. The Belgian tour for the English Theatre of Antwerp. When was that exactly? He tried to find some clue lurking somewhere in his brain. He remembered rehearsing in Antwerp for a few weeks before setting off round the country.   Then it hit him. He'd been in a bar, naturally, after rehearsals one night, watching the football. The European Cup Final. From just down the road in Brussels. The Heysel Stadium. That awful disaster. When was that? He pulled out his phone again. Within seconds it was there. The twenty-ninth of May, 1985. Bloody hell. Four days after this girl disappeared. And he was in Belgium. And had been for some days already, presumably. And would be for several months more. That was a long, tedious tour. It was only his commitment to drink every available Belgian beer that had kept him going. Especially when his Cathy was such a cow. He had no French or... the other one. Flemish. Always made him want to clear his throat. So he would have been out of the loop. Oblivious to British news. Just drinking, travelling, howling for Cathy, drinking, screwing (when possible) and drinking. No wonder he knew nothing about the disappearance.

Well well. He felt relieved. No-one had accused him of anything, but he knew this girl at the time she disappeared, and he would be bound to be of interest, wouldn't he? If they knew. Did they know? What if they did? He had an alibi. It wasn't him. But then he knew that. Didn't he? You don't forget murdering someone. That's what must have happened, presumably. Someone bumped her off and no-one found a body. Or a suspect. Until now. Well, whoever he is, his past has finally caught up with him.

Marcus realised he was hungry. That little flurry of activity and brain-dredging had given him an appetite. He picked up the remote control to turn off the television. There was some earnest acting going on between a nurse and what he took to be a doctor. He wondered if these two were at it off camera. If she turns out like mine, mate, you're in for it, he thought. Enjoy it while you can. He shut down the picture just as they appeared to be going in for the snog. That's enough of that, he thought.

He wandered into the kitchen and looked half-heartedly into the fridge. Not much there. Just some of Imogen's plant-based... What's the opposite of a delicacy? he wondered. Indelicacy? Inedible at any rate. A takeaway it must be then. No, not from that honking establishment below. No foul fowl for him.

Curry. That's what he fancied.

He checked he had his wallet and headed for the front door. As he opened it, he heard footsteps coming up the metal steps. He smiled, thinking Imogen was back, but as he stepped out onto the landing, he saw a tall, unfamiliar man of about his own age, followed by a younger woman, coming towards him. His first thought was to duck back into the flat and pretend he was out, but he soon realised he had been seen and switched on a broad smile.

'Marcus Thorn?' the grey-haired man enquired, pulling out a warrant card from his jacket pocket and holding it up to Marcus.

'Yes. 'Tis I. How may I be of assistance, officer?'

'I am Inspector Hutchinson, and this is Sergeant Moore. May we come in?'

'I was just intending to refuel, but I shall happily forego that pleasure until such time as I have furnished you with whatever information you seek. Pray enter.' He produced an extravagant flourish of his arm by way of an invitation for them to step inside.

Inspector Hutchinson knew better. 'No no. After you.'

'As you please.' Marcus went back into his flat and led the officers into his lounge. Sergeant Moore shut the door behind her.

Marcus gestured, again rather exaggeratedly, for them to sit, which they both did on the settee. Marcus went over to the single armchair. As he sat, he thought he'd pre-empt them. 'I have an inkling on what quest you come. Would it, perchance, pertain to events of our youths, sir? An unfortunate vanishing -?'

'Ellie Nelson. Yes.' Inspector Hutchinson had already tired of the theatrics. 'Do you know anything about her disappearance?'

No messing, Marcus thought. Straight to the point. Well, his conscience was clear. 'Alas, no. I have conducted an investigation of my own and have discovered that, at the time in question, I was overseas.'

Inspector Hutchinson raised an eyebrow.

'Well, more precisely, over the English Channel, sir. In the land of Poirot and Magritte. Of the waffle and the chocolate.'

'Belgium?' Sergeant Moore offered.

'Indeed, madam. In Belgium. Treading the boards in a dreadful adaptation, by a loony Walloon, of Miss Emily Brontë's classic tale *Wuthering Heights*. I, of course, was giving my Heathcliff.'

'Were you?' Inspector Hutchinson wondered how long this performance would continue. 'I shall of course verify this. Who was your employer?'

'The long-disbanded and little-mourned English Theatre of Antwerp, sir.'

Inspector Hutchinson made a note on his pad. 'And your relationship with Miss Nelson?'

'Relationship? I fear you have been misled. I had no relationship with the unfortunate young lady. She was a mere acquaintance. A fan, if you will. She sought me out and dallied in my vicinity over the course of a few weeks during the celebrated run of another production in which I featured; the bard's tragic romance, *Romeo and Juliet*.'

'At the Bullpit Theatre.' Again the Sergeant made a contribution.

'Indeed. A much-admired venue in its day. My Mercutio moved many.'

'I'm sure it did.' The Inspector needed answers. 'Given that you didn't seem surprised to see us, I take it you came across some news coverage on this matter?'

'This very evening, yes. On the broadcasting equipment you see before you.'

'Then you'll know some evidence has come to light. A diary.'

'So I heard. In which a mysterious gentleman featured. Have you identified the man?'

'We have. His name was Marcus. He could be found at the Bullpit.' Inspector Hutchinson let this information sink in, studying the once-admired actor's reaction.

'Me? She mentioned me?'

'She did.'

'What did she say about me?'

The Inspector noted how the language had become less

florid. 'That you were meeting her.'

'Meeting her? Where?'

'The bog.'

'The bog? I don't understand.'

'No? We hoped you could shed some light on where or what this bog might have been. Seeing as you were meeting Ellie there.'

'But I wasn't. I have no idea what this means. I hardly knew her. We never dated. I don't know why she would have said we were meeting.'

Sergeant Moore thought it was time she got involved. 'Could it be a synonym?'

Marcus and the Inspector both looked at her, perplexed.

The Sergeant shifted on the settee. 'Stand for something?'

Inspector Hutchinson realised what his Sergeant was asking. 'An acronym, Steph. I believe that is what you mean.'

Sergeant Moore started to colour, but ploughed on. 'Could it?'

Marcus had been compiling a list of synonyms of bog in his head, when he realised the policewoman was waiting for an answer, her head and neck covered in red patches. He glanced at the Inspector, who was looking at his junior, rather than at Marcus himself. He felt a pang of pity for the poor girl and became anxious to offer her something.

'B-O-G? Bag of gravel? Ball of glue? Bunch of-' Then it dawned on him. 'The Bunch of Grapes. That was my local.'

Inspector Hutchinson sat up. 'Was it?'

Marcus corrected him. 'Actually, it still is, or would be if I still drank. Only it's the Sack of Balls now.'

The Inspector looked doubtful.

'Haven't you seen it? It's just down the road,' Marcus added.

'The Sack of Balls?'

Marcus felt he needed to explain. 'A bit of a joke. Between me and Colin. The landlord.'

Inspector Hutchinson was clearly waiting for more.

'When Colin took over the licence, I was a regular in there, and I persuaded him he needed a name change. New management, new moniker. I confess I came up with the name. Childish, no doubt. But... Made us giggle.'

'But it was called the Bunch of Grapes in 1985?'

'Indeed. Early nineties, I think. The name change.'

'Well if this Bunch of Grapes was where you were to be found when you weren't at the Bullpit Theatre, then it makes perfect sense, I suppose,' said the Inspector, 'that Ellie should meet you there.'

'Well it might. If I had made such an arrangement. But I hadn't.'

Sergeant Moore felt another question coming on. 'How can you be sure? It was a long time ago and I believe you said you were a regular in this pub. So presumably you drank a fair bit.'

If only you knew, Marcus thought. I don't look like this now from sipping the odd dry sherry. 'That would not be an inaccurate statement.'

'So you may have forgotten.' The Sergeant felt her confidence growing.

Marcus was worried. He could very well have forgotten, but he didn't like the implications of admitting it. They'd have him down as a murderer. Then he remembered he had an alibi. 'Well, as I said, I was out of the country, so...'

'So you said. We will of course need to test the truth of that,' the Inspector said. 'Now, what can you tell me about postcards?'

'Postcards?' Marcus remembered postcards. 'What do you mean?'

'Do you remember receiving any from Ellie?'

'Actually, I do. Lots of them.'

'And what was the content of these postcards?'

'Scary stuff, as I recall. I think she had our future mapped out. As I said, we weren't in a relationship. So, all a bit weird and... scary.'

Inspector Hutchinson studied Marcus. 'Could she have made an arrangement to meet you in these postcards?'

'How would that work? I didn't send any back.'

'But she could have told you she would be in the Bunch of Grapes on the night in question.'

'I have no recollection of that. And that wouldn't prove I had actually met her.'

Sergeant Moore said, 'I thought you were always in there.'

Marcus considered this. 'Normally, yes. But I was away, remember.'

'So you say.' The Inspector stood up, putting away his notebook. 'Well, until we have confirmed your whereabouts on the night in question, there is not much point in continuing for now. We will, however, wish to speak to you again, so please don't stray far.' The Inspector fixed Marcus with a stare. He took out a card and handed it to Marcus. 'If you remember anything else, or have anything else you wish to say, please ring me.'

Marcus nodded.

'I take it you have a mobile phone?' the Inspector continued. Marcus nodded again. 'May I please have the number?'

'Do you have something I could write it on?'

Inspector Hutchinson fished out his notepad and a pen and handed them to Marcus.

'That's not how you spell Antwerp, you know.'

The Inspector was irritated by the man, but restricted his response to, 'The number please.'

Marcus scribbled it down and handed back the pad.

Inspector Hutchinson returned it to his pocket and turned to his colleague. 'Come along Steph. Let's leave Mr Thorn to his dining arrangements.'

The two police officers moved to the front door and Inspector Hutchinson opened it. When they were both outside, the Inspector looked back at Marcus, standing in the doorway. 'We'll be in touch soon. Please give it some thought, Mr Thorn. If there's anything you want to get off your chest...' Another hard look, then he turned and clattered off down the steps, Sergeant Moore following.

Marcus stood motionless in the doorway; his appetite gone. He felt sick. He watched his two visitors reach the foot of the stairs and walk over to a black Audi parked in the lane behind the row of shops. Inspector Hutchinson bent down to the driver's window and spoke to the two occupants. Marcus took them to be other plain clothes police officers, presumably brought along to intercept him if he tried to make a run for it. When the Inspector had said what he had to say, he and Sergeant Moore moved off to another car, got into it and drove away. The Audi remained. Marcus suddenly realised these officers must have been tasked with watching his flat. That Inspector must really be convinced he was guilty to deploy his manpower this way, with no evidence of his guilt whatsoever. He wasn't even being subtle about it. What had he done to warrant such behaviour? Were they going to follow him wherever he went? Should make for an interesting working day, he thought. Hope they have a mileage allowance. He let out a sigh, turned and re-entered his flat, closing the door behind him.

6

Imogen had had a very nice evening. She'd got Kai to take her to the Parrot Café, her favourite place to eat, where the vegetarian and vegan menu options suited her diet, and the brightly painted murals of colourful parrots and macaws always made her feel happy. Despite some very inviting meat-based choices, Kai had decided to let Imogen recommend something she enjoyed, and had been pleasantly surprised to have found her selection delicious. He had no idea what he was eating, but it had flavour and a kick and, the fact that it might earn him some Brownie points, only added to its appeal.

Now they were back on the street, after dark, slowly making progress in the general direction of Imogen's home, engaged in the sort of flirtatious banter that is only found in the early stages of a relationship, and weaving a meandering course such that they kept bumping into each other in that accidently-on-purpose way. When they reached a street corner, Imogen stopped and looked up at Kai.

'Well, that's me nearly home. Thank you for a lovely evening.'

'Oh. Sure you wouldn't like a coffee or something. It's Saturday night.'

'Yes, but I'm working tomorrow, unfortunately.'

'Fair enough. Nature of the job, I guess.'

'Yeah.'

So, where exactly is your place?'

'Why do you need to know?'

'So I can see you safely home.'

'What a gentleman. I'll be fine from here.'

'You sure?'

'Perfectly.'

Kai wanted to persist, but he was anxious not to upset her. 'If that's what you want.'

'It is.'

Well, if she was going to leave him now, he had to make sure he left her with something to remember him by. Her eyes were gazing into his, their dark brown centres sparkling with reflected streetlights. He pulled her towards himself. She didn't resist, indeed a smile played across her lips. The butterflies were on amphetamines in his stomach. Slowly he lowered his face towards her, his eyes not leaving hers. When their lips touched, he could swear an orchestra started playing somewhere. It felt so good, her lips were so soft and giving, he thought he might burst. He could have stayed like that all night, but eventually he slowly pulled away and refocussed on her eyes. She smiled.

'Goodnight.' She smiled again, turned and headed off down the side street. He watched her go, so bereft at her leaving it hurt. That walk again. So damned sexy. After a few yards she swung round to check he was watching, grinned to see he was, and turned down a lane behind the shops.

Kai stood there a while, staring at the air she'd just abandoned, a familiar throbbing in his trousers and a vice-like knot in his guts. He threw his head towards the stars and, so she didn't hear him, strangled what he wanted to scream. 'Yes!'

Imogen danced up the stairs to her flat feeling elated. Now that was how a date should be. Comfortable, playful, romantic, and leaving the promise of more, rather than a messy potential full stop. As there was no way she was going to take him into her father's flat, the messy outcome was never on the cards, but she realised, had her living arrangements been different…

Reaching the top of the stairs, she pulled out her keys and let herself into the flat. Almost immediately her father appeared from the lounge.

'Everything alright?' He looked dishevelled and haunted.

'Perfectly alright, thank you.'

'And?'

'And?'

'The date. Will you be seeing him again?'

'Maybe. If he calls.'

Marcus was crestfallen.

Imogen was in far too good a mood to let it bother her. 'You'll just have to get over it. What have you been up to? You look terrible.'

'Worse than usual, do you mean?'

'Really? What is it?'

'Did you notice a black Audi in the lane back there?'

'No. Oh, maybe.' She had other things on her mind than cars. Where was this going?

'Police. They're watching me.'

Imogen could see he wasn't joking. She knew he could be dramatic, but he did look awful, so she started to be alarmed herself. 'What do you mean?'

'They've been in here. This evening. Not those ones.' He gestured towards the back of the flat. 'Others. They think I'm a murderer.'

'What? You're going to have to explain. Sit down.' They went into the lounge and sat on the settee. 'From the beginning.'

Marcus told her everything that had happened and gave her the background that had led the police to suspect him. It inevitably meant he had to give her an idea of the sort of life he lived before he met her mother; not an easy conversation to have with your daughter.

When he'd finished, Imogen's head was spinning. So many questions were forming she didn't know where to begin.

'So, the only reason they think it might be you is because she said in her diary that she was meeting you that night?'

'Yes.'

'They have no other evidence.'

'No. They couldn't have. I didn't meet her.'

'Well what are you worrying for then?'

Marcus couldn't explain that. How could he tell her that he was such a heavy drinker he couldn't be sure what he had done?

'And you mentioned postcards she had sent you. Where did she send them?'

'To my flat. I lived in Prince Regent Mansions. You know, that block by the river.'

'How did you afford that?'

'It wasn't mine. I rented a room from a... well, not a friend... a bloke I was at drama school with. It was his flat. I think his parents owned the whole building. He was a yank. And a wanker. Total tosser.'

'Charming.'

'You didn't know him. Spoilt little rich kid. No friends. Thought he'd gain some kudos sharing a flat with one of the cool kids.'

'If you say so yourself.'

'It's true. What a cunt.'

Imogen was used to her father's colourful language and let it wash over her.

'Charged me an arm and a leg,' he continued, 'and insisted I keep paying when I was abroad for six months, if I wanted to keep the room. Even though he was rolling in it. Spent all his time smoking weed, and worse. Absolute fucking bat-faced cunt.'

'He looked like a bat?'

'Like a bat or hit with a bat. Same look.'

'So how long did you live with this delightful person?'

'Just till I went off to Belgium. I kept up the rent all the time I was there and, just before I came back, I received a letter from him telling me he'd changed his mind and the room was no longer available. Did I say he was a cunt?'

'You have a point. What was his name?'

'Howard Poot. The third, I believe. Howie.'

'So what happened to him?'

'No fucking idea. I never saw him again. Didn't even go back to collect my stuff. He probably went home to mummy and his millions. Atrocious actor too. Saw him playing a peasant in some Russian period piece once. Still had his fucking Rolex on.'

Something in what her father had told her rang vague bells for Imogen. The name. Howard Poot. Why was that name familiar?

'You wouldn't have a picture of him?'

'Of course not. Why would I have a picture of the piss flap?'

Imogen took out her phone and googled the name. There wasn't much, but one of the first links was to a press report of an incident that had happened a few months previously. A man of that name had been taken into psychiatric care, having tried to walk into Downing Street for his meeting with the Prime Minister to discuss future relations between 'our two peoples', as he put it. Then Imogen placed him. He was on one of her wards at work. She was currently working in St. Bernadette's Psychiatric Hospital for a few months of her F1 year. Drug-induced psychosis with delusions of grandeur. That was him.

'That's it. He's a patient. In Bernie's. Very unwell.'

Marcus didn't know how to take this news. It would not have been a remote disappointment to learn that he was dead, so having confirmation that not only was he still alive, but he was still to be found within a five mile radius of where he sat, made him slightly queasy. The fact that he was mad as a box of frogs was some consolation, and, given his penchant for mind-altering substances, not a total surprise. But what should he do with this information? It was Imogen who then sowed the seeds of a plan.

'So you were sharing a flat with this Howard Poot when this girl sent you all those postcards?'

'I was.'

'So he would also have seen them.'

'I suppose. Yes, actually, I have no doubt he would have read them. Entitled prick that he was.'

'So, if you didn't go and meet her, he could have. Couldn't he?'

Marcus considered this. The creep was jealous of him, he guessed. Didn't get much, no, didn't get *any* action himself.

'You need to tell this to the police.'

'Maybe. Aren't you working tomorrow?'

'Yes, I have to do one Sunday in four.'

'What time do you start?'

'Eight.'

'Could you get me into his ward?'

'What? No. What are you talking about? Tell the police.'

'They've made up their minds. I saw it in that Inspector's eyes. He's got it in for me.'

'I thought you had an alibi.'

'Yes, well, what if I don't. What if I didn't leave the country till after that night? I can't remember.'

'You're being paranoid, Dad. Anyway, I thought they were watching the flat.'

'Indeed they are.' He got up and went to the lounge windows, which were at the front of the building, and looked up and down the street. Being quite late now, there weren't many cars parked there. And of those that were, he couldn't see any with occupants.

He went over to the large, oak cupboard, opened the doors and then a drawer and started searching its contents. Finding what he was looking for, he held it up triumphantly. 'My salvation!'

'What are you on about?' Imogen was getting a little disturbed by his behaviour.

'These, my lovely, are the keys to the internal staircase. You know, the door at the end of the corridor out there? When your mother and I bought this flat, there was a bookshop below us. Do you remember it?'

'Vaguely.'

'You were very young. Well, we used to come up from the bookshop. This flat had belonged to Amelia who owned the shop, and she had internal stairs up to it. When she married her husband, that novelist, name escapes me, she moved into his place over by Wandsworth Common, and sold the flat to us. Because we were celebrities at the time, she was happy to let us use the stairway, to save us going all the way round the back to use what for her had just been a fire escape. We didn't have a car then, and it suited us. Anyway, when Amelia eventually sold the bookshop to Mr Tucker, or whoever, he didn't share her views on the stairs. He insisted, through his lawyers, we use the back stairs exclusively. However, because of fire regulations, he couldn't brick them up. And here are the keys.' He jangled them triumphantly. 'Amelia only gave them to us, not that lot downstairs, and we promised only to use them in an emergency. Like this.'

'So what are you thinking?'

'There's no-one watching the front of the building. I'm sure of it. They wouldn't know about the stairs. No-one comes into the chicken place before 8am. If I can get down there before then, I'm sure I'll be able to get out at some stage. I'm going to case the joint. See if there's anywhere to hide.'

Imogen couldn't believe what she was hearing. 'That's insane.'

'Look, I've had nothing to eat tonight. I'm going round to get something from them and my plan will then become clear.'

'You said you would never go near that place.'

'Needs must, Imogen. Needs must. Would you like anything?'

'No!'

'Very well.'

Marcus went to the front door and out onto the landing. The black Audi was still there. He made his way down the stairs and out into the lane. He saw the occupants of the Audi make a sudden movement, then look down as though busy with something. He strolled nonchalantly past them out into the side road, then round to the front of the building. As he pulled open the door of Ken Tucker's Fried Chicken, he spotted a head peek around the corner of the block and quickly withdraw.

Once inside the malodorous eatery, the presence of a small queue enabled him to survey his options. He could see the door to the stairway to his right in the corner of the eating area, which consisted of four small tables each with a couple of chairs, and, apart from having been painted yellow to match the walls, it otherwise looked functional. As he thought, the door handle was on the left and the door opened inwards, so he wouldn't be able to just open it a crack to see the entrance. He would need somewhere else to hide. Beside the door was one of those units with a bin inside, and a place where trays could be stacked at the top. He wandered over to it. He reckoned he could take out the bin, put it behind the stair door and, yes, he was convinced the unit was large enough for him to hide in the empty bin cupboard. All being well, they'll empty the bin later and clean the thing, he thought.

Satisfied with his reconnaissance, he joined the queue. He needed not to return empty-handed. He studied the board. What could he stomach? Oh, what the hell, he didn't need to actually eat it. When he reached the front of the queue and was confronted by the youth behind the counter, he pronounced, 'Do you have any chicken?'

Naturally, the boy was confused. 'This is a chicken restaurant.'

'So you say. How can we be sure? I'm sure I have detected the aroma of more pungent critters. Squirrel maybe. Dare I say rat?'

The boy became flustered. 'No, we only do chicken.'

'Very well, I'll have to take your word for that. Chicken it is then. Sandwich? Is that an option?'

'Chicken burger?'

'Curious notion, but fair enough. I'll take one.'

'Meal?'

'Not really, but it'll have to do.'

The lad didn't understand, but took it that this strange customer required fries and a drink too. 'What drink?'

'No drink for me, thank you.'

'But it's a meal.'

'So you say. However, I do not require any of your syrupy slop. The burger will suffice.'

'No fries then?'

'No. I do not require fries. Is this what Mr Tucker demands?

The hard sell?'

'Just a burger then?'

'Yes. Just a burger. Wasn't so hard really, was it?'

The boy placed the order. 'Four ninety-nine, please.'

Marcus found a five pound note and handed it over. As he did so, he saw the number 63 written on it and remembered where it had come from. He caught himself wiping his hand on his shirt. He became reflective. Did he need to challenge some of his attitudes? Was some internal rewiring necessary?

'There you go.'

Marcus was shaken from his contemplation. He was being handed a brown paper bag. How ironic, he thought, its resemblance to a sick bag.

'Much obliged.'

He took the bag and exited on to the street, not noticing the penny left for him on the counter. Once again, he had a good look at all the parked cars, then made the return journey to the back of the shops. He caught a fleeting glimpse of a retreating head at the corner again and, by the time he got round to the back lane, he was just in time to see the passenger door of the Audi being slammed shut and the occupant of the passenger seat affecting absorption in some invented task. He swung the bag of takeaway with his car-side arm as he passed to make sure his errand was understood, and made the ascent to his flat.

As soon as he had shut the door behind him, he felt elated, as though he had just been allowed onto the bus in Nazi-occupied Europe without falling for the Gestapo officer's English farewell. Gordon Jackson was an amateur.

'Imogen!' He looked into the lounge. His daughter was engrossed in her phone with a massive grin on her face. 'Everything okay?'

She looked up. 'Oh. Yeah. Just...'

'It's him, isn't it?'

'He's just thanking me for the evening. You know, being nice.'

'Bit keen, isn't he? You've only just left him.'

Imogen sent a reply, then turned to her father. 'I see you have your takeaway. Going to eat it?'

Opening the bag, Marcus looked suspiciously at the contents, took a sniff and gagged. He quickly crumpled up the bag, headed to the adjacent kitchen and binned it. Then he stuck his head through the hatch which linked the kitchen and lounge. 'It's going to work, by the way.'

Caught up with thoughts of her new beau, Imogen didn't immediately know what he meant. 'What is?'

'My cunning plan.'

'Oh, God. What are you thinking? What do you hope to achieve?'

'I'm going to confront him. Make a citizen's arrest, if necessary.'

'You won't get anywhere with him. He doesn't even know who he is.'

'Useful cover for a murderer, wouldn't you say?'

'Well, I'm not going to help you. I haven't worked my butt off all these years to be struck off before I've even got going.'

Marcus came back round into the lounge. 'Maybe you don't need to. They presumably allow visitors?'

'Family and friends, yes.'

'What are you saying? I'm an old friend.'

'Yeah. Right.'

'Just tell me what ward I need.'

Imogen sighed. 'Daffodil.'

He gave her a kiss on the cheek. 'Thank you, darling. Now you get to bed. Early start. I'll see you before you go. Night night.'

Imogen shrugged and headed for her bedroom. Marcus peered out of the window beside the front door. Still there. We're going through Harry, he thought, and retired himself.

7

Edward Nelson let himself in through his front door carrying a bag of shopping. He was puffing heavily from the effort of his excursion and he headed straight for the kitchen, dumped the bag on the table, and gratefully lowered himself on to his chair. Cynthia was still in her dressing gown making a pot of tea.

'Morning love. Early start for you,' she greeted him.

'Couldn't really sleep. And shops are open all hours now, so...'

'What did you get?'

Edward started to empty his shopping bag item by item. 'Marmite. Bourbons. Milk. Eggs. Paper.' When he announced this last item, his voice dropped.

Cynthia turned to see Edward holding up the newspaper and looking at the front cover through his magnifying glass. Her daughter's graduation photograph took up most of it under the headline, VOICE FROM THE PAST.

Cynthia was alarmed. 'Already? What are they playing at?'

'If you mean the police, it's not them. It's that stupid woman who came yesterday. Turns out she's a busybody.'

'Oh, Ted. He'll get away.'

'If it's been on the telly too. That's what I'm worried about.'

The Nelsons no longer had a television. They had lost interest in watching it, along with most other things, after Ellie disappeared, and eventually took it to a church sale.

'I hope they act fast, before he gets a chance.' With one hand on the worktop, Cynthia placed a cup of tea in front of her husband with the other. Then she got her own and made her way to her chair via all points of support available. Once seated she stared into her cup. 'He's got away with it for far too long.'

During the course of the sleepless night Edward had just passed, he had been tormented by his imagination. With thoughts of who his daughter really was. Had he missed something? Had he not really known her? Did she lead an entirely different life from the one she'd been brought up to? He had always done everything he could for her. Given her whatever she asked for, if at all possible. And she'd always seemed grateful and loving. How could he reconcile that Ellie with the one in the diary, who was out chasing after strange men and telling him nothing?

He looked towards his wife. He knew *her*. She held no surprises for him. He could understand her. 'She never told you anything?'

Cynthia looked up. 'Sorry?'

'Ellie. She didn't confide in you at all?'

'No dear. She didn't. I don't know why.'

'Did I do too much? Spoil her?'

Cynthia wondered if there might be some truth in that. He did dote on her. She always got her way. 'Of course not, Ted. Don't be silly.'

Edward sipped his tea. He was remembering when Ellie was little. All the hours they spent together out in the garage with the model railway. How she loved helping him build all the little houses along the line and would chatter away to him about all the people she imagined lived in this little town of their creation. Then he remembered that he hadn't been in the garage for years. That he'd lost interest in the railway along with everything else. He hadn't even thought of that. They'd need to clear that out as well, for the new owners. He couldn't face it.

'You alright, Ted?'

Edward looked up at his wife with rheumy eyes. 'Fine. Those people who are buying the house. They didn't show any interest in the garage, did they?'

'No. Don't think they had a car.'

Good, Edward thought. He wouldn't worry about that then. They could clear it out themselves if they ever wanted to use it.

53

This train operator had ceased business. It would be too painful to lay his eyes on any of those little houses again.

The garage was one of a row in a lane beyond their long back garden. While many owners had now got rid of the original double doors with a wired, frosted glass window in each, in favour of up and over modern affairs, Edward's remained. Such was his enthusiasm for his hobby, he had had mains power cables buried under his garden leading out to the distant garage, and providing for an elaborate set up on several levels that filled the entire space. The section in front of the doors was set high enough for them to duck under and sit in the middle of it all, which they did in all seasons, with the help of a Calor gas stove which sat in the middle with them.

Cynthia was reading the paper and all the history of her daughter's disappearance that the journalist had unearthed. It wasn't that there were inaccuracies in the article that irritated her, surprisingly there weren't, it was the tone. The way they were trying to make her trauma a source of public grief. The presumption that they understood how she felt, because they felt it too. She threw the paper down.

'I shouldn't have bought it. I'm sorry,' Edward said. 'It was her face. I couldn't help myself.'

'I'll get dressed.' Cynthia got herself to her feet, managed to reach her frame, and embarked on the long journey to the foot of the stairs, from where she would make her way laboriously up, step by painful step, clinging to the banister, before continuing the journey to her bedroom with the help of another walking frame she kept on that floor. Not for much longer, she thought. It's all on one level at Meadow View. This thought led to another and she found herself thinking of the very nice West Indian gentleman she had met when she was looking round the care home. Seymour, wasn't that his name? He said he came every day to visit his wife on the upper floor. The dementia floor. Well, if she ever needed to go up there, there was a lift. When she had reached the doorway, she turned to her husband. 'Ted, I don't suppose we can make the move this week now.

What do you think?'

'We'll see. Depends on the police really. I'm sure the home will be flexible. In the circumstances.'

When Cynthia had finally made it out of the kitchen, Edward got up too and started rummaging through a kitchen drawer. When he couldn't find what he was looking for, he tried other drawers, eventually giving up, shrugging, and setting about making them some breakfast.

8

Marcus slept fitfully. He imagined it had been much the same for those allied airmen in Stalag Luft III the night before they plunged down Harry. He rose early feeling ravenous. It wasn't often he skipped a meal and now he could eat, well, neither horse nor chicken, to be fair, but possibly... Following a brief detour to the bathroom, he arrived in the kitchen and descended on the fridge. He eyed Imogen's provender. He picked up a plate with some unidentifiable patties on it, and sniffed. Not unpleasant actually.

Soon he was enthusiastically cooking up a feast. He found some eggs, a tin of plum tomatoes and, in the freezer, some bread, and when Imogen poked her head round the kitchen door, drawn by the aroma, he was able to offer her a pretty decent plate of food.

Sitting at their small dining table in the lounge, Marcus devouring and Imogen more delicately ingesting the breakfast, talk naturally returned to the master plan of last night.

'So, run it by me again?' Imogen asked.

'Right. Well the stairs lead into the seating area downstairs, but I don't have a key to actually get out of the restaurant. I could get out the fire door at the back, but that would defeat the object, given that-' Remembering, he jumped up and hurried out into the corridor that linked the rooms and peered out of the window by the door once more. Interesting. Different car, but still clearly rozzers. He returned to his breakfast. 'Given that I'm still being watched. So, I have to wait till someone opens up, then hope they leave the keys in the front door while they go about their preparations for the day. Time it right and I'll be able to nip out without being seen. Obviously, I'll be leaving the door unlocked, but that can't be helped.'

'And if you *are* seen?'

'What are they going to do?'

'And if they *don't* leave the keys in the door?'

'I'll have to wait till opening time.'

'You're off your head. Well just leave me out of it. What's the penalty for evading the police?'

'No idea, but I haven't been charged with anything, so surely I'm a free man. For now.'

Imogen looked at her father with rather more worry than pity, and got up. 'I'd better be going.' She took her plate through to the kitchen and put it in the dishwasher, then stuck her head through the hatch. 'Thanks for breakfast. Nice.'

'You're most welcome.'

Marcus heard Imogen go into the bathroom and after a few minutes she was leaving the flat.

'Bye.'

'See you later.' Then he quickly added, 'Tonight'.

The door slammed.

At ten to eight precisely, having checked he was fully equipped, Marcus pulled out the keys to the stairway, identified the one for the upper door and fed it into the lock. At first it resisted his attempt to turn it and he cursed himself for not checking it last night, but following a little wiggle it finally budged and the door creaked inwards. He put his hand around the doorframe and found the light switch. He flicked it on, momentarily there was light, then a little ping and darkness once more. He peered down the stairs expecting there to be at least some light spilling round the lower door, but it was pitch black. Oh well. No time to change the bulb, so he took out his phone and turned on the torch. Retrieving the keys from the door he directed the beam down the long-unused stairs. There was plenty of dust and cobwebs, but no other horrors he could see, so he started the decent. When he reached the foot of the stairs, he found the second key and slotted that home. This time the lock turned easily and he pulled out the key and returned the pair to his pocket. Okay. Time to make a bid for freedom. He pushed down the handle and gave the door a tug. It appeared to be stuck, so he looked at the door and its surroundings by the light of his phone torch and, when satisfied he was sure where everything was without the aid of light, he switched off the torch, put the phone in his pocket, and, by touch alone, took hold of the door handle with both hands and gave it a heftier tug. Still not budging. Then he remembered the yellow paint on the other side and realised the problem. To be fair, he had the only keys, so they had no option but to paint the door closed. This would require some serious effort. He once again applied both hands to the handle, then placed one foot against each door jamb and leaned his whole weight backwards. When this was unsuccessful, he lifted his right leg and planted his foot alongside the handle, then once more leaned back while simultaneously straightening his leg. There was a sudden crack and he fell back against the stairs bathed in a blinding yellow light, the hard edges of the stairs hacking his spine, the edge of the door biting into his inner thigh and his wrists being violently twisted sideways. The multi-pronged insult was exquisitely painful.

After several seconds of immobility, his face crumpled against both the pain and the light, he slowly got to his feet and peered into the restaurant. The morning sun was streaming through the large windows of the shop front and bouncing off the yellow walls. When eventually his pupils had shrunk to pinholes, he was able to see that there was no sign of life within, and no keys in the door. Just as well given the entrance he had just made.

As planned, he went straight to the bin cupboard and removed the bin. He took it through to place it behind the stair door, but the bin was large and the space cramped, so he had to put it onto the stairs, hold it in place with his left hand and pull the door closed with his right, letting go of the bin when the door met his left arm and hearing the bin slide to the floor behind it. He pulled the door shut, but didn't lock it at this stage. Puffing, he then crouched down and backed into the cupboard. He had to put a hand behind him to pull the flap that hung from the top forward while he got his head in, but once behind it, he was able to reach forward and pull the door closed. It was tight, but he could just sit with his knees to his chest. He pushed the flap forward a little and was pleased to see he had a perfectly good view of the front door without making himself obvious. Then, his back, thigh and wrists throbbing and perspiration running down his face, he sat waiting.

He hadn't been in there long before a whole new world of agony crept upon him. He was far too old for such contortions. Please God someone comes soon.

He was at the point of giving up, so painful had this situation become, when he heard a key in the lock. Cracking open the flap, he saw the young man from last night coming in the door carrying a takeaway cup of coffee. He let the flap close and waited. He was about to push it forward again when it violently swung inwards, cracking him under the nose, and the paper coffee cup fell between his legs, splashing a considerable amount of undrunk coffee onto his crotch. He bit his lip as his eyes started to water.

As soon as he heard noises coming from the kitchen, he kicked open the cupboard door and eased himself out, dragging the coffee cup with him and mopping up the remaining coffee with the seat of his trousers. Brilliant, the keys were in the front door. He tried to get to his feet, but found his entire body had seized up, so he had to roll on to his hands and knees and heave himself upright with the aid of the cupboard door. He shuffled over to the stair door to get the bin, but when he tried to open the door he found the bin was wedged between the door and the foot of the stairs, so he had to snake a pulsating arm around the door and persuade the bin to slide back up the stairs while he inched the door open. When, finally, he had freed the irksome receptacle, as quickly as he could he replaced it in its cupboard, threw the coffee cup into it, locked the stairway door, pocketed the key and headed towards the front door. As quickly as he could wasn't remotely quick however, as he found any movement excruciatingly painful and difficult. When he eventually reached the door, he glanced back to see the youthful employee eyeing him open-mouthed, wondering how an incontinent tramp had gained access. Marcus hauled open the door, shouted 'Rentokil!' and staggered into the street, doing his best to straighten up and make progress away from his humiliation.

9

Despite his early start, it was approaching ten o'clock by the time Marcus arrived at the gates of St. Bernadette's Psychiatric Hospital. The intervening couple of hours had involved travelling, certainly, and where that involved walking, it had continued to be a laboured process, but he had also had a couple of diversions along the way. First amongst these was a detour into a department store to acquire replacement clothing for his lower half. Obviously, he couldn't attempt to enter the hospital with so large a stain in so incriminating a location. He would run the risk of being taken for a patient and permanently detained, he thought. Besides it had been a miserable journey to the store, so damp and heavy were his trousers and boxers, and so mortifying the looks of pity and disgust to which he had been subject along the way.

Freshened and dehumidified he had returned to the street. He had sat a while on a bench to review his plans. Things had started pretty ineptly he had had to concede. He had not put enough planning into the enterprise, he realised, and he didn't wish to repeat the mistake.

Whilst engaged in this one-man strategy meeting, he'd had another of those more and more infrequent occurrences these days, when a member of the public recognises something in his features, but cannot actually place him. On this occasion, an elderly lady in need of smaller plates or fewer sittings had parked her considerable bulk beside him on the bench, and proceeded to simply stare at him until such time as the answer came or her next meal called. Marcus had tried to ignore her and concentrate on his preparations, but had found this impossible.

He had turned to her and smiled. While once this would have disarmed most, the ravages of time and alcohol on his features, skin and teeth, induced a quite different response. Her chin was precipitately withdrawn into the folds of her neck while she simultaneously emitted a short, low cry of alarm. She might well have jumped back too, had jumping back been in her repertoire.

'Sorry,' Marcus had felt compelled to offer. 'Are you alright?'

'What happened?' was as much as the woman could return.

Unsure what else he could do to relieve her suffering, Marcus had got up to move away, when the woman spoke again.

'Weren't you nice?'

Despite knowing his own actions had led him to this moment, the question nevertheless cut deep. He may no longer look 'nice', but he hoped he was not without redeeming features. He had brought up a small child on his own and worked long hours to see her through medical school. Had he not earned a little redemption? Admittedly, there had not been an immediate abandonment of his current course when the child's mother had deserted them. After all, in doing so she had not only left him to bring up Imogen alone, she had also caused him to lose his lucrative and high-profile job, because, when she had asked to be written out of *Primary Care*, the producers had decided to write him out too, and send the pair of them off to Milton Keynes. In truth, it was a perfect excuse for them. He was already starting to lose his looks, and his drinking was making his behaviour ever more unpredictable.

He had subsequently had a period of wallowing in self-pity, and redoubled his efforts to drink himself into oblivion, until the moment he had his conversion, not on the road to Damascus, but on the road to hell.

He had woken one morning staring at the ceiling, with a vicious hangover and a stench of vomit in the air. Hearing a noise beside his bed, he had turned to see his eight-year-old daughter with a bowl of water and a towel, trying to clear the erstwhile contents of his stomach from the carpet. This was his rock bottom. Ever since he had tried to make amends. He was not now a perfect human being, but he was doing his best.

'No madam. I was not,' he had replied. 'But I'm working on it.' With which he had continued his painful progress towards the tube.

When, eventually, he had arrived at the underground station which served St. Bernadette's, as soon as he had emerged into the street, he had ducked into a small supermarket and reappeared with grapes and a bottle of Lucozade. That's what you do, isn't it?

Now he was standing looking up at the imposing facade of the hospital. It was a Victorian building of staggering ugliness. In what twisted world would an architect, tasked with accommodating distressed and bewildered souls, design this hellish edifice? Surely it was purpose built to add to their distress and terror. Its dark grey walls towered over the surrounding suburban streets, and were topped with castellations and turrets. Why? It's a hospital.

Marcus, who was himself reasonably sane, found he was feeling anxious as he crunched up the gravel path, between quite pleasant lawns, and approached the enormous front doors. Maybe that was just because of his mission, but he didn't think so. As he got closer to the entrance, he saw that there was a more human-sized door within the right-hand monster, beside which there was a bell. This he pressed. He heard a jangling from somewhere deep within, and, after a good thirty seconds, he heard a bolt sliding across inside, and a grey-haired woman dressed in grey poked her grey face around the door.

'Can I help you?'

Marcus got the distinct impression that they didn't get many visitors here.

'I've come to see Howie.' He smiled. The woman backed off. He must remember not to do that.

Eyeing his offerings, the woman sought clarification. 'Howie?'

'Howard Poot. Daffodil ward.'

The woman seemed very surprised. What Marcus didn't know was that his old flatmate had not had a single visitor in all the months he had been in residence. No family, no friends.

'He's very unwell, you know. I'm not sure he'll know you. Are you family?'

'Friend,' he lied.

'Well, come in. I'll find out how things currently stand.' She stood aside to let him in, then closed the door behind him, sliding the bolt back into place. 'If you'll just wait in there, I'll contact his ward.' She indicated a door across the hall marked *Visitors*. 'Who shall I say wants to see him?'

'Marcus Thorn.'

The woman momentarily froze and stared at him, the name ringing a bell left silent by his face. Unable to make a connection between the evidence of her eyes and ears, she turned and disappeared into a side room.

Marcus crossed the hallway and opened the door to the visitors' room. Inside was an arrangement of chairs around the perimeter and a coffee machine at the end opposite the window. There were no other visitors. He sat on one of the chairs clutching his gifts. He looked up at the high ceiling and bare walls. What a depressing place, he thought. How does Imogen cope?

After a few minutes, the door opened and the grey lady entered. 'Mr Poot is calm at the moment, so if you want to go up, you're welcome to, but if he becomes agitated, could you press this and someone will come.' She handed him a small device with a central button attached to a lanyard. 'Just put it round your neck. But don't forget to return it when you leave.'

'Okay. Thank you.' He put it over his head.

'Daffodil ward is on the first floor at the back of the building. Come with me. I'll show you where to go.'

Marcus followed her back into the hall, where the woman pointed down the corridor that led away towards the back of the building.

'About half way down there, on the left, you'll find a lift. Take it to the first floor and turn left when you get out. The ward is straight ahead. Press the buzzer. They're expecting you.'

Marcus thanked her again and headed towards the lift.

When he arrived at Daffodil Ward and did as instructed by pushing in the button, the door almost immediately opened and a cheery face looked at him, clouded a little, peered over his shoulder to scan the corridor, then looked at him once more with some confusion.

'Marcus Thorn?' the forty something nurse enquired doubtfully in a soft Irish accent.

'Indeed. 'Tis I.'

'Well, you've... Come in. Howard is it you're after?'

'If you'd be so kind. An old mucker of mine.'

The nurse closed the door and assumed a confidential tone. 'You may find him a little changed from when you last saw him. When was that, by the way?'

'It's been a while, to be fair. But I have no doubt we'll pick up where we left off.'

'Well, maybe, but don't be disappointed if he doesn't know you. He's in the day-room. I see Jane gave you an alarm. Hopefully won't be needed, but better safe than sorry. Follow me.' She led him down a corridor with what looked like individual patient rooms on either side, till she came to the room which identified itself as the day-room. Opening the door, she stuck her head in and greeted the occupants. 'Morning everyone. Visitor for Howard.' She turned back to Marcus. 'In you go. I'll be around the ward if you need me. Sister Mary Scanlon, by the way,' she said, tapping her badge and moving away.

'Thank you kindly, Sister.' Marcus started to smile, decided against it and settled for a wink instead. If Mary Scanlon found this odd, she didn't show it, and headed about her duties with brisk purpose.

Marcus turned towards the day-room and stepped inside. A brief scan of the room revealed three occupants. To his right, a fairly young woman with thinning hair was twisting and pulling at her locks, while conducting a conversation with no-one in particular in a conspiratorial voice. Straight ahead a large black man was sitting quietly reading. Looking to his left, Marcus at first was about to leave the room to ask why he had been misled, but, taking a second look at this third patient, he suddenly realised he had not been. What had thrown him was the hair. Where once it had hung red and lank, now it was pure white and standing on end as though its owner were in the throes of electrocution, an impression only added to by the wild staring eyes. He could not have looked madder. It was only the chiropteran features that identified Howard Poot.

Marcus steeled himself and approached. 'Howie. Good to see you. Long time, no see. How's it going?'

Poot frowned, the woman stepped up her hair abuse and the black man broke wind loudly, then shifted his position with a look of satisfaction suggesting he'd said all that needed saying.

Marcus persevered. 'Don't suppose you expected to see me again, eh?' Nothing. 'Howie? Eh?'

Slowly Poot turned his head towards Marcus, the wild eyes finally focussing on his face. He stared at him hard. Marcus felt uneasy. He tried to lighten matters. 'We've neither of us fared particularly well at the hands of Father Time, have we? An excess of excess, perchance.'

When still no response was forthcoming, Marcus offered the grapes. Poot looked at them with alarm and pressed himself back into his armchair.

'They're grapes, Howie. Thought you might like them.'

Poot's whole body suddenly started shaking and a voice both high-pitched and nasal shrieked from his mouth. 'How did you get in here? Where's my security detail?'

Marcus was not a little alarmed. 'Sorry?'

'Do not threaten the President of the United States of America with your fiendish foreign weaponry, you asshole. I'll have you eliminated.'

'They're just grapes, Howie. Look.' He put the bottle of Lucozade on a side table and started pulling off grapes and eating them.

Poot laughed scornfully. 'You really think I'm gonna fall for that one? Do you take me for a schmuck?'

This was not going well. Marcus decided to remove the offending fruit and took them over to a bin in the corner and dropped them in. 'There. All gone. No need to distress yourself.' He turned back to his old flatmate and found he had got up and was studying the bottle on the side table suspiciously.

'I've seen these before, you know. Think you can sneak one of these in without me noticing? What do you take me for?'

'A loony,' Marcus found himself saying aloud.

'What did you call me?'

'Sorry. Nothing. It's just a bottle of Lucozade. Honestly.'

'Do you think the President of the United States of America is crazy?'

Now there's a question, Marcus thought. 'Not at all,' was what he said. 'Come on, Howie. Forget the bottle.' He dispatched it the way of the fruit. 'Don't you remember me? Marcus. You rented me a room in Prince Regent Mansions. Way back. Drama school days.'

Poot went quiet. He was staring again. There appeared to be some conflict betrayed in his eyes. A fight between reality and delusion. An attempt to reconcile the dangerous assassin before him with some stirred memory. His own perceived identity with another humbler being. Slowly he drew nearer to Marcus, tiny step after tiny step, all the while staring and processing, until their faces were inches apart. Marcus could smell the rancid breath. He fingered the button on the alarm round his neck. Was it going to be necessary to seek help? Then Poot stopped, and his wide eyes scoured the face before him for several seconds. He sniffed, as though enlisting another sense might be helpful, which was most disconcerting for Marcus. This was followed by another prolonged and extremely uncomfortable stare. Marcus was on the verge of diffusing the tension with some quip, when Poot leaned in. At first Marcus had the alarming thought that he was about to be kissed by the crusty lips, but they bypassed both mouth and cheek and came to rest hovering over his left ear. At first all he was aware of was hot damp breath, but then, faintly and hardly voiced at all, Marcus heard words. Three of them. 'She was mine.'

Before Marcus could react, the volume button was spun to maximum and the patient switched to a chilling scream that almost knocked Marcus off his feet and left him reeling. This in turn alarmed the other patients, and the young woman joined in the screaming, now tugging chunks of hair out with both hands. The large, black man appeared to have evacuated his entire bowel contents and was standing looking at his soiled sweat pants in great distress. Marcus pressed his alarm and the cavalry arrived in time to prevent the US President carrying out his threat of elimination with a side table. Two male nurses took hold of Poot's arms and disarmed him, then held him down while Mary Scanlon administered a shot to his left buttock. Things calmed down rapidly after that.

Once she was happy that no violence was going to happen on her watch, Sister Scanlon turned to Marcus. 'You okay?'

'Yes. Thank you.'

'Maybe best if you left, eh?'

Marcus was not going to argue. He'd had quite a fright, and an awful stench was now pervading the room. He took off the life-saving alarm and handed it to the Sister.

'Can you find your way out, do you think?' she asked gently.

'I think so. Thank you. Bye.' He turned and headed to the door. Pulling it open, he turned back to survey the carnage. Mary Scanlon smiled at him. 'Bit messier in the real world, eh?'

Marcus realised he'd been placed. 'Indeed.' He risked a tight smile and left the day-room.

10

Edward and Cynthia had just finished their breakfast when the doorbell rang.

'On a Sunday morning? Who can that be?' Cynthia asked.

Edward knew there was only one way to find out and set off to solve the mystery. He opened the front door to reveal Sergeant Stephanie Moore, who smiled at Edward's enormously magnified right eye.

'Hope you don't mind me calling like this, but I wanted to keep you up to date with our progress. May I come in?'

'Of course.' Edward shuffled back and let her enter. 'Go through to the kitchen. Cynthia's in there.'

As Sergeant Moore did as she was told, Edward shut the front door and went into the front room to get a chair for his guest. Stephanie Moore poked her head into the kitchen and greeted Cynthia.

'Oh, it's you. Have you any news?' Cynthia was immediately animated.

'Some. Not a great deal, but I thought you'd want to know.'

Edward placed the chair for the policewoman and they both sat.

Sergeant Moore continued. 'We've found the Marcus Ellie wrote about. He's Marcus Thorn. He was an actor she had a thing about. You might remember him from *Primary Care*.'

The Nelsons looked at her blankly.

'*Primary Care*? You know, that television show? The health centre? He was Matthew Hope. The pharmacist?' The sergeant couldn't understand why they were showing no recognition. It was such a high-profile show and only fairly recently axed.

'We don't watch TV. We don't have one.' Cynthia explained.

Not for the first time Sergeant Moore felt foolish. And insensitive. 'I'm so sorry. I just assumed. Most people... Sorry.'

'Have you arrested him?' Edward asked.

'Unfortunately, we don't have grounds. But we're working on it. If and when we do, we'll have to pass it over to CID. At the moment we don't know a crime has been committed. People do go missing all the time, I'm afraid, and it isn't always as the result of a crime.'

Edward was shocked. 'There's no other explanation. She wouldn't just have gone off.'

'I'm sure you're right, Mr Nelson. But we have no evidence of that. However, as I say, we're working on it. Inspector Hutchinson is like a dog with a bone on this one. He's taking it personally. He won't rest until he's cleared this up for you, and, if a crime has been committed, as you believe, until whoever was responsible is banged up.'

Edward scowled, but said no more.

'I was also hoping to just have a little chat with you about Ellie,' Sergeant Moore continued. 'If that's okay.'

To just split an infinitive, Edward thought, but kept his counsel.

'What do you want to know?' Cynthia was anxious to help.

'Well, the diary has given us a bit of a sense of the kind of person Ellie was, but it would be really helpful to hear more about her from you. When you're trying to work out what might have happened, it's so useful if you have a fair idea how a person would be likely to react in any given situation. If you had to describe the kind of person she was, what would you say?'

Cynthia gave it some thought, then had a go. 'Well, she was a very determined girl. She always wanted to succeed at whatever she put her mind to. She wouldn't take no for an answer.'

Edward didn't like the way this made her sound. 'She was a winner. That's no bad way to be in life.'

'Of course not,' Sergeant Moore said.

'She got a first class honours degree, you know,' Cynthia

added.

'Very impressive,' the Sergeant admitted. 'But she wasn't working at the time she disappeared. That must have been hard for her.'

'It was,' Cynthia agreed. 'But she was trying really hard to find a job. I'm sure it wouldn't have been long, if...' She trailed off and found herself getting tearful yet again. After all these years.

'I'm sorry, Mrs Nelson. I really don't want to upset you.'

'It's okay, dear. I know. You're just doing your job.'

Sergeant Moore didn't want to waste valuable information gathering time, but nor did she wish to cause distress, so she switched tack. 'Would I be right in thinking you'd all been away on holiday shortly before Ellie's disappearance?'

'We had,' Cynthia agreed. 'Cromer. Nice beach holiday.'

'And were you aware of Ellie sending postcards while she was there?'

'She might have done. She was always writing. Didn't she mention that in the diary?'

'She did, but I was just wondering if you might have read any of them, that's all.'

'Oh no, dear. She wouldn't have let me do that. Especially not if they were, you know, personal.'

'Yes, I think they were. To this Marcus.'

The mention of the name made Edward's hackles rise. The thought of his beloved daughter sending 'personal' postcards to this depraved man was intolerable. He got up and put the kettle on to try to calm his churning emotions, then started clearing the breakfast things. Not an easy operation when you can't really see what you're doing. As plates and cups were bashed about and spoons dropped and searched for, Sergeant Moore ploughed on.

'Was it usual for Ellie to go on holiday with you at this stage?'

'Not really,' Cynthia admitted. 'She had gone off with university friends during the summer breaks, but now she'd finished university and was trying to find a job. I think I'm right in saying she hadn't really wanted to come away with us. I think we persuaded her because we thought she needed a break from all the stress. And it was nice to have her with us for one last...' She had set herself off again. Edward handed her a sheet of kitchen roll and she blew her nose loudly on it, then dabbed her eyes with the uncontaminated corners.

'I'm so sorry, Mrs Nelson. I know this is hard.' Stephanie Moore was feeling bad. 'Look, I'll leave it for now. I've put you through enough for today. I know Inspector Hutchinson is going to be talking to... that man again. I'll keep you up to date with any developments.'

Cynthia was feeling stupid. She wanted to help. She just couldn't control the effect it had on her. 'I'm sorry.'

'Don't be daft. It's perfectly understandable. I'm dragging it all up again.' Then the Sergeant had an idea. 'Look. Maybe you could take a leaf out of Ellie's book, sort of thing. You know, write it all down. Anything that would help us get a fuller picture of her. Anything that might be helpful.'

'Oh. Okay. I suppose I could.'

'Thank you, Mrs Nelson. If you would. I'll maybe pop back tomorrow. I'll let myself out.' Sergeant Moore got up and picked up her chair.

'You might as well leave that there for now, dear,' Cynthia said. 'I'm sure we'll be needing it again.'

'Sure. Good idea. Well, bye then.' The policewoman nodded and made her exit.

When he heard the front door close, Edward stopped what he was doing and gave a long sigh. This was all so hard. He heard a familiar buzzing sound and lifted his magnifying glass. The buzzing stopped and Edward spied the fly sitting on top of the butter in its dish. He carefully reached behind him and got hold of the newspaper. Rolling it up so his daughter's face was buried inside, he gripped one end and, imagining the loathsome insect was this Marcus, he brought the weapon down hard on it, splattering both fly and butter and breaking the dish. Despite the damage he felt a sense of satisfaction.

'Got you, you bastard.'

'Edward! What are you doing?'

'Eradicating a pest. It won't be bothering us any more. Have you finished with that?' He took the screwed up soggy kitchen towel from his wife and picked up the dying fly with it. He squashed it viciously between his thumb and forefinger, enjoying the crunching, squishing combination of bursting insect and snot. Then he pulled open a door under the worktop and threw the bolus forcefully down into the bin. 'Dead. Good riddance.'

Cynthia looked with some concern at her husband's back. When she then saw his shoulders start to heave and his head start to drop, she struggled to her feet and wrapped her arms around him, resting her head on his back, while Edward silently sobbed.

11

As Marcus stepped on to the gravel outside the hospital and heard the bolt slide behind him, he was thankful to be back in the fresh air. He had never liked regular hospitals, but psychiatric ones were, it seemed, another level of misery. He had not looked after himself he knew and hoped, now that he had quit the booze, that his liver would function sufficiently well to see him through for the foreseeable future, and not necessitate him ever being an in-patient. And God forbid he should ever need the services of one of these places he thought, as he looked back at the hideous building.

He headed straight for the underground. He had already had quite enough for one day. On a typical Sunday he might have put in a couple of hours in the cab, but not today he thought. Home and feet up, that was his plan. That was the beauty of being your own boss. Now that Imogen was earning, having no mortgage, he only needed to keep his income ticking over to cover his bills. Besides, he had some serious thinking to do. What was that nutjob on about? How was she his? She wasn't even *his*, Marcus's, but at least he knew her, after a fashion. What claim did that pitiful Poot have on the poor girl? Surely that was an admission that he got his hands on her. He must be responsible for her disappearance. Obviously been dangerously mad for years.

Back on home ground, Marcus glanced through the window of the chicken restaurant as he passed. Still they came to take their chances with the dubious product. Inexplicable. The bewildered boy had a few colleagues with him now and was far too busy to notice him, but Marcus put his head down and pressed on, rounding the two corners that brought him into the back lane.

The black Audi was back. As Marcus swept serenely past, he noticed in his peripheral vision two faces turned towards him. Did he imagine it or were they open-mouthed? As he started to climb the stairs, his body reminded him he'd given it a bit of a battering earlier and the ascent was laboured.

Once inside, he lowered himself on to the settee and slipped off his shoes. He pulled out his phone and sent Imogen a text, then lay down. He had to actually lift his legs up with his hands as his back was too weak and painful without the assistance. Once horizontal, it was a matter of seconds before he was fast asleep.

The doorbell woke him again, and, when he checked his watch, he saw that he had been sleeping for a few hours. He struggled to his feet, seriously stiff and uncomfortable, and slowly made his way to the door. Before he had got there the bell rang again.

'Alright. I'm coming.' It's Sunday for fuck's sake, he thought. He opened the door and found Inspector Hutchinson blocking the light. 'Oh. You again.'

'Yes. Me again. Is that a problem?'

'No, no. I don't observe the Sabbath either. Do come in.' He led the Inspector through to the lounge and they both sat. 'How may I assist?'

'Been out?'

'Erm. Yes. I have actually. How did you know?' He was feeling mischievous.

'Just a question.'

'Oh, I thought perhaps you were spying on me.'

'What time did you go out?'

'Didn't they tell you?'

'Who?'

'Your spies.'

'Just answer the question, please.'

'This morning. After breakfast. Eight-ish. They were probably having a lie in.'

There were a couple of officers to whom Inspector Hutchinson would certainly be giving a good bollocking, but he wasn't admitting anything. Not least because he hadn't sought approval for the surveillance, as he had no grounds to receive it. He knew he was taking a risk, not following correct procedures, but he was on to something with this man, he felt sure of it, and he didn't want him evading him.

'Listen to me, Mr Thorn. You won't help yourself by getting smart. I have been making enquiries, and it turns out you do not have an alibi for the night of Saturday 25th May, 1985. You and your fellow cast members all took the 1pm ferry to Zeebrugge on the Sunday, the following day. It turns out those Belgians keep thorough records. Records I have since verified with the ferry company.'

Shit, Marcus thought. It was what he feared. This policeman was going to stitch him up. He had no idea what he was doing on the Saturday night, but he hoped to God he was nowhere near the Bunch of Grapes. 'Well I must have stayed in and got an early night. You know, what with travelling the next day.'

'You were going to Belgium. Not exactly the other side of the world.'

'I'd still have needed to pack. I was away for months.'

Inspector Hutchinson eyed him scornfully. Time to approach from another angle. Unbalance him. 'Your wife. Fleur. Can you tell me where she is?'

Really been doing his homework, Marcus thought. 'I can't. But how is this relevant?'

'Well when did you last see her?'

'A long time ago. Around the millennium. Not long after we both finished in our show. *Primary Care.*'

'And where did she go?'

'She didn't tell us. Just left a note saying she needed some space, or some such bollocks, and skedaddled, never to darken our door again.'

'You have this note?'

'No, I do not. Not exactly a souvenir to treasure.'

'So you weren't sorry to see her go?'

Marcus was about to provide a glib reply when he was taken by surprise that he felt he couldn't. That there was no easy answer to this question. It was true their marriage had been strained for some time. Fleur had seemed very unhappy and the intimacy of their relationship, which had once been wonderful and intense, had not been good since... well... since Imogen had come along. And then the stupid woman had asked to leave the show. What an idiotic decision. She was approaching forty and in well-paid, high-profile work. Work she had been allowed to continue after having a baby. A baby they'd even written in to the show so her absence was minimal. Why walk away? And not even to cash in on her celebrity and pursue other perhaps more challenging work, if she felt under stimulated. No, she fucks off to fucking Outer Mongolia or some such to find herself or what-ever, leaving her four-year-old child behind. What a bitch. Both stupid and callous. So why should he be sorry? Sorry for Imogen, sure. The poor kid didn't deserve that, even if he did.

'I wish she hadn't,' was the reply he found himself giving. 'It was...difficult.'

Inspector Hutchinson was studying Marcus intently. 'If you were me, what would you think if confronted by a man who was involved with two women, both of whom disappeared? With-out trace?'

'I was not involved with one of those women, remember.'

'So you say. Doesn't look good though, does it?'

He knew it. He was going to pin everything on him. Marcus was beginning to panic. Now he thinks I killed Fleur, he thought. 'Are you seriously saying you can't find any trace of my wife? You've done all the searches?'

'I have. There is no record of her ever resurfacing after she left you. Anywhere.'

Oh, for fuck's sake. Where the hell did she go? 'How can you know that already? It was only yesterday this all kicked off.'

'I've been busy. I'm going to put this case to bed. That's a promise, Mr Thorn.'

That's a threat, Marcus thought. An undisguised threat. What was he going to do? Should he mention Poot yet? Would Hutchinson know about him, having been such a busy boy? He didn't want to throw away his investigative advantage, if the policeman had not already unearthed that connection. He needed to see what he could find on the mad Yank. That's why he had texted Imogen. To see if she could confirm his address.

Inspector Hutchinson was still giving Marcus a hard stare, which he tried not to break when his phone rang. He found, however, he couldn't answer the phone without looking at it, and Marcus was grateful for the respite. The Inspector then got up and went to the door, and, following a brief whispered exchange that Marcus couldn't follow, came back with Sergeant Moore in tow.

'Sergeant Moore has joined us,' the Inspector unnecessarily informed his host.

'So I see.'

'Hello Mr Thorn,' the policewoman said as she sat on the settee next to her senior officer.

'Where was I?' Inspector Hutchinson continued.

Making threats, Marcus thought. To innocent people. Jumping to wrong conclusions.

'Yes. Your wife, Mr Thorn. Sergeant Moore has discovered that she was not using her real name. Tell Mr Thorn what you found out, Steph?'

The Sergeant pulled out a notebook. 'Your wife's real name was Julie Christie. Apparently, that name was already taken. '

Both men looked at the policewoman in disbelief. Apparently, they were getting too old.

'I was aware of this, yes,' Marcus admitted. 'She had to change it for Equity, so she preferred to be known by her new name. It was easier that way. It was all I ever called her from the beginning.'

'But it has Julie Christie on all official documents?' Inspector Hutchinson asked with a pained expression, as the implications of this new information finally dawned on him.

'It had. Until we got married. Then she became Mrs Julie Thorn.' Marcus realised the busy boy had been barking up the wrong tree, and enjoyed the fact that he was going to have to repeat his searches. 'I'm sure there are a lot of Julie Thorns out there. You'll no doubt find one in a nunnery somewhere.'

Inspector Hutchinson was seething. He couldn't believe he had made such a school boy error. He was shattered as he had been up most of the night trawling databases, and the prospect of revisiting the whole process was soul-destroying. But revisit it he would. He stood up and loomed over his prey. Sergeant Moore jumped up too.

'Come on Sergeant.' The Inspector fixed Marcus with one last witherer. 'I'll be back.'

Marcus tried not to smirk and let the police officers find their own way out. He would have struggled to get up again anyway. When he heard the door shut, he allowed himself a chuckle and leaned back in his armchair a little relieved. At least this gave him more time.

After a few minutes of quiet contemplation, Marcus felt the familiar pangs and rumblings that alerted him his stomach needed filling. He really must do some shopping, he thought. Living off takeaways was incompatible with his attempt to reach old age and perhaps spend some time with grandchildren. This thought led him back to Imogen's date of the previous night. He imagined a brood of coffee-coloured kids running around his flat. What's the problem with that? He realised he had no reasonable answer to his own question and pulled out his phone. His current incapacity was his excuse, and he phoned his favourite pizza firm and ordered the Mega Meat Feast Combo.

A couple of hours later, his belly Mega-stuffed, he was sitting flicking channels looking for something worth watching, when he hit a news channel and that picture again of squinting Ellie Nelson. This station had managed to extract a little more information from its source, and as Imogen came into the lounge, the newsreader was explaining about the escritoire and the secret drawer.

'Hello darling. Hard day?'

'Not too bad. Is this about that girl you knew?'

'Yes.'

'Sounds like an interesting piece of furniture. I'd have liked something like that. Hide things from you.'

'What have you got to hide?'

'I do have a private life.'

'And I have never poked round your room in search of it. Ever.'

'Good.'

'The old bill have been round again. They're after me. They've found out I was still here on the night in question.'

'It doesn't matter. If you didn't do it, what can they do?'

Marcus looked at his daughter in disbelief. 'Do you think a miscarriage of justice is an abstract concept? Tell that to the Guildford Four.'

'How did you get on up at Bernie's?'

'Complete bloody lunatic.'

'I told you.'

'Yes, well there are degrees of insanity. Did you get it?'

'The address? Do you want me to lose my job?'

'Of course not. It's just an address. So you didn't?'

'How could I allow my father to die in prison?' She pulled a piece of paper from the cover of her mobile phone and handed it to Marcus.

'Yes!' Marcus exclaimed as soon as he saw what was written on the paper, and he got to his feet and kissed his daughter on the forehead. He then made his way to his all-in-one office, the large cupboard against the wall, and rooted around in drawers until he found what he was looking for. 'I thought I did,' he said as he held up more keys.

'You still have the keys to his flat?'

'I do. And I have every right to use them. He still has my stuff and he owes me six months' rent.'

'What if he changed the locks?'

'Then I'm buggered. You'd better hope for your old man's sake he hasn't.'

'And when are you going to attempt this act of stupidity?'

'How stupid?'

'Er, the police? Don't you think they'll be checking out your American friend themselves?'

'Don't bank on it. They're not the nation's finest. Trust me.'

'So when?'

'In the morning. After a bit of R and R and with a foolproof plan in place.'

'Is this going to involve the chicken place again? How did that go, by the way?'

'Not quite as smoothly as I'd hoped, to be honest, but our friends out back were oblivious, so successfully.'

Imogen shook her head and walked from the room. 'I'm going to have a shower. Going out.'

'On a Sunday night?' Marcus called after her and followed her into the corridor.

'Off tomorrow,' his daughter replied as she shut herself in her bedroom.

Well that'll be our colonial friend again then, I suppose, Marcus thought. Two nights in a row. Clearly serious. Clearly something he was going to have to get used to.

He was still standing in the corridor when Imogen re-emerged in a dressing gown. 'He's calling for me and I'm running late. Could you entertain him till I'm ready?' She disappeared into the bathroom before he could object. He was coming here? Didn't he get a say in this? Obviously not. He was wondering just how he would fulfil his brief, when a shadow crossed the window and the doorbell rang. Great. Marcus opened the door. A nervous looking Kai Holding was standing on the landing. He smiled at Marcus.

'Hello, sir. Is Immy ready?'

'Far from it, young man. Would you care to cross the threshold and partake of a little light lubrication while we await her emergence?'

Kai was nervous enough, and passing the time of day with this strange man was not the relaxant he required. Nevertheless, he accepted the invitation and entered the flat.

'Sit yourself in there.' Marcus gestured to the lounge. 'What tickles your fancy?'

'Oh, well, what do you have?'

'To be frank, bugger all, sir. But I could probably rustle up a cup of something. I no longer stock fermented intoxicants owing to my own personal failings, and I am sorry that this deprives my guests of the pleasure. However, guests are infrequent and hence the deprivation likewise infrequent. I crave your indulgence on this occasion.'

Kai thought he had the gist of the message. 'Coffee?' he ventured.

'A good choice, sir. I believe I have the relevant ingredients.' He disappeared into the kitchen and Kai entered the lounge. He looked around, getting a feel for the home of his new obsession. Sitting on the settee, he looked at a large painting on the wall opposite. It was colourful and he supposed quite accomplished, but he couldn't fathom what it was supposed to represent. He was just starting to relax and look forward to seeing Imogen when a voice boomed from over his shoulder, 'Milk?' Kai swung his head round to see the grizzled features of his host poking through a hatch a few inches from his own.

'Oh, no, black's fine.'

'Is it? If you say so.' And the gargoyle withdrew.

Kai turned back to the painting. He then inched down the settee to put some distance between himself and the hatch. He was replaying the words he'd just heard and interrogating their meaning, when Marcus reappeared in the doorway with a steaming cup of coffee. Kai took the cup as he was handed it.

'Thank you.'

Marcus sat in the armchair and appraised his guest. Kai squirmed and sipped his drink.

'Whither wander you this even?' Marcus enquired.

'Erm, eating out somewhere, I think. Immy's choice. Is that what-'

'Indeed? Two nights on the bounce?'

'Yes. Immy's not working tomorrow.'

'So I gather. And you?'

'I am, but...'

'But?'

'But I'm owed some time off, so...'

'So?'

Bloody third degree, Kai thought. Still, better not upset the man. 'I could phone in. If...

'If?'

'If necessary.'

'Necessary? How so?'

'If it's a late night and...'

'And?'

Oh, for God's sake. What did he want him to say? 'And it looks like I'd be too tired. For work.'

'Tire easily, do you?'

'No, but I do need sleep.'

'Sleep, yes. Best to sleep.'

What was the man driving at? How was Immy the fruit of this freak's loins? Maybe he should deflect this inquisition. 'I was admiring your painting.'

'Ah. The Grist. Damned fine piece, don't you think? Cost an arm and a leg. Are you familiar with the artist?'

Kai wasn't sure if Grist was the artist or the work. 'No,' was the safest and most honest reply.

'Hector Grist. Love his stuff.'

'What's it called?' Might get a clue to what I'm looking at, Kai thought.

'*The Transience of Love.*'

Nope. Not useful. 'Great.' Help!

'Not finding it a bit graphic?'

Kai looked harder. What was he missing?

'Doesn't leave much to the imagination, does it?' Marcus

grinned horrifically.

Kai thought imagination was all he had to go on. Marcus suddenly thought better of titillating the young man, what with his daughter showering down the corridor and having no wish to encourage him in that way.

'How's the coffee?'

'Fine. Thank you.'

'So, what services do you render to acquire remuneration?'

'My job?'

'Indeed.'

'Advertising.'

'Ah. The art of the conman. Selling a dream to sell crap. Not that I did not once myself sell my soul to keep the wolf from the door.'

'How do you mean?'

'Breakfast cereal. Chocky Wockies. Remember them?'

'I think so.'

'The bowl of chocolatey crunch that sees you through to lunch. Delivered à la Robert Newton while I grimaced at the camera, having dug up the packet from my stash of buried treasure. Not my finest hour, but it kept me in ale.'

'I'd like to think we are delivering something a little more sophisticated these days.'

'Would you? How touching.'

Kai was wondering how long this torture would last, when Imogen swept into the lounge radiating fragrance and comeliness. 'Sorry to keep you waiting. You two getting along?'

Kai jumped up grinning from ear to ear from relief and to see that his memory from last night was, if anything, underestimating her allure. 'Yeah. You ready then?'

'I am. Bit rushed, but take me as you find me.'

This was an invitation Kai would gladly have accepted had not her father been glowering up at him with his meanest mien. 'Let's go then.' Then to Marcus, 'Thanks for the coffee.'

'You're welcome.' Marcus's face gave the lie to his words.

Kai went to open the front door. Imogen looked at her father quizzically.

'What?'

'I hope you've not been mean to him,' she said *sotto voce*.

Marcus affected wounded innocence. Imogen frowned at him and followed Kai out. When he heard the front door shut, Marcus got himself upright and made his way into the hall. He peered through the window and saw Imogen and Kai walking away from the foot of the stairs. The boy had his hand on the small of his daughter's back. His face clouded. As he watched them move off down the back lane, they passed the black Audi. Have they really nothing better to do? he thought. Well, once more unto the breach, crying thank God for Harry, to abridge the bard.

12

For the second time in his life Kai Holding leaned on the door of the Sack of Balls. He allowed Imogen to enter and followed her in. Colin's face lit up as he saw his favourite young lady, then darkened when he saw who she was with.

'Hello Colin. We're back,' Imogen announced as she arrived at the bar. 'Remember Kai.'

Colin nodded curtly at him.

'Don't worry. I've established he's not a weirdo. I think.'

Colin took a small pile of coins from a shelf behind the bar and put them down in front of Kai. 'Your change.'

Kai looked at the money. Initially he had no idea why he had been given it, then he remembered the twenty pounds he had laid on the bar for last night's round. 'Oh, I didn't expect change. Keep it.'

'No, you're all right.'

Odd, Kai thought. Why was he bothering to give him what was really very little money? Was that it? Did he see it as an insult? But it wasn't supposed to be a tip. He was just giving enough to cover the round and he didn't want to hang around for change. There was something strange going on here. Was this a race thing too? The man didn't want to feel indebted to him? Kai shrugged and pocketed the coins. 'What are you having?' he asked Imogen.

'A glass of wine, I think. White.'

'A glass of your finest white wine please landlord. And a pint of the Krugelhoffer for me.'

When they both had a drink in front of them, Kai waved his bank card at the machine Colin was holding out and, without meeting the man's eyes, lifted his pint and turned away. With Imogen at his shoulder clutching her drink, he escorted her to the same table as the night before and, this time, he slid in beside her on the banquette.

'Cheers.' He clinked glasses with his date. 'Here's looking at you.'

'Kid.'

'Immy.'

'Anything original?'

'Felt right.'

'Did it?'

' Sorry. Just... It's very nice to be looking at you again.' Kai smiled and looked into Imogen's eyes. The effect was intoxicating. He was smitten. 'How are you feeling today?'

'Fine. You?'

'Very fine. Busy day?'

'Not too bad.' She was remembering the aftermath of her father's visit. Being called to assess Howard Poot and the shambles left behind. 'Soon be over. Moving into F2 soon. Then things will really hot up. A and E next.'

'Wow. Tough, eh?'

'Maybe.' She was sort of looking forward to it, but not without a little nervousness. In many ways it would be more straightforward than psychiatry. More definite outcomes. Still, not a subject for tonight. 'Sorry about Dad. Was he too weird?'

Kai laughed. 'Some dude. How do you cope?'

'All I've ever known.'

'How old were you when your mum went?'

'Four.'

'You do remember her then?'

She did. Perhaps not clearly. There were not many definite images she could recall. It was more the feelings. The very real sense of being loved. And protected. Of being cuddled. And laughing a lot. That was why it was all so devastating when she left. It didn't make any sense to her. Why would her mother, who, as far as she was aware had been a good mother to her, suddenly just go? Abandon her. There was not much laughter after that. For a long time.

'Must have been awful when she went.'

Imogen shrugged and looked at her drink. Kai could see it was a sensitive subject, even after so long. 'Sorry. I shouldn't have -'

'No. It's fine. Long time ago.'

'Pretty unusual though. That way round. I could imagine your dad doing it.'

'He's been great. When he eventually got the hang of it.' She wasn't going to go into the hellish years she spent before Marcus stopped drinking. All her early schooling was against a backdrop of his appalling alcoholism. She wasn't even sure how he maintained custody of her. He must have turned on the charm when he needed to. She didn't see so much of it herself then. Sometimes. There were moments of tenderness. Maudlin, self-pitying tenderness, but enough to keep her from feeling totally bereft. But since the drinking stopped, he'd really made an effort, and she loved him for that.

'He thinks the police believe he killed her,' she said, after a short pause.

'What? Do *you*?'

'Of course not. She definitely left.'

'How do you know? You were only four.' Kai was becoming alarmed.

'She left a note.'

'How do you remember that?'

'I still have it.'

'Really? What did she say?'

Imogen knew it off by heart. Ever since she had picked the crumpled paper from the bin where her father had thrown it, she had looked at it many times. At first, of course, she couldn't read it, but, as soon as she could, she had tried to divine its true meaning beyond the obvious message.

Marcus. You're making things impossible. I have to get away. You don't need to know where. I can't cope at the moment and I need time to work out what to do. I can't believe I'm trusting you, but you are in charge of Imogen for now while I sort a few things out. Can you please take that responsibility seriously and love that child? She adores you. Me, not so much. This is your chance to step up and be a father. Don't blow it. Fleur.' Imogen looked at Kai. There were tears in her eyes. Kai had no choice but to slide along and put his arms round her. She let him and rested her head on his chest.

'I'm sorry. That must really hurt.' He rested his cheek on the top of her head. He was going to look after this girl. Thorn's time was up.

Imogen pulled away a little and looked up at Kai again. 'Don't you think it sounds like she was coming back?'

Kai had to agree. 'I did get that impression, yes.'

Imogen had never shared this with anyone. No-one, not even her father, knew she had the note. She was trusting this boy with the most intimate and raw of all her emotions. She didn't know if this was wise, but she felt a great sense of relief. Instinctively she felt she could trust him with this knowledge. 'I wonder what changed.'

Kai was wondering if Thorn had found her and the police were right, but he kept that to himself. 'She must have had her reasons.'

'Something must have happened. I'm sure she meant to come back. That's what has kept me from hating her all these years.'

Kai became aware that the eagle-eyed landlord was a spectator to this intimate scene. He hated this. 'Shall we wander?'

Imogen smiled and dabbed her eyes on her sleeve. 'Okay.'

They got up and, without even a glance at Colin, left the pub, Imogen holding tightly to Kai's arm with both her hands, as though drawing strength from him.

13

Without really thinking about it, Kai and Imogen had found themselves in the Parrot Café once more. Surrounded by the cheerful murals, Imogen had filled Kai in on everything Marcus had told her with regard to the case of the missing girl in the nineteen eighties, and why this had now led the police to their door. By the end of the account, Kai was seriously concerned that the woman he wanted to spend the rest of his life with was living with a serial killer, and he was determined to remove her from danger as soon as possible. He couldn't let her go back there alone tonight, but nor was he going to jeopardise the relationship by being too pushy. He needn't have worried as Imogen had already decided that she wasn't going to let him leave her tonight. She wanted to spend the night with his arms around her. Sharing with him her memories of her mother had left her feeling vulnerable. She had needed *her* then; she needed *him* now.

After they had finished eating, Imogen had gone to the toilet and taken the opportunity to phone her dad. She wanted him forewarned that she would not be coming back alone tonight, and to extract a promise that he would not be weird about it. She was, after all, a grown woman with a right to a private life. Naturally, he was not happy, but she had managed to get the assurances she needed, and she returned to the table with a delicious smile on her face that Kai couldn't truly appreciate, but which he gratefully received.

As they strolled back, they had already graduated from the early awkwardness of the previous night to a comfortable intimacy; Kai's arm round her shoulders, hers round his waist.

They stopped frequently so they could kiss.

When they passed Ken Tucker's Fried Chicken and reached the corner of the block, Kai was preparing to have to let her go. But as Imogen pulled away from a prolonged smooch, she put her hand on the back of his neck and pulled him down so she could whisper in his ear. The invitation she then gave him set his heart hammering in his chest.

'Are you sure?' he said. Praise the Lord, he thought.

They scampered up the metal stairs, an allegro percussion echoing from the nearby walls. Once inside the flat, all Kai wanted to do was keep Imogen away from her deranged father and shut himself in her room with her, but they were obliged to exchange some niceties with their host, who appeared to be sitting in silence in the lounge.

'Everything alright?' Imogen asked.

'Absolutely fine. Why shouldn't it be?'

Remember, not weird, she thought. 'Good. We'll turn in then. See you tomorrow?'

'I guess.'

'Goodnight,' Kai offered. Marcus just looked at him deadpan, then turned away.

Kai followed Imogen down the corridor to the end, and she opened her bedroom door.

'Where's the loo?' Kai asked. Imogen pointed to a door opposite and a little further down the shorter arm of the L-shaped corridor, and he nipped through it. While he made himself comfortable and prepared for his eagerly anticipated night, Imogen got ready for bed.

When Kai pulled open the bathroom door to leave, he found Marcus blocking his path.

'Got a condom?' he whispered.

Kai was freaked out. 'Yes thanks.'

'Well use it. Okay?'

'I will.' He squeezed past the strange and possibly murderous brute and let himself into Imogen's room. He was a little shaken by this encounter, but as soon as he had closed the bedroom door behind him and he looked towards the bed, he had no thoughts for anyone but Imogen. It was warm, so she had removed the duvet from the bed entirely, along with all her clothes, and was lying invitingly on her back on the bed, propped up on her pillows, with one knee up. She looked magnificent, the shy expression on her face somewhat at odds with her brazen nudity. Kai had never felt luckier or hornier, and he quickly undressed and rolled onto the bed beside her. He wanted this to be sensational, so he was silently telling himself to take his time. He kissed her slowly and passionately. He felt her hand on his shoulder. She pulled him closer so their bodies touched. The heat and softness of her skin was wonderful. He lifted his head and looked deeply into her eyes. Was this what love felt like? It was most certainly what lust felt like. He realised he hadn't got a condom ready, and was about to break away to get one, when he saw that Imogen was holding one ready for him, already out of its packet. He smiled. What a girl. He went to take it, but she said, 'Allow me', and pushed him gently over on to his back.

When Kai woke, light was streaming through gaps around the curtains, and he found the duvet pulled up over his lower half and Imogen curled up at his side. How different this was to some of his previous dates. She was adorable and he wasn't running anywhere. He lay watching her sleeping. Suddenly there was a knock at the door and Imogen stirred. She smiled to see Kai's face, but quickly looked as concerned as he did.

'What is it?' she called out.

'Coffee,' came her father's reply.

Imogen jumped up and grabbed her dressing gown from the back of her door. Kai pulled the duvet over himself. When Imogen opened the door, she saw a smiling Marcus holding a tray with two mugs of coffee, one black one white, and a plate of buttered toast. She gave him a quizzical look, thanked him and took the tray from him and laid it on the bed, kicking the door closed with her foot.

'It seems we have room service,' she said. 'Not sure what that's all about, but I'll take it in the spirit it was offered. Good morning, by the way.'

'Morning.' Kai smiled at her.

Smiling back, Imogen handed him the black coffee, and took the white one and got back into bed with it. This was the first day of the rest of their lives and it was starting rather well. They may not always have nights as synchronous as that one, but that will always be their first and they both knew it had been special.

When they had finished the coffees and toast, it didn't take much more than a little eye contact before they were making love again. Less urgently, but no less passionately.

Eventually they emerged from the room. They could hear Marcus pottering about in the kitchen, from where aromas of cooking were drifting, and, while Kai popped into the bathroom, Imogen went to investigate what her father was up to.

'We've had toast, remember.' She could see and smell a smorgasbord of breakfast treats in preparation - her father had clearly been shopping - and, glancing through the hatch, she could see the table was laid for three.

'I'm sure you've worked up an appetite,' Marcus said archly.

Oh, please. Not my own father, she thought. Couldn't he just pretend they'd only been sleeping? Anyway, why was he being so nice? Bit of a change from his surliness last night. 'Everything alright?'

'Absolutely. New day, new plan. When will you be ready for this?'

'A shower would be nice. Can you give us, what, twenty minutes?'

'No problem. Let me know when to put the eggs on?'

'Sure.' Imogen returned to her bedroom bemused.

It was after nine when they all sat down to eat. Kai was still wary of Marcus, but he gratefully and graciously accepted the offerings and filled his belly. When their plates were empty, Marcus gathered them up, and then his behaviour became clear.

'I had a little boon to crave,' he started.

The two young lovers looked at him expectantly.

'You know this business with the boys in blue, watching my every move? Well, I've thought of a way you could assist my escape.'

Imogen was cringing inside and hoping Kai would not react badly.

'I need a distraction,' Marcus continued. 'If you happened to be in the takeaway downstairs when I wish to effect my egress, one of you could linger by the lower door and alert me when the coast is clear with a judicious tap on the timber. T'other one could distract the staff and signal when said tap should be administered. What do you say?'

It didn't feel dangerous or particularly irksome, so, after looking at each other to gauge the other's response, Imogen and Kai agreed to the plan. Of course, Kai didn't know why Marcus wanted to get out unseen, but, if Imogen wanted to assist her father, he was happy to go along with her. He could always alert the police later if he thought he was trying to evade justice.

'Excellent.' Marcus was delighted his plan was coming together.

While Imogen and Kai cleared the table and stacked the dishwasher, Marcus made sure he had everything he needed. Stairway keys, check. Poot's flat keys, check. One bag for the removal of evidence, check. When he was satisfied that he was ready, he sent the other two out the front door and started his descent. He had changed the light bulb, so he had no trouble seeing on this occasion, and arrived behind the lower door to await the signal. Once he had the key in the lock and his hand on it, he flicked off the light again and waited in the dark. This time some light was spilling round the door, so the darkness was not so profound.

When Imogen and Kai entered the takeaway, they bought themselves coffees and went to sit at one of the tables near the stair door. They waited till there were no other customers in the restaurant, and as they did so, Imogen explained the part of the story she hadn't given Kai about Howard Poot and his flat, his mental health and her father's conviction that this man was involved in the disappearance of the girl. And how he believed the police were trying to pin it on him, so wanted to gather his own evidence to exonerate himself. Kai listened with interest, but his concern for Imogen's safety was not diminished. Her father sounded as barking as she said the American was, and thus equally likely to be guilty.

Eventually there was a lull when the last customer left and none came in, so Kai looked across at the counter and waited till one of the two staff there withdrew. Then he and Imogen jumped up and Kai went to the counter while Imogen waited by the stair door. Kai requested some tap water, because he could see that the sink was in the kitchen and the young woman would have to desert the counter to get it. As soon as she did so, he signalled to Imogen who tapped on the door. She heard the key turn and her father emerged blinking into the light. When the woman came back with the water, Marcus just looked like a customer who had entered in her absence and seemed to know these other two. Kai handed Marcus the water, he took a swig, then they all exited into the street.

Once outside, Marcus thanked his accomplices for their assistance. 'Worked like a dream.'

'Yes. I hope the rest does.' Imogen was feeling anxious.

'What could possibly go wrong? We know Poot's safely locked up.'

'What if he doesn't live alone?'

Marcus thought this unlikely, but he assured his daughter he would be careful. Imogen didn't feel she could leave him to do it alone. 'Would you like a lookout?'

'I'm sure that's not necessary, but if it's what you want, I'll gratefully accept the offer.'

Kai looked at Imogen a little alarmed. He had phoned his work to take the day off, so he wasn't letting her out of his sight. Especially not to engage in potentially hazardous activity. 'I'll come with you.'

Imogen looked up at Kai and smiled. 'You sure?'

'One hundred percent.'

Marcus looked at his two young confederates and felt a little touched by their support. 'Your assistance is greatly appreciated. Follow me then.' And the three amigos set off towards the river.

As soon as they arrived at the main entrance to Prince Regent Mansions, Marcus saw his first problem. While in his day there had been a simple Yale lock, the key for which he had in his pocket, now there was a sophisticated card operated system. Not that he would have known how it worked had it not had the words PRESENT CARD HERE etched on the reader. He, of course, had no such item.

'Great. It's a waiting game then. We need a kind neighbour.'

'Hadn't you better push the buzzer to see if there's anyone in?' Imogen suggested.

'Perhaps a sensible precaution, granted.' Marcus looked at the board of surnames, numbers and buttons and saw his one-time flatmate's name by flat 2/1, as he remembered. He pressed the corresponding button and waited. No reply. He tried again. Still nothing. 'See. Your fears are unfounded, my dear.'

Imogen didn't feel this was conclusive evidence, but she felt a little calmer all the same. Just then the front door was opened from within by an elderly but sprightly lady whom Marcus fancied he recalled from his days in residence, but he decided against that tack in his pursuit of entry. Keeping his smile to a minimum, he addressed the departing resident. 'Ah, madam?'

The woman looked up at Marcus in some alarm, but the sight of the two younger people with him, whose smiles were more generous and attractive, eased some of her anxiety.

'So sorry to trouble you,' Marcus continued. 'I was bringing my young companions to visit their ailing uncle, but I have inadvertently left my entry card in another jacket. May we take the opportunity of your departure to affect our ingress?'

The lady was not untroubled by doubts, but the ongoing reassurance of the pretty young smiles and her own politeness won out over caution, and she held open the door to allow their passage.

'I am much obliged to you madam. Your kindness will not go unrewarded, I have no doubt.'

The woman smiled uncertainly as she let go of the door and set off down the road.

'Marvellous,' Marcus announced. 'Your performances were exemplary, my dears. And so, to the ascent.'

Imogen thought it best to remind her father of their function in this enterprise. 'We are here to look out for trouble, remember? Maybe we should station ourselves over there by the river. I can call you if anyone comes.'

'Good idea. You do that. Leave the dirty work to me.'

Imogen and Kai left Marcus to it and crossed the road. There was a bench the other side of the small tributary of the Thames, so they walked a little down the road to where a footbridge allowed them to cross the waterway, and then returned to sit on the bench, looking across at the front door of the block. Two young lovers sitting by a river. What could be less suspicious?

Meanwhile, Marcus was climbing to the second floor. The last time he had done this it would have been a breeze. Now, the effects of age and yesterday's exertions, meant he arrived breathless at flat 2/1 as his two allies assumed their watch. As he did so, he reached into the canvas bag he had slung over his shoulder and produced a pair of yellow kitchen gloves, which he eased on to his hands.

At first glance the door appeared as he remembered it. It had possibly been repainted over the years, but there were no obvious differences. He was relieved to see this door still had a Yale lock on the right with a mortise lock a foot or two below it. Fishing out the keys from his pocket with his gloved fingers, he took hold of the longest one first and slotted it into the lower lock. Now the moment of truth. He twisted it anti-clockwise. It wouldn't budge. Damn. His heart sank. Almost as an afterthought, and with no expectation of success, he turned it clockwise. The key rotated and the bolt slid into place. It hadn't been locked. Great. He reopened it. If that lock was the same, hopefully the other one was too. Selecting the Yale key with the red sleeve over the head, which distinguished it from the sleeveless one for the now defunct street door lock, he slid it into the upper keyway. He took a deep breath and turned it. It moved, and, with a small nudge, the door opened inwards with a squeal of protest from the hinges.

Marcus's delight was swiftly overwhelmed by an atrocious odour which assaulted his nostrils. What in God's name did that freak get up to in here? It was dark inside, so he switched on the light. This revealed a filthy, litter-strewn hallway, which had clearly not been acquainted with broom nor vacuum cleaner in a long time. The walls were streaked in places with various dried fluids, what looked like blood conspicuous amongst them. Bracing himself, he shut the door behind him and surrendered to the fetid interior. Most of the doors off this hall were closed. Was that why it was so dark? Marcus moved down the hall to the lounge. This door was open, but the room was nevertheless in darkness, the curtains being drawn tightly together. Switching on the light, a truly shocking scene of squalor was illuminated. The floor and all surfaces had multiple items of rubbish, many cans and bottles and decaying matter, scattered over them, and revolting stains were festering on the carpet and couches. Across the coffee table, amongst further dross, were strewn an array of the drug-taker's paraphernalia - spoons, cigarette papers, lighters et cetera - and, most alarming of all, used needles. Quite apart from the stench, Marcus wanted to leave as soon as possible to avoid coming to harm. But he had to focus on his mission.

Treading carefully, he picked his way through the garbage. He wanted to look in a large dresser against the wall which he remembered was Poot's preferred repository. Mindful of the need not to disturb any more than was absolutely necessary, in order not to leave a record of his presence, when he arrived at this filthy piece of furniture, he started carefully sliding open the various drawers in search of his evidence. He was at once taken aback that the contents of these drawers were in a much more ordered state than anything on open surfaces. The third drawer he opened caused him to take a sharp intake of breath; ill-advised in the rank air. On top of what appeared to be a pile of letters, he saw his name and this address written in a curly hand on a postcard. There were several more beneath it. Hallelujah! That was easier than he had expected. He had no idea why Poot would have kept them, but he was mighty glad he had.

As he reached into the drawer and tried to pick up the cards with his rubbery fingers, he was suddenly stopped in his tracks by a loud buzzing sound. Someone was at the door. He scrabbled for his phone, but found, once he had it in his hand, that he couldn't operate it with the gloves on. Balancing it on the edge of the dresser, where there was no more than a thick layer of dust, he was about to remove a glove, when the phone emitted his chosen ringtone; *Hey There* by Rosemary Clooney. It also vibrated, which caused it to topple into a grey soup of indeterminate composition on the revolting carpet. Shit. He reached down and retrieved it from the puddle as Ms Clooney sang 'Love never made a fool of you'. Brushing off some of the clinging goo, he placed it more securely on the dresser while he ripped off a glove. Then, picking it up again with the still gloved hand, he managed to accept the call, Ms Clooney getting no further than 'Throw a crumb to you.' Putting the still contaminated phone to his ear, he heard his daughter's agitated voice demanding to know why he took so long to answer.

'It's a delicate operation, Imogen.' The buzzer sounded again, a more prolonged blast. 'Who is that at the door?'

'So it is that flat? I think she's a policewoman.'

'Fuck flaps. Are you sure?'

'She's with a cop in uniform.'

'Great.'

'She looks like she's speaking to someone now. On the intercom. Now she's sending the other one out into the street. He's looking up at the building. And waving. Oh no, she's got in the front door.'

'Oh, fuck fuck fuck.'

'She presumably can't get into the flat. If you don't open the door.'

'I'm hardly going to do that, am I? What do you take me for? Shit!' Realising he had to act fast, he tiptoed into the hall, switching off the lounge light first. Then he had just switched off the hall light, when there was a loud knock on the door and the letterbox was lifted. He threw himself to one side and pinned himself to the wall by the door, desperate to avoid detection.

'Hello. Is anybody in?' a female voice enquired through the slot. 'I'm Sergeant Moore. Police. If you're there, could you please open the door?'

Her, Marcus thought. What's that? He realised he had his phone in his hand and he could hear Imogen's frantic voice. Quickly he ended the call, hoping it hadn't been loud enough for the policewoman to hear.

The letterbox closed and Marcus held his breath praying she'd go now. Suddenly it flew open again and a beam of light shone through, picking out various items of trash as it swung from side to side. He pressed himself harder into the wall, holding in his belly and flattening his shoulder bag against it to avoid the beam. Eventually the swinging torchlight was extinguished, and the letterbox snapped shut. Marcus could hear Sergeant Moore talking to someone else, presumably the other officer, describing the state of the flat. Then the voices became fainter and he realised they were leaving. He raised his phone and rang his daughter.

'I think they're coming out. Can you confirm?' he said when she answered.

'Are you okay?'

'Fine. Are they?'

'Wait a minute. I think... Yes, here they come. They're getting back into their car. They're talking. Putting on seatbelts. And they're off. Thank God for that.'

'I wholeheartedly concur, my dear. Thank fucking God.'

'Are you coming out now?'

'I can't yet. Not till I have completed my mission.'

'Well hurry up. I don't like this. What if they come back with reinforcements and break in?'

'Can they do that?'

'I don't know. Just hurry up.'

'I will. Bye.' He ended the call and pocketed the phone. Flicking the light on again, he picked his way back to the lounge, switched on that light and returned to the dresser. He pulled on the removed glove again and tried to pick up the pile of postcards. It wasn't easy with the gloves on, so he started sliding one card at a time off the top of the pile and reading them. It was very much as he remembered; gushing declarations of love and excitement. What had he said to her to make her feel this way? He knew he could be a bit of a charmer when he wanted to be persuasive, but surely not with this girl. After he had read each one, he dropped it into his shoulder bag. Eventually he picked up and read the card on which the fateful meeting was proposed. She was desperate to see him. To kiss him. To make love to him. She would come straight to the Bunch of Grapes as soon as she got back from her holiday, and she would be his to do with as he wished. Bloody hell. Still terrifying.

Dropping this card into the bag too, he then shoved both hands into the drawer, managed to scoop up the remaining postcards, and deposited the handful into the bag. Now, did he want to see if any of his stuff was still here? Not really. He was after incriminating evidence on Poot, so he'd better have a look in the rest of the flat.

Stepping over the detritus, he made his way back out into the hall and crossed to what had been Poot's room. This time when he opened the door the curtains were pulled back and the room flooded with daylight. Unlike the rest of the flat, this room was reasonably tidy. He was about to start looking through wardrobes and drawers for anything he could find that might tie Poot to this missing girl, when he became aware of what he had at first thought was just some picture above the bed. Now he could see it was a collage of photographs arranged in a large frame. While that in itself was not particularly noteworthy, what suddenly took his breath away was realising the subject of the photos. Of every photo. It was his wife. Fleur. Dozens of photographs, cut from newspapers, magazines and other sources, of Fleur. His deserting wife. What the...? He recognised many of them. He had been in many himself, but he was not included in the crops. What had Poot to do with Fleur? He didn't know her. Was this some fixation on himself? Did Poot want what he had? Did he meet up with that Ellie and do away with her, then turn his attentions to his wife. Dear God, could he have had anything to do with her leaving?

It was all too overwhelming. This was one sick individual. Marcus remembered that Hutchinson suspected *him* of killing both women, and now the thought that Fleur might actually be dead, and at the hands of that psycho, was too distressing. It was only now it dawned on him that he hadn't really given up on her. Seeing the many images of her looking at him, he realised his anger with her had masked his feelings. His love for her. He sat on the end of the bed and experienced a kind of catharsis as these repressed emotions were released.

He was snapped back to the present when Rosemary Clooney started singing to him again.

'Are you coming,' Imogen wanted to know.

'Yes. Give me five.' He hung up.

Standing up, he smoothed the bed covers to remove the indent he'd made, and left the room, taking one more look at the collage as he closed the door. Realising the evidence was stacking up against Poot, and with no wish to incriminate himself, he decided to return the postcards to the drawer in the dresser. Let the police discover them. He didn't know what he had been thinking anyway.

Switching off the light, he repositioned the lounge door more or less where he had found it, and went to leave the flat. The last door on the left before the front door was his old room. He was mindful of the possibility that the police might return, but curiosity got the better of him, and he opened that door. He immediately wished he hadn't. The stench which hit him was truly appalling. The room was lit by a dim bedside light which revealed a gruesome sight. Lying on the bed, in a state of on-going decomposition, was what he took, from its size and the length of the hair, to be a female body. For a moment he had the awful thought it might be Fleur and, with a hand over his mouth and nose, he flicked on the overhead light. Although this made the sight all the more horrendous - a profusion of wriggling maggots evident on the unclothed parts and clearly equally active beneath a t-shirt and sweatpants - he could see that the hair, though predominantly white, retained enough red hairs to ease his fears. And, in any case, if Poot had done harm to his wife, it would have been years ago, and this poor woman had clearly met her end much more recently. He flicked off the light and quickly closed the door to contain the many flies which filled the room. Reeling from this grim discovery and his mixed emotions, he opened the front door, switched off the last light, and pulled the door closed behind him.

He quickly descended the stairs and left the building, pulling off the gloves once outside and stuffing them in his bag. Imogen and Kai jumped to their feet when they saw him and hurried round over the bridge to meet him. They could see immediately that something was wrong, but Marcus just gestured for them to follow him and marched off down the street.

14

After Sergeant Moore had left, Cynthia Nelson had spent most of Sunday, and now much of Monday morning, putting on paper her memories of her daughter. She had found the words flowed easily, as through tears, but with happy memories too, she presented the girl she remembered for the police to discover. Edward had chipped in with thoughts and recollections of his own, and what Cynthia now held in her hand was a portrait of a person with enormous potential and determination who could have achieved anything to which she had put her mind. A girl who would not give up until she had attained whatever goal she had set herself.

Laying the sheets of writing paper down on the kitchen table and tidying them into a neat little stack, she turned to her husband.

'Ted? I think it's time.'

'What do you mean?'

'We should make the move now. They've said the room's ready. It's not as if the police can't still speak to us. There's nothing here now. We can't live in a shell of a house.'

'What about the remaining furniture?'

'There's really not very much. Let the new people have it. If they want it.'

'Okay dear. If that's what you want. I'll let the home know. When did you have in mind?'

'Let's do it tomorrow. Help me pack up what we're taking this afternoon and I'll see if Dennis can take us over with it all in his van in the morning.' Satisfied that a decision had now been taken, Cynthia started to get to her feet, when the doorbell rang.

'Could you get that, Ted?'

It was Stephanie Moore again, as promised. She followed Edward back into the kitchen and sat at the table. Edward put the kettle on.

Cynthia, who had sat herself back down, gestured to the little pile of paper in front of her. 'There it is.'

'That's so kind of you, Mrs Nelson. You never know how useful it might be.' Sergeant Moore gathered together the sheets and slipped them into her jacket pocket.

'Any more news?' Cynthia asked.

'Not really. We have found out where Mr Thorn used to live at the time, but I haven't had chance to speak with his flatmate yet. It seems he still lives there.'

The Nelsons were surprised by this information, and a little encouraged. After so long a time, it was unexpected that such a connection still existed.

'That's wonderful. Maybe he can shed some light on what that man was up to that night.' Cynthia realised she was getting her hopes up and tried to temper them.

Sergeant Moore was equally keen not to raise any false expectations. 'We'll see. He wasn't in this morning when I called round.' She remembered the state of the flat and what this suggested about the present condition of Mr Howard Poot, and was under no illusions that this might well not be a very profitable lead.

'We're going to move into Meadow View care home tomorrow, Sergeant,' Cynthia informed the policewoman. 'Will you still be happy to pop by and keep us in the picture?'

'Oh. Okay. Not a problem. Are you ready now then?'

'More or less. Just mainly the kitchen units to empty. Not that we'll be needing most of what's there. The rest is just clothes and a few ornaments and stuff that we've already got in boxes.'

'How will you get it all over to the home?'

'Oh, we know a man with a van. Son of a friend of mine. He's already been really helpful with selling the furniture.'

'That's good. Oh, talking of furniture. What about the esca- esci- the desk?'

Cynthia realised she hadn't considered this. 'Have you finished with it?'

'I think so. What would you like us to do with it?'

Cynthia wasn't sure. Given how that woman who wanted to buy it had behaved, she wasn't too keen to let her have it now. But she still had the problem of not having room for it where she was going. Although, maybe she should wait till she was in there. There might be space if they got rid of something else. It would be nice to have this piece of Ellie with them. 'Would you mind holding on to it for now, and I'll think about it?'

'Of course. Get yourself settled in first.'

Edward crashed a cup on to a saucer and turned round. 'I take it you didn't find any more secret drawers?'

'No, Mr Nelson. That seems to have been the only one. Very clever though. Look, I won't stay for a cuppa.' She stood up. 'We all have plenty to be getting on with. I'll leave you to your packing. Thanks for this.' She patted the papers in her pocket. 'I'll be in touch soon.' The policewoman was in two minds whether to return her chair to the front room, but settled for leaving it where it was and making her way out to the front door.

'Thank you, Stephanie,' Cynthia called after her. 'We're very grateful for your efforts.'

'My pleasure.' And the front door shut.

'Nice girl,' Cynthia said to her husband.

'I suppose,' Edward replied. 'Shall we get on with packing up then? Have a cuppa later?'

'Probably best.' Cynthia struggled up again and took hold of her walking frame. As she made her way slowly out into the hall, intent on making the journey upstairs to pack her suitcases, Edward pulled a drawer out of the kitchen units and emptied its contents on to the table. He set about picking through them with the aid of his magnifying glass.

15

All the way back to his flat Marcus didn't say a word, just marched on like a man possessed, head down and eyes haunted. Imogen tried to elicit some explanation for her father's behaviour, but, when he paused and threw up his breakfast over a garden wall, she realised now was not the time.

As they approached the flat and passed the black Audi, Marcus noticed nothing, but Imogen was aware of a degree of panic within.

Once inside the flat, Imogen asked Kai if he could put the kettle on, and she got her father to sit down in the lounge.

'I think you're in a bit of shock, Dad. What happened back there?'

Marcus looked at his daughter. She thought he might cry, but he turned and stared out the window.

It wasn't until Kai brought in a tray of coffees and placed it on the coffee table that Marcus turned back, to see where the aroma was coming from. He looked up at Kai and stared straight into his eyes. Kai was a little alarmed as he didn't say anything at first, just kept looking at him, but eventually Marcus gave a weak smile and said, 'Thank you. That was nice of you.'

'What happened, Dad?' Imogen tried again.

Marcus stared out of the window once more and said quietly, 'There's a dead woman in that flat.'

Imogen was at once alarmed. 'Oh, my God. Are you sure?'

'Sure of what?'

She realised it was a stupid question. 'You'll have to call the police.'

'How can I?'

She could see his point.

Kai realised Marcus was not behaving like a serial killer, and tried to help. 'The police are already looking into the flat, aren't they? They just need to get in and they'll find the...the...the body.'

Marcus considered this. 'But they have no reason to force their way in.'

'What was the state of the body?' Imogen asked, switching into professional mode.

Marcus didn't really care to remember. 'Awful.'

'Maggots?'

Marcus nodded.

'Then it must have smelled?'

Marcus still had the foul odour in his nose. 'It did.' He gagged.

'So it must be apparent to neighbours. Surely?'

Marcus shrugged. He hadn't noticed it till he opened the flat door.

'What if you call the police pretending to be a concerned neighbour and report the smell?' Kai suggested.

'They'd want to know who I was.' Marcus didn't see how this would work.

'Say you wish to remain anonymous because you don't want to cause any trouble with your neighbours,' Imogen offered. 'And call from a payphone.'

Marcus realised he had to do something, not only because it could get the police off his back, but also for the sake of the poor woman. But he also knew he was being watched, and couldn't just go out to find a payphone.

'I'll go,' Kai said.

Imogen looked at Kai and smiled. 'Thank you.'

'What was the flat number?'

'Two/one,' Marcus told him. 'It might be an idea to tell them you heard Mr Poot is in hospital. Speed things up.'

'Okay. I'll be back,' and he got up and left the flat.

'Really appreciate this', Marcus called after him.

'He's alright, isn't he?' Imogen said to her father when the door had shut.

Marcus looked at her. 'He does seem to be, yes.'

Imogen smiled and hugged him.

They sat like that for a while in silence. Then Marcus suddenly said, 'I thought it was your mother. For a moment.'

Imogen looked at her father in horror. 'What? Why?'

Marcus told her about the photos. She looked at him in disbelief and confusion.

'I know,' he said. 'I don't know what he had to do with her. Maybe he was just a fan. But he would have known she was my wife. So it's definitely weird. Anyway, it looked like she was a redhead.'

'Well surely there's a little more than that to rule out it being Mum. Like the fact the woman has only been dead a couple of weeks, given the state of decomposition.'

'Absolutely,' Marcus agreed.

Imogen became thoughtful. 'What colour was Mum's hair?'

'What? Blonde, you know it was.'

'But that was out of a bottle surely?'

'Well, yes. But she wasn't a redhead.'

Imogen didn't feel comfortable exploring any further how he knew this, and changed the subject. 'Was there any indication how she'd died?'

'I really didn't look too closely.'

'No. But it can't have been anything to do with Mr Poot. He's been in Bernie's for months now.'

Marcus realised this was true, but there was plenty of other evidence of illegal activity in that flat, so Poot had many questions to answer, and he'd rather the police turned their attention on him.

The doorbell rang and Imogen jumped up to let Kai back in.

'All done,' he announced as he entered.

'What did they say?' Imogen asked.

'They just thanked me for the call and said they'd look into it.'

Marcus let out a sigh. He was relieved something might now

be resolved for whoever that woman was, but he realised if she had died from natural causes, it may still not help him. And given Poot's state of mind, the police weren't going to get far with him anyway. Suddenly he made a decision and stood up.

'I'm going to get out on the road. Can't sit here all day brooding.'

Imogen was concerned. 'Are you sure? You've had a shock, Dad.'

'I know, but I want to see how those guys out back play it. It'll take my mind off that image. Hopefully.' He checked he had his car keys, and went out the front door. 'See you later.'

When the door shut, Imogen and Kai looked at each other. All of a sudden they were unexpectedly alone together in the flat. No Marcus cramping their style. Although an awful thing had just happened, it had happened to Marcus, not them. The dominant image for each of them was each other. Kai pulled Imogen to him.

'You okay?' he asked her.

'Yeah. Fine. Thanks for making that call.'

'Not a problem.'

'Well, what now?' Imogen was pretty sure she knew what Kai was thinking.

Kai couldn't believe he suddenly had her all to himself. He realised they had already pretty thoroughly explored each other that morning, and he didn't want to push his luck, but when Imogen planted a soft kiss on his lips and took him by the hand, he knew his luck was holding, and he let her lead him through to her bedroom, the denim of his jeans stretching further with each step.

16

Inspector Richard Hutchinson was at his desk on a caffeine-fuelled mission. He had already worked through most of the night and, after catching a few hours' sleep in the morning, had now been hard at it for most of Monday. He had covered a lot of ground, but he had found relatively little. He felt confident he had identified the right Julie Christie, but, as with Fleur Hardy, there was no trace of her in the twenty-first century. In fact, she appeared to have disappeared twice. She grew up in Basildon, and there were records of her birth in 1962 and subsequent schooling, then one police caution in London in 1980 for possession of drugs, but nothing between then and joining the British Actors' Equity Association in 1989, when she started a job in a regional repertory theatre. He planned to visit this company and see what light could be shed on her missing history. As for her future post-Thorn, well, she didn't appear to have one. And that was as he suspected. All he needed was some tangible evidence of criminality and he could set the CID on that loathsome luvvy. After all, he knew the man was guilty, he could feel it in every fibre of his body. He knew it from the moment he stepped into his flat. When you've put in the number of years he had, you develop a sixth sense.

Picking up his mobile, he called Sergeant Moore. 'Steph. Any plans this evening? ... Good. Fancy a trip down to Surrey for a little culture? ... I'll explain on the way. Meet you out front in ten.' He pocketed his phone and started shutting down his computer and tidying his desk.

As they approached the Rattigan Theatre and drew up in one

of only a few vacant parking spaces, Stephanie Moore knew as much as her boss about the mystery of Julie Christie. In return, the Inspector had been put in the picture about Thorn's flat-mate Howard Poot and his Sergeant's visit to his flat. It was approaching 7pm and the two police officers could see from a large poster by the main entrance that tonight was the opening night of a play called *The Lady Vanishes*. How apt.

As instructed, they walked down the side of the theatre until they reached the Stage Door, identified as such by a painted sign. Inspector Hutchinson pushed it open and approached a desk within a little booth, with a grey-haired man of around eighty sitting behind it, a look of panic on his pink face. The Inspector pulled out his warrant card and flashed it at the man. 'I called earlier.'

'Oh yes, Inspector Hutchinson.' His voice was light and effeminate. 'You'll have to forgive us. We are about to open a new show and things are pretty fraught at this minute. One of our cast is having a mini nervous breakdown and refusing to perform unless changes are made to some of the staging.'

'I see. Well we don't want to get in the way,' the Inspector replied. 'We just wanted a word with Willy Milligan.'

'Yes, that's me. But I'm not sure if I dare leave my post.'

'I see. So you are doorman and...?'

'Well, quite a few things really. I've been here a long time and turned my hand to most things over the years.'

'It's your long service which leads us here,' Inspector Hutchinson explained. 'We are particularly interested in the year 1989. Do you remember a young lady called Fleur Hardy?

The pink face lit up. 'Indeed I do. Lovely Fleur. I wonder what happened to her?'

'As do we, Mr Milligan. Hence we are looking into her past and wondering how she came to work here.'

'She was my ASM. When she started.'

'Your ASM?'

'I was Company Manager back then and we took her on as an acting Assistant Stage Manager. She went on to take on more and more acting roles. She was very good.'

'But where did you find her? What had she done before?'

The old man looked down apparently in search of an answer. 'You know, I really can't remember. I think we gave her an Equity card, so presumably she was just starting out.'

'But she would have been twenty-seven at that time. She must have been doing something beforehand.'

'Yes. She must.' Willy Milligan shook his head, unable to offer more.

Inspector Hutchinson was hoping he hadn't had a wasted journey. 'Well, who actually employed her? They must have seen a CV or something.'

'Ooh, well that must have been Ralph. Ralph Messiter. He was Artistic Director back then.'

'And where might we find him?' He pulled out his notebook.

Before Willy Milligan could answer, a young man with slicked back hair and braces flounced through, declaring, 'Well you can stick your production up your hairy arses. I'm out of here,' and exited through the Stage Door. Willy Milligan looked distraught and struggled to his feet, as a young lady with headphones round her neck, presumably some sort of present-day stage manager Inspector Hutchinson imagined, rushed after him, throwing the old man a look of despair.

'You must forgive me, Inspector,' the old man apologised, and came round through a door and doddered after the other two.

Hutchinson looked at his Sergeant. 'Another world, eh Steph? What's the matter?'

'Nothing.' But something was very much the matter. That was Simon Tanqueray. She'd seen his picture on the poster. He was the strong, silent, ex-SAS soldier Mark Argyll in her favourite soap, *Mafeking Road*. Nothing like this foul-mouthed diva. Devastating.

It wasn't long before the Stage Door opened again and all three re-entered, the two adults offering soothing words and promises.

'I will speak to Graham right now, Simon. I'm sure he can make some tweaks,' the young woman was saying.

'Well I shall be in my dressing room, and I shall not set foot on that stage unless and until little Miss Fishface learns who the star of this show is.' Then he disappeared through a door, followed by the young woman, and was gone. Willy Milligan came back round behind his desk.

'I'm so sorry. It's these television stars. We have to use them more and more these days. You know, bums on seats. No class unfortunately. Too much money being thrown at them. Think they... Well, there it is. The modern world, I suppose.'

'I'm sure you're right, Mr Milligan.' The Inspector was keen to get the old man to refocus. 'Mr Lassiter did you say?' He was standing with his pencil hovering over his notebook.

'Pardon? Oh, no, Messiter. Ralph.'

'Okay. And where would we find him now?'

'Actually, he's here tonight. This production is something of a celebration. It's fifty years since we opened, with this same play, and Ralph was its director back then.'

'He'll be knocking on a bit himself then, I guess,' the Inspector said.

'Indeed he is. He has a few years on me.'

'Well how might we get to speak to him?'

Just then a breathless female voice came through a speaker high on the wall. 'Ladies and gentlemen. This is your fifteen minute call. Fifteen minutes please.' Before the speaker went silent again a male voice could be heard wailing, 'I'm an award-winning director-', then it clicked off. Willy Milligan shrugged apologetically.

'Mr Messiter?' Again the Inspector tried to take control of the agenda.

'Yes. Ralph. Well he'll be going into the auditorium soon. Could you wait till later?'

'How much later?'

'Well there's a twenty-minute interval. Should be about eight twenty-five. All being well. He'll be in the Circle Bar then.

We've cordoned off a little VIP area.'

Inspector Hutchinson looked to his Sergeant. 'Fancy a bite to eat?'

This was a welcome suggestion and Stephanie Moore readily agreed.

'We shall be in the Circle Bar by 8.20 then. Thank you for your help. Oh, how will we recognise Mr Messiter?'

'Ah, well there's a large picture of him in the foyer, straight ahead as you enter. You can't miss it.'

'Excellent. Come on Sergeant. I saw a pub as we approached.'

As the two officers exited the Stage Door, the public address system crackled back into life. 'First aider to dressing room number one please. First aid to dressing room one.'

As the two replete police officers pulled open the front doors of the Rattigan Theatre, they saw on the wall ahead a rakish look- ing gentleman, with a strong jaw and a buttonhole, in a black and white photo of some vintage. They followed the signs to the Circle Bar and showed their warrant cards to the bar staff as they entered. This was clearly the calm before the storm and the bar- tenders were preparing for the onslaught. Various drinks were already poured and distributed around the room, with pieces of paper tucked under each collection indicating whose pre-order each was. Inspector Hutchinson looked across to the cordoned off area at one end of the bar and headed over to it, followed by his Sergeant. Stepping over the rope, the two of them sat con- spicuously at a table and waited.

It wasn't long before a brief smattering of applause could be heard from within the auditorium, and doors were flung open and people started flowing into the bar. The police officers looked around for the face in the foyer, allowing for what time had since done to the features. Eventually, when the bar was full and the VIP area filling, they spotted a tall but stooped gentle- man in a linen suit, with very little hair and a stick, but still cut- ting a bit of a dash, who was heading over towards them accom- panied by a much younger woman. An usher unhooked the rope and showed him to his table, where two glasses of champagne awaited him and his companion. Inspector Hutchinson rose as he approached and took his chair over to join them, Sergeant Moore hovering nearby.

'Ralph Messiter?' the Inspector asked as he placed his chair beside the old gentleman.

'Who's asking? Have we met?'

The Inspector presented his warrant card. 'I'm sorry to spoil your evening, but I need to ask you some questions on a matter of some urgency.'

'Spoil it? You might actually enhance it. Couldn't get much worse, to be honest.' He took a large sip of champagne. 'What can I do for you?'

'We're enquiring about a young woman you employed some years ago.'

'Child support, is it? Can she prove it?'

'No, nothing like that.'

'Phew.'

'Fleur Hardy née Julie Christie.'

'Knew them both. Lovely ladies.'

'They are the same woman. We believe she became Fleur Hardy when you employed her and she joined Equity.'

'Is that so? I'll take your word for that.'

'So you don't remember employing her?'

'Which one?'

'Fleur Hardy.' Inspector Hutchinson feared this was hopeless.

'Indeed I do. Gorgeous young lady. Everything where it should be, if you see what I mean. Turned out to be a cracking little actress too.'

'You sound surprised.'

'A happy bonus.'

'So, on what basis did you employ her? What had she done before?'

'What basis? She was divine. What other basis is there?'

Sergeant Moore was quietly stewing behind her boss, wondering how old a man needs to become before you can no longer call him out on his sexism.

'Weren't you employing her as a stage manager?'

'Assistant, I believe. Not too demanding. Props and stuff, you know. Any shortcomings adequately compensated for.' He chuckled and took another swig of champagne.

Sergeant Moore could remain silent no longer. 'Are you saying you didn't see a CV or any references?'

'Her tits were her reference.' More chuckling. The female companion rolled her eyes indulgently.

It was clear they were not going to get anywhere with this man. He represented a time when men could employ on a whim and dismiss on the same grounds. Employment law was an alien concept.

Inspector Hutchinson had one more attempt. 'So, would you have any records from that time which might shed some light on her background?'

'Doubt it. Might have some production shots which shed some light on her backside.' This one really amused him.

Sergeant Moore was already on her way out. Inspector Hutchinson thanked him for what help he'd given and stood up himself. 'Enjoy the rest of the show.'

'Ha. Unlikely.' The old man drained his glass and looked expectantly at his companion, who hurried to get him a top up.

Outside the theatre Inspector Hutchinson rejoined his Sergeant, who was pacing up and down the car park trying to calm herself.

'Sorry to have dragged you down here, Steph.'

'Do you think there have ever been any complaints about that man? Could we look into it?'

'I don't know, but we can look.'

'Thank you.'

Stephanie Moore was looking at the poster again. Specifically at *Mafeking Road*'s Mark Argyll. What a twat. Men.

As they got into the car, Sergeant Moore could see down the side of the theatre. Outside the Stage Door the young stage manager from earlier was trying to keep apart Simon Tanqueray and a woman she took to be Miss Fishface. The latter looked to be getting the better of the encounter, the heroic Tanqueray cowering on the tarmac. Willy Milligan tottered out and tried to assist. Sergeant Moore considered intervening, but thought better of it. The last image the policewoman saw as she got into the car was poor old Mr Milligan toppling on to the prone actor as his co-star tried to kick him where he lay.

17

Marcus had kept himself busy most of the day ferrying people around South London, with the constant entertainment of the cops in the black Audi, whose lamentably poor tailing technique offered some amusement. While his passengers were not today receiving the usual Marcus Thorn performance, for the most part he did keep the morning's gruesome image at bay.

By early evening he even found his appetite returning, so when he received a call from Imogen asking if he would be back for dinner, he told her he'd be home by eight.

When he dropped off his last fare and turned for home, he suddenly realised he was no longer being followed, and when he pulled up in his parking space, he sat for a while to see if they showed up. Eventually he got out of the car and looked up and down the lane. No, definitely not there. Does this mean they've been stood down? he thought. Have they turned their attentions on Poot? But as he turned to head up to his flat, with a squeal of tyres the black Audi swung into the lane, and he dropped his head and set off up the stairs.

As he opened the door to his flat, he was first met by a wonderfully piquant aroma from the kitchen, then by his wonderfully pretty daughter.

'You okay?' she asked.

'I'm fine. That smells good. Your adman gone home?'

'He's just getting some wine. Do you mind?'

'Him or the wine?'

'Both.'

'Neither. But keep me upwind of the latter. After today.'

'Would you rather we didn't drink?'

'Not at all.'

'Kai will be going home after dinner.'

'Fair enough.' He headed to the bathroom.

Imogen reapplied herself to her preparations. She thought her father still seemed a little subdued, and she hoped there would be no long-term repercussions from the trauma.

When Marcus returned, he stopped at the kitchen door. 'Should I sit at the table?'

'Yes. It's nearly ready.'

The doorbell rang and Imogen put down the spoon she was holding, but before she could get to the door, Marcus had opened it.

'Good evening, young man. Welcome back. I trust you found an adequate vintage locally.'

Kai looked at the bottle in his hand and shrugged. 'We'll see.'

'You two go through. Won't be long.' Imogen returned to the kitchen.

The two men went into the lounge and sat at the table. Kai was dreading the anticipated awkwardness, but he found Marcus preoccupied, almost unaware of Kai's presence.

'How are you feeling?' Kai found himself asking, as he poured two glasses of wine.

If Marcus found this a very twenty-first century question for one man to ask another, he didn't show it. He merely raised his head as though surprised he was not alone, and shrugged. 'Not too bad. You?'

Me? Kai thought. Fantastic. But he couldn't say that. 'Fine. How was work? Busy?'

'Pretty steady, yes.' And Marcus slipped back into his shell and stared at his cutlery.

Kai was unsure whether to continue the small talk, but it proved unnecessary as Imogen called through the hatch, 'Could you put this on the table, Kai?' and he jumped up and brought the steaming bowl of rice over, where he was joined by Imogen with a large pot of what smelled like curry.

'Hope you like it veggie,' she said as she placed it in the

middle of the table, and Kai smiled. It could have been card-board and it wouldn't have bothered him. Marcus too seemed unperturbed.

'Help yourselves.' Imogen handed Kai a serving spoon, and he set about filling his plate. Marcus waited in turn, then followed suit.

Soon they were all eating, but conversation was not exactly flowing. Imogen assumed she knew why her father was not talk-ative, but it wasn't what she imagined. Yes, the gruesome sight of a decomposing corpse was certainly there at the back of his mind, but it was Fleur whose face had been dominating his thoughts all day. He hadn't seen her for twenty years. Years in which she symbolized all that had gone wrong in his life. Today, however, something had changed. It was still true that her leav-ing had kicked the stuffing out of him, but his moment alone with her pictures on Poot's bed had for some reason removed the dreadful, debilitating hate that had eaten away at him for so long. Or perhaps that was not an accurate interpretation of what had happened. Perhaps what had actually happened was that he recognised that it was never really hate at all, but the far more tragic and equally overpowering emotion of love sun-dered. He still loved her, but she was no longer there to be loved or to love him back. And having believed for so long that Fleur was the cause of this pain, had made it feel like hate. As soon as he allowed himself to remove the blame from her, to consider that perhaps it was not her intention to abandon him, he recog-nised the emotion for what it was. This in turn had led him to reflect on his own behaviour leading up to her disappearance, which shifted the blame somewhat on to himself.

Kai and Imogen were discussing the specifics of her recipe, when Marcus suddenly said, 'She was a wonderful woman, you know. Your mother.'

Imogen felt this like a kick to the stomach. She found her-self coughing up the mouthful of food she was in the process of swallowing. What had he just said? Throughout her entire life she had never heard him say a single positive thing about her mother. She felt her eyes pricking and tears welling up.

Marcus saw the effect his words had had and placed his hand on his daughter's. 'I'm sorry. I understand that must come as a shock. That I admit that. But she was, and I haven't allowed myself to acknowledge it for so long.'

'But why?' was all Imogen could say.

'Why?' He realised what she was asking. 'Oh. Poot. The thought that he might have something to do with her disappearance. That she hadn't intended not to come back to us.'

Kai looked at Imogen. She knew what he was thinking. She weighed up whether now was the time. Seeing the softness in her father's face as he thought of her mother, she made the decision.

'Dad?'

Marcus looked at her. 'What is it?'

'You remember that note Mum left?'

'Yes.'

'I still have it.'

Marcus was astounded. He didn't even know she was aware of it, let alone that she had kept it. Hadn't he got rid of it? 'Really?'

'Do you want to see it? I think it backs up what you're thinking.'

Marcus was stunned. That wasn't how he remembered it at all. 'Please.' His voice cracked as he spoke.

Imogen got up and left the room. Kai looked at Marcus and offered a little smile of encouragement. Marcus's emotions were in turmoil, and he suddenly felt a warmth towards this boy, but he was in too much shock to question it. When Imogen came back into the room holding a piece of paper, he looked at it suspiciously. Could this really be from Fleur? But when he took the note and unfolded it, he recognised it as the one that had precipitated his decline. He read it through, as if for the first time, its meaning appearing so much at odds with his memory. When he had gone over it for a third time, he looked up at Imogen. There were tears in his eyes.

'I wonder where she was going,' was all he said.

'Me too,' Imogen replied. 'But she does sound as though she's coming back, doesn't she?'

Marcus remembered the purse he'd found in the bedroom, with all her bank cards. She would have had no access to money. Hadn't it been obvious she had been coming back? Well, not at the time. He was a drunken idiot, incapable of following the logic. She had left him, and the fact she didn't reappear proved it.

He looked deep into his daughter's eyes. He was realising she had had this knowledge all these years. This completely different interpretation of Fleur's going, and he felt awful. So, so guilty. He tried to speak, but he couldn't. Tears were now streaming down his face and he didn't care that Kai was witness to them. Imogen put her arms round her father and joined in. Kai inspected his empty plate.

Eventually Imogen pulled back and looked at her father. He seemed exhausted. What a day it had been.

'Has everyone had enough to eat?' she asked, trying to recover herself. Marcus and Kai nodded, and she started to clear the table. Kai joined in and they both headed through to the kitchen carrying plates and dishes. Marcus, left alone at the table, wiped his face on his sleeve. He looked up at the Grist on the wall. *Transience of Love* indeed. What the fuck did he know? Love endures. Even when you don't recognise it. He looked at the open bottle of red wine on the table and the two half-filled glasses. Remembering how any little emotional hiccup would have once been his excuse to drain the bottle, he picked it up and looked at the label, almost tempting himself to drink it. Having read the risible description of what subtleties awaited the drinker's palate, he placed the bottle back down on the table. Hint of pretension would be more accurate, he thought, and got to his feet. Leaving the room, he paused at the kitchen door and looked in on Imogen and Kai, rinsing the plates and loading the dishwasher.

'I'm going to turn in,' he announced. 'Shattered. Need an early night.'

'Oh. Okay,' Imogen replied. 'Kai's about to go.'

Not sure of the relevance of this, Marcus said, 'Is that so? Well, goodnight, Kai. Thanks for your help today.' And he headed down the corridor and round the bend to his room.

Kai closed the dishwasher and turned to Imogen. 'Shall we finish our wine first?'

Imogen smiled and followed Kai through to the lounge, where they took their glasses and sat on the settee.

'Thank you for a wonderful day.' Kai raised his glass. 'To your Mum. Wherever she is.'

Imogen wasn't sure if this was appropriate, but she clinked her glass with his and took a sip.

'Pretty intense day though,' he continued, putting his arm round Imogen and looking up at the indecipherable painting on the wall. Something to do with love wasn't it? He stared at it, wondering if it was perhaps an indicator of the emotion. Only manifest to those in its thrall. What if he relaxed his gaze and stared through the painting, like with one of those magic eye pictures, where the image suddenly jumps out at you in 3D. He tried this, but no tumescent phallus or gaping lady parts revealed themselves. He sipped his wine and placed the glass on the coffee table. He turned to Imogen, who was deep in thought. She looked sad, but so beautiful he didn't need any painting to tell him what he felt so powerfully. He knew he had to go home, but leaving was going to be difficult.

Suddenly Imogen turned her head and looked up at him intently. 'Am I safe?'

'Safe?'

'With you.'

At first Kai was taken aback, but from the intensity of her eyes searching his, he realised what she meant. Given how he was feeling himself, he could empathise with her moment of insecurity, and he took the glass of wine out of her hand and placed it beside his on the coffee table. Then he turned and straddled her on the couch, a knee either side, and took her face in his hands. Looking her in the eye with an equal fire he said, 'Totally. I have never felt this way before. Am I?'

She smiled. 'Absolutely.'

Kai kissed her and felt he was falling back in space. Was this why they called it falling in love? When he eventually and reluctantly pulled away, she said gently. 'Now go.'

Why did they have to work? Leaving was the exact opposite of what he wanted. He never wanted to be apart from her. But he smiled and got to his feet. Having drained his glass, he pulled her up to him. He gave her a tight hug, then kissed her neck. She took his hand and led him to the door. Opening it, she tiptoed and gave him one last kiss, then pushed him out on to the landing. He punched his heart to indicate his feelings, then turned and headed down the stairs. At the bottom he turned back to see she was still standing by the door. He blew her a kiss, which she returned, before going back into the flat and closing the door.

Kai stood there a while looking up at the closed door, hoping it might open again, then unenthusiastically headed away down the lane, as a blue Vauxhall drew up, and a black Audi drove away.

18

Tuesday dawned wet and overcast. This was the end of an era for the Nelsons, and they had only had a couple of hours to gather together the last of what possessions they wanted to take with them, before Dennis would be arriving with his van to take them over to Meadow View.

On the kitchen floor sat several cardboard boxes filled with crockery and pots and pans, and other redundant items in need of disposal. On the windowsill were all the household keys, labelled with little tags to identify them. Edward had done his best with the vacuum cleaner to leave the place in reasonable order, and that was now standing by the boxes in the kitchen in need of another home.

Now Edward and Cynthia were sitting on their two kitchen chairs in the front room, waiting for Dennis. Edward had managed to get the kitchen table in there too.

'He'll be here any minute, Ted,' Cynthia said. 'Is there anything we've forgotten.'

'Don't think so.'

Cynthia looked around the room, it's walls now bare and the floor like a junk shop, remembering the days when it was the hub of their family life. When a little Ellie would sit between them on the sofa as they watched TV. Children's programmes like Trumpton, Camberwick Green and Blue Peter, and family ones like The Golden Shot and The Generation Game, when Ellie was so good at remembering what had been on the conveyor belt. British television had not moved on from this era for the Nelsons.

When the doorbell rang, Edward let Dennis in.

'We've packed up all the kitchen things, Dennis,' Cynthia told him. 'Are you sure you're okay to get them to a jumble sale?'

'It's not a problem, Mrs Nelson. I've got a few things of my own. I'll maybe do a car boot. Shall we get those things in first, and what you need at the back?'

Cynthia looked apologetically at him, sorry she couldn't help. Edward showed willing, but Dennis stood him down. 'Leave it to me.' And he went into the kitchen and came back with a large and heavy box of plates. Edward thought he should, at least, hold the door for him, which he did for the entire operation, as an increasingly sweaty Dennis went back and forth, the rain drops indistinguishable from the perspiration on his balding head, right up until he had brought down the last of the suitcases and filled the floor of the van.

When Dennis came back into the house for the last time, he announced, 'That's us. Are you ready?'

Cynthia looked at Edward. So, they were really going. She felt overwhelmed by sadness to be leaving, even though she knew she had no choice. Putting both hands on her Zimmer, she struggled to her feet. 'Would you bring the other frame, Dennis?'

Dennis picked up the second frame, which was also standing in the front room, and headed out to the van with it. Cynthia set out after him, and Edward went to have one last look in the kitchen.

Surveying the array of keys on the windowsill through his magnifying glass, he picked up one of the front door keys. He had realised he would need to drop it into the estate agent. Then he saw a tag identifying the lone garage key, which had been with all the other spare keys in the tin under the stairs. Where the one which used to be in the kitchen drawer had gone, he had no idea.

Once out on the doorstep, he closed the door behind him. His eyesight didn't allow him to see Dennis struggling to help Cynthia up into the cab of his van. This was probably just as well as it wasn't going smoothly, and when it looked like the poor woman might fall out again, Dennis had no choice but to shove her in with a hand under an ample buttock. By the time Edward had reached the van, Cynthia was seated centrally in the cab recovering her dignity, and he was able to pull himself up beside her.

'Everyone ok?' Dennis asked as he put on his seatbelt.

'We're fine,' Cynthia said, but she wasn't feeling it.

'Could we go via the estate agent?' Edward asked Dennis.

'Absolutely.' Dennis was more than happy to oblige.

Taking a last look at the house, Cynthia's eyes filled with tears, blurring the view. 'Let's go,' she said.

Dennis did as he was told, started the engine and pulled away, with only a slight clatter from the back.

19

Following the previous night's abortive trip into theatreland, Stephanie Moore arrived into work wondering if she had time to do a little search for Mr Ralph Messiter in the police databases. She felt she owed it to the sisterhood. However, she found Inspector Hutchinson pacing up and down by her desk.

'Ah, there you are,' he said when he turned and saw her. 'Something's come up. Today we have a hospital visit.'

'Know how to show a girl a good time, don't you?' Sergeant Moore replied, then internally admonished herself for the inherent sexism in her own attempt at humour.

'That flat you went to yesterday? Howard Poot's? Thorn's old flat?'

'Yes yes.'

'We've had reports of unpleasant odours coming from it.'

Sergeant Moore remembered the smell through the letterbox. Should she have perhaps mentioned this?

Hutchinson continued, 'And it turns out Mr Poot has been detained under the Mental Health Act for some months. I want to visit him and borrow his keys, so we can look into it. Makes life a bit easier that way, doesn't it? I realise we could, and maybe should, just break the door down, but if we're quick about it, it shouldn't make a significant difference.'

'Oh. Okay boss. Are we going now?'

'No time like the present.'

She had been hoping to get a coffee first, but she could see the Inspector had had little sleep and quite enough caffeine for both of them, so she dutifully trotted after him as he strode towards the stairs.

Pulling up outside St. Bernadette's Psychiatric Hospital, both police officers were struck by its ugliness. Inspector Hutchinson had had cause to visit in the past, over the course of his career, but this was his Sergeant's first encounter.

'Now, these places can be a bit challenging, if you're not used to them,' Richard Hutchinson explained. 'Nothing really prepares you for what a loss of marbles can do to a person.'

They got out of the car and the Inspector marched up the gravel towards the entrance. Sergeant Moore had to break into a little trot to keep up with him. Having rung the bell, the Inspector drummed his fingers against his thighs as he waited. Eventually the door was opened by a woman as grey as the day, and both officers flashed their warrant cards.

Once inside, the grey lady, Jane, directed them to the lifts, and they found their way to Daffodil Ward. Sister Mary Scanlon opened the door to them.

'Won't you come in, officers? Lucky old Howard. Two visits in as many days. What's he done to deserve this?'

Eager to get on, the Inspector didn't register the significance of this. 'How is he today?' he asked.

'A little subdued. We've had to up his medication.'

'Have you? May we see him?'

The Sister led them through to Howard Poot's room. He was propped up on his bed, his hair as white and erect as Marcus had found it, and his eyelids drooping.

'Howard, would you look at who's come to see you. These two police officers would like a word.'

There was no discernible reaction, so Inspector Hutchinson approached the bed. Mary Scanlon waited by the door in case she was needed.

'Good morning, Mr Poot. I'm Inspector Richard Hutchinson. I was hoping to speak to you about Marcus Thorn.'

Despite the sedation, that name seemed to cut through, and the eyes opened a little more, and Poot's head turned slowly towards the policeman.

'Do you remember Marcus Thorn?' he continued. 'He used to

live in your flat.'

Poot was now staring at Inspector Hutchinson, but not really focussing on him. This was disconcerting.

'We're enquiring about a missing girl, Ellie Nelson, and Thorn's possible involvement in it. We wondered if you had any memory of her disappearance.'

Poot was having an internal struggle again. His eyes were becoming wilder. Sister Scanlon was getting anxious. She hoped the sedation was sufficient. She looked down the corridor and beckoned someone.

'Is there anything you can tell us?' the Inspector continued.

Poot was still wrestling with something. Then he seemed to be trying to speak. His mouth kept opening, and his tongue was flopping about, but nothing was coming out except spittle. Despite this, Inspector Hutchinson leant in, trying to catch any words which might be forthcoming. Gradually the tension spread throughout Poot's body and his fists became clenched. Suddenly he was vocalising. It was nothing more than a strangled note being forced through his vocal cords. The volume was increasing.

Mary Scanlon had a quick word with another nurse, who hurried away.

It was now almost a squawk that was coming from Poot. Stephanie Moore looked to the nurse for reassurance, but the Sister's expression offered none. Inspector Hutchinson too was becoming alarmed. It was now a quite hideous sound the man was making. The tongue started flicking about at the same time. Then the single sound became two sounds, punctuated by the flapping tongue. At its crescendo, the entire ward could hear a screeching 'Ellie-Ellie-Ellie-Ellie-Ellie-Ellie', which finally ended when Poot's whole body started thrashing about, and his voice was choked off by his clenching jaws.

The other nurse had returned with a drugs trolley and a male nurse. Sister Scanlon quickly found and prepared a diazepam enema. The other nurses flipped Poot on to his side and held him there, while the Sister pulled down his pyjama bottom and administered the solution.

Gradually Poot's body started to relax, and the thrashing ceased.

When she was satisfied the fit was over, Mary Scanlon looked up at the police officers.

'It would seem visitors don't agree with Howard. I can't put him through this again.'

The two police officers were shaken, but Inspector Hutchinson hadn't lost sight of the purpose of his visit.

'Could we get those keys?'

Mary Scanlon asked the other nurses to keep an eye on Poot, then led the police officers down to a locked room. Opening it, she retrieved Poot's keys from a locker assigned to him, and handed them over.

'Thank you.' Inspector Hutchinson put them in his pocket. 'I'm very sorry if we've caused a problem for you.'

'Can't be helped, I suppose. You have a job to do. I'll show you out.' And she led them back to the ward entrance, and saw them out to the lift. As they got in, the Sister said, 'At least he didn't attack you like he did Mr Thorn.'

Hutchinson grabbed the door to stop it closing. 'He was here?'

'On Sunday. I thought I said.'

The Inspector let the door close. He looked at his Sergeant with narrowed eyes and slapped the button for the ground floor.

Once outside in the drizzle, he stomped down the gravel, Stephanie once more jogging along behind. As soon as they had shut the car doors, Hutchinson started the engine and drove off at speed, his Sergeant hastily strapping herself in.

'Are we going to the flat then?' she asked.

'Naturally. That was the plan, wasn't it?'

'I guess.' She still hadn't had a coffee. Actually, she could use something stronger after that little episode, but that wasn't going to happen, so she just sat back in silence and didn't utter another word until they drew up outside Prince Regent Mansions.

'It's a right mess in there, you know boss,' she said.

'Having just met the owner, that doesn't surprise me.' Inspector Hutchinson jumped out of the car and fished out the keys. He saw the card reader and presented the card attached to the key ring, as requested. The door gave a click and he pushed it open. Sergeant Moore just made it to the door in time to stop it closing again, and she hurried up the stairs after her boss.

Having seen through the letterbox the previous day, and having had a hit of the smell, she wasn't looking forward to the next bit. Hutchinson had already located the correct key and was turning it as Stephanie Moore arrived. As soon as the stench hit the Inspector, he knew what it was. He had put in a few years in CID, and had become well acquainted with the smell of death.

'You'd better prepare yourself, Steph. Something has died in here.' He flicked on the light and surveyed the squalor. He moved down the corridor in search of the source of the odour, and realised, awful though it still was, it was worse by the front door, so he returned to the first door he had passed. Satisfied that this was where it was coming from, he opened it. Sergeant Moore could see past him what was on the bed and, when he switched on the light and the full horror was revealed, she turned and retched. She was glad she hadn't had anything this morning, as she had nothing to bring up.

'Go and call CID would you, Steph? This one's for them.' He could see an empty syringe lying beside the bed, beneath the dangling, dripping hand.

Sergeant Moore was only too grateful to get out of the flat, and she rushed down the stairs and out into the fresh air. She had, of course, seen dead bodies before, but never one in this state.

Realising this was a potential crime scene, Hutchinson knew he too should withdraw, but he had every intention of coming back in when the team arrived. He was confident that, with his previous experience, and given his involvement in this case already, he could get himself assigned to it. But, for now, he switched off the light and closed the bedroom door again, then did the same in the hall. He went to join his Sergeant out the front of the building.

He found her sitting in the car with the door open. She didn't look good.

'Did you manage to call?'

She nodded. 'They're on their way.'

'Good.' He was concerned for his Sergeant. 'Take the car. Go back to the station. I'll wait here. Would you like to talk to someone?'

She shook her head and took the car key she was being handed, then went round to the driver's side and drove off.

With no-one to impress any more, Inspector Hutchinson crossed the road and threw up in the river.

20

Marcus had woken early after a dream-filled night in which Fleur featured heavily. Now that his attitude to her had softened, he found his subconscious spewing forth scene after scene in which he and Fleur were happy and loved-up, and when he had finally found himself back in his lonely bed, he looked across at the space she had once occupied and felt bereft. This was some sort of delayed grief and all the more powerful for it.

Not wanting to stay in bed with this aching void, he had got up and gone out to work before Imogen had even emerged from her room. So early was it that, for the first couple of hours, it was a blue Vauxhall that he found in his rear-view mirror, but at some point a switch had been made, and he suddenly became aware that the familiar black Audi was tailing him once more.

None of his passengers was getting much chat from him today, his mind was too preoccupied with thoughts of Fleur and Poot and what the connection between them could possibly be. His imagination was in overdrive, and it got to the point where he wanted to head back to the hospital and shake some answers out of that deranged dope head. All that prevented him from attempting it was the presence of the Audi.

Around lunchtime, he was sitting outside the tube station waiting for another fare, when his phone rang. It was Imogen. She was concerned for him, having not seen him in the morning, and he assured her he was fine and not to worry. He was getting on with things and everything would become clear in the end, he had no doubt. He considered asking her to look in on Poot to see if she could get something out of him, but he realised this wouldn't be fair on her, and he certainly didn't want to get her in any sort of trouble, or indeed for her to trigger any more violence from him. So he dismissed the idea, repeated that he was fine and told her to get back to work and stop worrying.

As he ended the call, he noticed the little envelope icon pop up on his phone to indicate an incoming e-mail, so he opened the app. It was from that stupid DNA company for whom Imogen had made him spit into that tube. What did they want? He opened the message and was informed his results were in. Oh yes? Did he care? But curiosity got the better of him and he followed the link to their website to see what they had to say. He was presented with a pie chart representing the different regions of the world they reckoned his DNA had originated, and a list with the percentages of each he supposedly had. The bulk appeared to come from Great Britain. Well there's a surprise, he thought. It was the second largest slice of the pie that caused him to effect a double take he would have been proud to reproduce on camera. This was crazy. They were clearly just making stuff up for the money. No way did he have 24% African-Caribbean DNA. That was ludicrous. He was a white man. Anyone could see. He looked at himself in his rear-view mirror. Just a bit tanned. It was summer. But he knew he had not spent much time in the sun and, after the draining experiences he had just been through, the fact he had any colour at all told its own story.

He found himself thinking of his mother, something he avoided. There was another woman he had hardened his heart against. He hadn't seen her since his late teens, when he'd flounced out in a fit of adolescent pique because she had the temerity to question whether drama school was really the right choice for him. She was a millstone round his neck. Why could she not recognise his genius? Well he wasn't letting her hold him back. Over the years she had made attempts to reconcile with him, but he was having none of it, and she had eventually given up.

What was happening to him? Why was he suddenly feeling sad about her? He realised he didn't even know if she was still alive. What sort of man was he? Indeed, what sort of man was his father? A black one it would seem. He'd never known him. He didn't think the man had even been in a proper relationship with his mother. Just some sordid one-night stand, presumably. No wonder he'd turned out as he had.

These uncomfortable thoughts were interrupted when the rear door of his car was opened and another customer climbed in, and he was soon heading off again through the familiar streets, the black Audi in his wake.

However, it would seem that once a can of worms is opened, those slimy little blighters just keep wriggling through your grey matter with no intention of returning whence they came. He just could not suppress the images of his mother that continually presented themselves to him, nor shake off the gnawing sadness he was feeling. So tormenting did these thoughts become that, when he dropped off a customer only a few streets from his childhood home, he found himself heading towards it, rather than back towards his base. He had no plan, he just felt drawn in that direction. As he turned into Asquith Road, a street of small terraced houses, and approached number 63, he started to feel a little queasy, and he realised his heart was beating rather fast. This was ridiculous.

From the outside, the house didn't appear to have changed much in all the years since he had slammed that door behind him, *en route* to fame and fortune. He pulled up across the road in a space that had miraculously just been vacated. That was definitely a change. Cars lined both sides of the road with often only a few inches between them. His mum didn't have a car back then, nor did most of her neighbours.

Switching off the engine, he sat looking across the road at the house. It looked cared for and neat and tidy. There were a few mature shrubs in the small front garden, all equally well-maintained. Surely his mother didn't still live here though. Should he find out? Was he ready for that? He decided he wasn't. After all, he'd only today allowed himself even to think of the woman. Visiting her was a massive leap further into the...well, not unknown. Once known, long forgotten.

He started the engine and noticed an old black man slowly walking towards him on the opposite side of the road. He remembered this as a totally white street. Had that all changed now? There he went again. He was hard-wired to think that way. Well, if that DNA stuff was true, he had to start thinking differently now. No, that wasn't good enough. Whether or not it was true, he needed to think differently. For Imogen and her new boyfriend. Because he had no good reason not to.

He was about to pull away, when he saw the man take out a bunch of keys and turn in to number 63, where he opened the door and entered, closing the door behind him. Well, he guessed that answered that. His mother was probably long gone. He engaged first gear and drove away.

The mournful feeling was still with him he realised, but now his thoughts returned to his immediate situation. As the beautiful face of Fleur Hardy came back to him, bringing with it the feelings with which he woke, he checked his rear-view mirror, and it dawned on him there was no sign of the black Audi. He had sat for some minutes opposite his old house and there was no sign of it there either, he realised. Finally, they must have found that body and switched tack. He felt at once both a sense of relief and great tiredness, and decided to head back to his flat.

As he pulled into his parking space behind Ken Tucker's Fried Chicken, he became conscious that the song *Ebony and Ivory* was playing in his head, and he smiled ruefully to himself as he climbed out of the car. Again he looked up and down the back lane, then headed up the stairs to his flat. Once outside his door he turned back just to be sure, but the lane was still empty. They did appear to have lost interest in him.

Once inside, he sat down on the settee, picked up the remote control and turned on the television. He flicked through looking for a news channel, in case there were any developments, but having tried several, it became clear that they had all lost interest again, presumably because they had nothing new to add. He continued his search until suddenly confronted with Fleur's face, in close up, as Millie Moffat. It was one of those channels showing reruns of ancient shows, clearly. She was confiding in one of the receptionists her feelings for Matthew Hope. It would have been filmed during those glorious early days of their own relationship, Marcus realised. Seeing her animated, rather than just in the photographs on Poot's wall, and hearing her voice again, he was suddenly overwhelmed by emotion, and he wanted the woman back in his arms so badly. Drawn to the television, he slid off the settee on to his knees and crawled across to it, where he sat on his heels staring at the screen as though worshipping at her altar.

When Fleur had left him, overnight his sex life had come to an end. He had a daughter to look after and a drink habit to take to the next level, there was no time for that. Even once he had hauled himself up on to the wagon, his opportunities were few, and he learned to accept that this was how it was for him now, although what he and his right hand got up to was nobody's business but theirs, albeit their relationship was intermittent. Anyway, hadn't womankind been more than generous to him already. But after the rollercoaster of the last few days, and given that he couldn't jump through the screen and reassert his conjugal rights, he found the understanding vaginal substitute at the end of his right arm spontaneously strumming to an up-tempo beat in the middle of his lounge. When the inevitable had happened, he dropped his head onto his chest and wept like a baby.

21

By the time the CID team had arrived at Prince Regent Mansions, Inspector Richard Hutchinson was over his little episode of fragility. He had spoken with his superiors, who had acceded to his request to be included in the investigation, and he had let the detectives into Poot's flat, where the grizzly process of examining the corpse had begun, while he and other officers went through the rest of the flat with a fine-tooth comb.

When he had entered Howard Poot's bedroom, the sight of the collage of photographs of Fleur Hardy had sent chills up his spine. He couldn't help himself imagining he would be immortalised as the man who tracked down a prolific serial killer. However, he couldn't fit Marcus Thorn into this theory. It would appear that he might be innocent after all. This realisation, however, was not the reason he had stood down his surveillance team; he had already made that call while he was waiting outside, in light of his discovery that they were unaware that Thorn had visited Poot in hospital. What was the point of them? He was pushing his luck anyway tying his men up this way without authorisation.

He had also found Ellie's postcards. Why would Poot still have these neatly stacked in a drawer? But there was clearly nothing there to place Thorn at the Bunch of Grapes on the night in question, just evidence of a young woman with a fixation on the man.

After several hours of painstaking work, a multitude of evidence was bagged up and labelled, and samples from the body had been dispatched. While there was plenty of evidence of drug use in the flat, there were no actual drugs to be found.

Traces were detectable, but no stashes. What could it all mean? The evidence suggested the deceased had been injecting drugs, but with Poot detained, she might well have been alone. Hutchinson had already looked for CCTV cameras, but the building didn't appear to have any. He had had to settle for sending a couple of constables off to interview the neighbours in search of any accounts of comings and goings to and from the flat. They were also instructed to tease out which had alerted them to the smell.

Late that night Hutchinson had finally got a lift back to the station. He had been home to catch a few hours' sleep, and was now back at his desk on the Wednesday morning going through the various statements from Poot's neighbours. He knew it would be a few days before they would have all the results back from the samples, but in the meantime, he must keep at it, gathering his evidence. He really needed to get something out of Howard Poot. There was the information he needed, but the man was so conveniently insane.

The theme of the neighbour statements seemed to be that it had all been quiet from flat 2/1 for some time. Probably since Poot had been detained. Before that it had not been unusual to see people coming and going at all hours and to hear strange noises and raised voices from within, but nobody had seen anyone come in or out for months. And no-one was owning up to being the mystery caller. One woman had let some people into the building the previous day, but she didn't know which flat they were visiting, although she had been a little alarmed by the older man of the party. He could well have been a drug dealer, she thought. As a precaution, Hutchinson had sent one of the constables back to find out which neighbour had had visitors on Monday morning, but he wasn't too hopeful this was useful. After all, the woman had been dead for weeks.

There was a knock on the door.

'Come.'

Stephanie Moore entered. 'Morning boss.'

'Steph. Are you okay now?'

'Fine boss. How did it go?'

'As you know, it was truly awful in there, but I'm on the team and we've got to be closer to a resolution for Ellie and Fleur.' He told her what he'd found. 'I'll have to assign you to something else now, but you can still liaise with the families, if that's okay.'

'Of course.' Despite her trauma of the day before, Sergeant Moore still couldn't let the Ralph Messiter thing go. Given what appeared to have happened to those women at the hands of Poot, she wasn't about to let that old lech get away with his behaviour towards her gender. Not if there was anything out there in the records to help. 'Could I spend a little time looking into Messiter?'

'Who? Oh, that theatre director. Go on then. I'll let you know when I need you.'

'Thanks boss.' And she went back to her desk.

Hutchinson decided he wasn't going to get any further sat at *his* desk. It may be futile, but he had to try getting through to Poot. They didn't have enough to arrest him yet, but he had better warn the hospital that he was a person of interest. He would clear it with the senior investigating officer, DCI Shah.

Within half an hour he was crunching up the gravel once again, the brooding grey walls all the more sinister for the dull, overcast day. When the same grey face as the previous day peered round the door in answer to the bell, it registered recognition, and the Inspector was let in.

The door to Daffodil ward was again opened by Sister Mary Scanlon, whose cheerful face clouded when she saw who it was.

'Oh, is it you, Inspector? I hope you haven't come to upset old Howard again.'

'That is not my intention. But I have reason to believe Mr Poot has been up to things he should not have been, and I have to try again with him. I'll go as carefully as I can.'

The Sister let him in. 'As it happens, he does seem a little more with it today. He actually asked for a coffee this morning. That seizure seems to have had an unexpected effect on his brain function. It may not last, but now may be the time to try.

142

But I'd better check with Imogen first.'

'Imogen?'

'Doctor Thorn. She's doing a round at the moment.'

'Oh, okay.' He was encouraged by Poot's reported condition, and he hoped this doctor was not going to stand in his way.

Sister Scanlon had led the policeman down to the central nurses' station, and she asked him to wait there while she found this doctor. While she was gone, he stood and listened to the crazy soundtrack of strange laughter, shouts and moans that came from all directions, and watched a large black gentleman shambling by clutching a book, who then pushed open a door, farted from the effort, chuckled and let the door close behind him.

Hearing footsteps coming from the opposite direction, the Inspector turned to see a pretty, dark-haired young woman striding towards him, followed by the Sister. She extended a hand.

'Imogen Thorn.'

'Inspector Richard Hutchinson. Pleased to meet you.' They shook hands.

'I understand you would like a word with Mr Poot.' You're not the only one, she thought.

'Yes, would that be okay? We think he may have been a bit of a naughty boy and really need some answers from him.'

Imogen most definitely didn't want to stand in his way, her father's freedom might depend on it, but she had at least to appear to be making a professional judgement on the wisdom of this.

'He's had a nasty seizure, as you know, so he is going to be a little delicate today. If you could be as gentle as possible with him. Any sign of distress from him, please don't push it.'

'Okay. I'll go easy.'

'Perhaps I should be with you. Is that okay?' Professionally she had every right to ask this, but she knew if the policeman knew her connection, he might give a different answer. And, of course, she should be coming clean that she was the daughter of one of his suspects, but she'd given her name and, if he couldn't work it out, perhaps her dad was right; he wasn't the Met's brightest.

Inspector Hutchinson considered the request. He didn't really want witnesses to the questions he needed to ask, but neither did he wish to be alone if the man kicked off again, so he agreed.

Imogen thanked him and led the policeman towards Poot's room. Sister Scanlon went and fetched the drugs trolley and followed on behind.

Howard Poot was sitting up in bed staring out of the window when they reached the room.

'Good morning, Howard,' Imogen said as she entered. 'How are you feeling today?'

The patient slowly turned his head. Seeing Imogen's face, he visibly relaxed.

'This is Inspector Hutchinson. I believe you've already met. He would like to ask you some more questions. He's promised to be gentle. He knows you're not well.'

Poot had started to tense as soon as he registered the policeman, but Imogen's words soothed him somewhat.

Hutchinson pulled up a chair and sat beside the bed. Imogen stood over him smiling reassuringly at Poot, her effect on her patient clear to see. Pulling out his notebook, the policeman considered what his first question should be, given he might not get many in before a return to bedlam. He decided not to start with a question. He would give him some information and see how he reacted.

'Hello Mr Poot. I'm afraid I have to give you some bad news. We have had to pay a visit to your flat. I have to tell you that we have found a body there.' This was just the sort of information he didn't want overheard, but he wasn't to know this doctor was ahead of him on this news. 'Do you have a flatmate?'

Poot considered the question as though it were the most perplexing conundrum anyone had ever had to solve. He kept looking to Imogen for reassurance. Finally, he shook his head and let out a sigh, defeated.

Great start, Hutchinson was thinking. Okay. 'Could you please tell me why you have all those pictures of Fleur Hardy on your bedroom wall?'

The name triggered a flicker of recognition across Poot's face. He started muttering something to himself and smiling.

'What are you saying?' Inspector Hutchinson asked.

Poot looked up as though taken by surprise the officer was there.

The Inspector tried again. 'I was asking why it is that you have all those pictures of Fleur Hardy on your wall?'

Suddenly it was as if the clouds had parted, and Poot seemed to understand what he was being asked. His expression changed to one of contempt for the man who would ask such a dumb question. In his nasal American drawl, he spat out, 'Do you expect me to look at *her*?'

As this was the first thing Hutchinson had heard the man say, he was taken aback as much by the voice and accent as he was by the aggression in the reply. He had assumed the man was British.

'Look at who?' he asked.

'What?' Poot squawked.

'Who else would you be looking at?'

Poot considered this, but his mind had clearly become fragmented again. The questions were no longer making sense.

Hutchinson persevered. 'You implied there was someone else? Is that your flatmate? Your girlfriend?'

Poot had lost focus. He seemed preoccupied once more with some internal life. The Inspector was finding the whole process very frustrating, but he was anxious not to trigger another of the man's attacks, so he tried another approach.

'She was very attractive that Fleur Hardy, wasn't she? Did you ever meet her, Mr Poot?' Hutchinson wasn't sure he was getting through to the man. 'Mr Poot? Fleur Hardy? Did you meet her?'

The repetition of the name appeared to have registered this time. Poot looked back at the policeman, but without focus.

His lips were moving and he was making faint sounds. Suddenly Hutchinson realised he was singing, tunelessly and raspingly, but singing. Leaning in, the Inspector caught what the words were. 'Happy birthday, Mr President, happy birthday to you', over and over again.

'You like Marilyn Monroe, Mr Poot? Is that it? Is that why you like Fleur Hardy?'

Poot abruptly stopped singing and turned to the policeman with a gimlet eye. Then, so loudly it knocked Hutchinson back, he screeched, 'He took her,' and the convulsions started again.

Imogen signalled to Mary Scanlon, who prepared another diazepam enema, and a male nurse suddenly appeared who helped Imogen hold Poot down while the Sister administered it. All the while Imogen reassured the patient that all was well and not to distress himself, until the drug had done its job and the seizure petered out.

Inspector Hutchinson had withdrawn to the door while the staff did what they had to do. He had to accept that that was a far as today's interview was going, but he didn't like it. He needed to know what the man was on about. As Imogen slowly stepped back from the bed, satisfied her patient was in no immediate danger, she turned to the Inspector.

'I'm sorry that happened again,' Hutchinson told her. 'You do understand I have to do this? There's a dead woman in this man's flat.'

'I do,' Imogen replied. 'But you're going to have to leave it now.'

He nodded. 'Thank you. I'll find my way out.' And he left the room.

Sister Scanlon looked at Imogen. She was not happy. Imogen gave her a sympathetic smile, but didn't apologise for allowing it.

The Inspector found his way out of the building and stomped down the gravel. He was so frustrated it hurt. What did the man mean? Who took whom? Is it Thorn he's referring to? Were they in it together?

Slamming his car door, he paused to consider his next course of action. Until those results came back, he wasn't going to know who the woman in the flat was, and maybe not even then, so what should he do in the meantime? He decided, as he was supposed to be working as part of a team, he had better report back to DCI Shah, so he started the car and headed to Poot's flat.

22

Seymour McKenzie had arrived in Britain from Barbados in the late 1950s to seek his fortune in the land of his father, but, despite all that centuries old white DNA asserting its superiority in every cell of his body, it was his black skin that everyone saw, and it was a shock to the average Londoner to see Seymour and his compatriots walking their streets in search of work and accommodation. But the British government wanted them to rebuild the economy following the devastation of the war, especially in London, so where was the welcome? Seymour had a job to come to, having been recruited in Barbados by London Transport, and he started as a bus conductor as soon as he had found accommodation, a job he managed to keep right through to his retirement, thanks to London's affection for the Routemaster bus, and his exemplary service.

It was during the course of his work that Seymour had met young Kitty Thorn. Every morning she would board his bus on her way to work and give him a shy smile when he came to take her fare. She wasn't like so many of the other girls. She met his eye and thanked him politely when he handed over her change. He always looked forward to arriving at her stop in the morning and would be looking ahead down the street as he approached to make sure she was waiting at the bus stop. But for many weeks that was the extent of their interaction. He was working and grateful for the opportunity to do so, and he didn't want to jeopardise that by being inappropriate with his customers. Besides, he had been given plenty of warning by less polite male passengers that he was not one of them, and not even to look at their girls.

Kitty Thorn had liked it when he looked at her, and when he allowed himself to return her smile, she felt joyous. She could sense however that he was being careful, and after many weeks of these brief exchanges, it became clear to her that she was never going to get to know him better unless she herself became proactive. So one August Friday morning, her heart pounding in her chest, when she got up to leave the bus, she faked a little stumble as she stepped down onto the rear platform where Seymour was standing, and when he instinctively reached forward to save her from falling, she slipped a little note into his hand, side-stepped him and deftly jumped off the bus before anyone had any idea what had just happened. Seymour could feel the eyes of some of the young men on him, and he wondered what would have happened had he actually got his hands on the girl, but he had also been quick thinking enough, when he had felt the paper in his hand, to turn his back to the passengers and slip it inside his jacket.

For the rest of his shift he kept running his hand over the jacket, feeling the note crackle against his chest, but never daring to take it out again, until he had finally finished for the day and could head back to the little house he shared with several other Barbadians. Alone in the room he shared with two others, he pulled out the note and read it.

Hello Mr Conductor

Thank you for reading this. My name is Kitty Thorn and I hope you don't think   me too forward for writing this to you, but I see you every day and you look so   kind and I know we will never get the chance to talk on the bus. I don't even know your name. I know I am taking a chance in doing this, because you may   not wish to have anything to do with me, and I am still going to need to get on   your bus every day, so I really hope you will not be upset about it. If I told you   I will be in Brockwell Park by the clock tower at 2pm this Sunday, might you   find your way there to meet me? I do hope so.

149

Yours,
Kitty

Seymour re-read the note several times. He felt light-headed. He wasn't sure how to react. Naturally he was flattered that this sweet young lady had taken an interest in him, and he was certainly very interested in her, but could he really go and meet her? He knew being seen with a white girl was asking for trouble, and he really didn't want trouble, but surely not to do so would be cowardice. Furthermore, he was going to have to see her again at work anyway, and he couldn't bear the thought that she would be upset with him for standing her up.

So it was that when Kitty approached the clock tower two days later, there was her lovely conductor waiting for her in his Sunday best, despite the summer heat. At first they only had eyes for each other, but after the initial shy exchanges, in which Kitty discovered Seymour's name - she found it strange but cute - they became aware of whispering and looks, not just from white people, and decided to take a stroll in the hope of finding some privacy. This was to be the pattern of all their subsequent encounters.

Over the course of several months they met secretly, and behaved as though unknown to each other on the bus. They both quite enjoyed this clandestine courtship, but their feelings for each other were deepening and they knew they couldn't keep each other secret forever. Things came to a head a few weeks after their first escape to Brighton, where, in a rundown bed and breakfast owned by a rundown man too grateful for business to object to their race mix, they had first spent the night together. They tried to be careful and avoid the risk, but their desire for each other had got the better of the flimsy latex, and when Kitty didn't have her usual regular period, she knew she was in trouble.

Seymour declared at once he would marry her, and immediately set about buying a house. He had a good job and had been working for three years by now and spending very little, so he was able to come up with a deposit and secure a mortgage on a little terraced house. Kitty was delighted when he told her. They must arrange the wedding at once. But she hadn't told her parents anything. She still lived with them and they would have to know her plans, not least because she was still only twenty and couldn't get married without their permission.

One night when she got home from work, she asked them to sit down, then told them the whole story. It didn't go well. To be fair, it wasn't going well when they were still assuming the boy was white, but when she showed them a picture of Seymour, as if to underline their difference from this person, what colour they had drained from their faces. Her father was adamant she could not possibly marry this man. Her mother just cried. A lot. When Kitty eventually ran up to her bedroom, also in tears, she thought her life was over.

The following morning she left for work without saying a word to her parents, and once on the bus, looked towards Seymour in despair. For him it was unbearable that he couldn't ask her what the matter was. And when Kitty got home from work, she went straight to her room and cried her heart out.

What Kitty didn't know was that, during the course of that day, her father had made a phone call from his office. He had an old army friend in quite a senior position within London Transport. The following day when she got on her bus, Kitty almost fell into her seat when she saw a strange man with the ticket machine round his neck. Where was Seymour? So desperate was she that she asked this man where the usual conductor was. All he knew was he had been asked to swap routes.

Back home that evening she had confronted her parents. What had they done? It was explained to her in no uncertain terms that she was to forget about this man, that if she tried to contact him, he would lose his job and have to return home, and that she could not possibly keep the child. Knowing how much Seymour treasured his job and how much his family in Barbados depended on the money he sent home, she decided, despite her breaking heart, she would somehow have to accept that she couldn't see him again. But killing their child or taking it away from her at birth? She could not accept that.

From this point on, a state of war existed in the Thorn household, and Kitty put up the strongest defence imaginable against the threat to her unborn child. She knew her parents would be committing a crime if they tried to get the pregnancy terminated, but it soon became clear that was not their plan. No, they intended to find it a new mother. Kitty, however, knew that she would turn twenty-one before the baby arrived, and determined that she would be gone from her parents lives as soon as that day came. How and where she would live was an enormous worry, naturally, but she would find a way.

Meanwhile, Seymour was in his own private hell. He had been told that Kitty had changed her mind about him and didn't want any more to do with him. That she could have had such a sudden and complete about-face overnight might seem unbelievable to many, but Seymour was an immigrant who had experienced the hostility of the natives, and he allowed himself to be convinced this might be true. If it were not, then surely she would contact him.

As the days passed, Seymour learnt to accept he had lost the girl he loved, and to adjust to his new route and routine. He decided, however, to complete the purchase of the house. It may no longer be his marital home, but he had hundreds of compatriots in need of accommodation who were struggling to find any in the face of an increasingly hostile private rental sector. He could cover his mortgage renting out rooms. But something was still troubling him. Was Kitty going to have their child? Was he to be a father? If so, how could he not support that child? That was not the way he had been brought up. He would have to do his duty.

A few months after the traumatic parting of the ways, Seymour decided a little covert surveillance was required. At the depot, he showed his replacement on Kitty's bus the picture of her he had, and persuaded the man to let him know if she appeared to be pregnant. When he received the report back that she certainly did appear to be in that condition, Seymour decided he had to make contact and assure her that he would see the child was supported. And was there anything he could do now? For a small consideration, his go-between delivered the letter.

When Kitty was handed it with her ticket, she was at first confused, then quickly slipped it into her handbag and looked about hoping no-one had seen. As soon as she arrived at work, she dashed into the toilets and locked herself in a cubicle. She pulled out the letter with a shaking hand and read. It was quite formally written, with no declarations of love, but she could hear the kindness in the words, and he clearly wanted the best for her and their baby. The formality, taken with the fact that he had utilised this clandestine delivery method, convinced Kitty that Seymour was just being dutiful, and no longer had any romantic interest in her. He, of course, believed she had no interest in him, and wrote accordingly.

That night in her bedroom, Kitty set about writing a reply to the man she had lost. She too kept it formal, but, with no real expectation that he could help, she explained her need to escape her family home as soon as she turned twenty-one. As she handed her letter over in the morning with her bus fare, the substitute conductor rolled his eyes. She gave him an imploring look, and he reluctantly put it in his pocket.

Every subsequent morning for several days, Kitty would look expectantly towards the conductor when she boarded her bus, not because she expected a solution from Seymour, but just because she wanted to hear from him. After a week or so of disappointment, one morning she was handed a small package. A present? Surely not.

When she was eventually able to open it away from prying eyes, she discovered it contained a key on a London Transport key ring and a long letter of explanation. Seymour had bought that house he had found. It was in need of quite a bit of work - that was why he could afford it - and he had spent many weekends and evenings doing it up, with the intention of moving in and renting out the other two bedrooms. But her need was greater than his, so he had found a couple of Barbadian nurses to rent rooms, and she could have one too for herself and the child. There would be no rent to pay and he would make sure she had an allowance too. She couldn't believe what she was reading. How could he afford this? Didn't he have to send money home? And where was *he* going to live? The truth was that he was going to take every hour of overtime he could get and live like a monk, but he didn't trouble her with this information.

So it was that, as soon as Kitty turned twenty-one, she packed a suitcase, left a note to tell her parents she'd moved out, and, before they were even up, put the case in a second-hand pram she had bought the previous day and hidden overnight in the back garden, and wheeled it the several streets over to the address she had been given - 63, Asquith Road.

And so began Kitty's life as a single mother-to-be and, soon enough, as a single mum. Her housemates proved to be ideal girls to have around, and saw her through the whole process of bringing a child into the world. When she had to give up work, she found she could get by on her savings and the money Seymour sent her.

When the child, little Marcus, was about six months old, the two nurses announced that the boy needed his own bedroom now, and they were going to move on, but if Kitty didn't want to be alone, they would see if they could find someone to take one of the bedrooms. While Kitty would have been perfectly happy to be alone with her child, whom she doted on, she was worried that Seymour would need the rental income, so she let them find her a new housemate. The new girl, Fiona, was also a nurse, but this time a white one, and older. She was Scottish and quite religious, and Marcus would grow up knowing her as Auntie Fi.

Throughout all this, and for all the years Kitty raised her child in his house, she never saw her landlord. If ever any little jobs were needed on the property, there was another man she could summon who would rectify the issue, but never the man she would still dearly love to have seen.

This tragic state of affairs was finally resolved when the boy, now a headstrong and arrogant young man of eighteen, had walked out on his distraught mother and never returned. When news of this had reached Seymour, he had sent Kitty a letter of support asking if he could do anything to help. Given that so many years had now passed, and attitudes were slowly changing, she dared to ask in her reply if it would be possible that she might see Seymour. When he turned up on her doorstep, holding a bunch of roses, and smiled sweetly at her, she didn't even wait to hear him tell her he had never stopped loving her; she knew it from his eyes, and she threw herself on him and let his embrace support her trembling legs.

Seymour had finally then moved into his own house, and the long-delayed wedding had taken place, with Fiona and Seymour's sister Gloria as bridesmaids. Naturally, Kitty had wanted Marcus at the wedding; but she couldn't find him. When she had eventually discovered his drama school, she had written to him there to let him know about his father and their marriage; but she wasn't to know he callously binned it unopened as soon as he had left the school office.

Now an octogenarian, Seymour had had a wonderful forty-year marriage to his Kitty. But for the last few years she had been suffering the awful memory loss of Alzheimer's disease, and now she was confined to a specialist floor of a local care home, where her distressing symptoms could be more safely managed. And he, ever-dutiful, would walk over to see her every morning, and pass the bulk of the day beside her, attending to her needs, holding her hand and generally attempting to have her feel his love and support. Then he would make his way back to his empty house alone.

When he arrived at the gates of Meadow View care home this bright Thursday morning, he looked up at Kitty's floor, to see if she might be looking down on him from her lounge, but he could only see one of her fellow residents, her hair in disarray and her nightdress open to her waist, desperately trying to open the windows to make her escape. Of course he felt great pity for the poor woman, but he wondered at the wisdom of corralling together all these similarly confused and distressed people, given that none of them had the insight to know they had this common affliction, and each believed the others were malign agents intent on their persecution and harm. Perhaps it would be better to mix them in with the mentally sound residents on the ground floor, who would better understand their behaviour, but he realised this would be unfair to those people, who had their own infirmities to cope with, and who did not deserve their liberty restricted.

As he exited the lift on to the first floor, he headed for the lounge as usual, knowing that he may not find his wife there, as she was wont to wander in search of her sanity. But as he entered the lounge, on this occasion Kitty was sitting in an armchair, the remnants of her breakfast on her chin and blouse, staring without focus into the middle distance, a look of some anguish on her face.

'Hello, Kitty. How are you this lovely day?' he asked as he approached her.

Kitty turned her head towards him and waved a hand in his general direction, as though swatting away a fly, a frown on her face, and turned her attention to her skirt, the hem of which she started to tug. Used to such a greeting, Seymour found himself a chair and brought it over to sit beside his wife. Sitting down quietly, he simply waited till she returned from whatever distressing thoughts she was having, and till he no longer represented whatever villain she took him for. Eventually she looked up and gave him a look of delight, which swiftly changed to one of great distress. She grabbed hold of him and pulled him towards herself, and sobbed into his chest.

'Where were you?' she wailed through her tears. 'They wouldn't let me go, and they wanted to... I told them it was mine, but... Who do they think...? I didn't know if you knew who I was...'

'It's alright, Kitty my love. I'm here now. I won't let them get you.' And he patted her back and kissed her cheek, then held her tightly to himself, till her fears subsided.

23

Ever since the discovery of the body in Poot's flat, Marcus had entered a waiting phase over which he had no control. He was no longer being watched, but he didn't know if he was in the clear. No-one was telling him anything. He had continued to put in the hours in the cab and carry on as normally as possible, but now he had a new flatmate to contend with, as Kai, unable to cope with staying in North London while the woman of his dreams resided in the South, had arrived on Tuesday night with a suitcase and taken up residence in Imogen's room. It wasn't an ambush, Imogen had asked first, but Marcus felt he had no choice but to allow it. After all, he was genuinely grateful for the help the boy had given the day before.

Throughout Wednesday and all through the night, while still obsessed by Fleur, he also couldn't shake off thoughts of his mother. For the first twenty-five years or so since walking out on her, he had his drink to dampen down any feelings for her. Then his anger towards Fleur had hardened his heart against all women. But now the anger had gone towards his wife, it seemed his mother was allowed into his heart too.

When he woke on Thursday, he had decided he was going to have to do something about it, and spent the morning while out on the road trying to formulate a plan of action to locate her, or at least learn of her fate. Finally, he realised that, if she had stayed in the same area, she would probably have stayed registered with the same doctor. He knew where that had been back in the seventies, so he had better start there.

Early in the afternoon, he headed for the surgery. When he started to enquire of the young receptionist if Kitty Thorn was still registered there, it soon became clear that, owing to confidentiality rules, she was not going to be helpful. Fortunately, his former celebrity came to the rescue, as, overhearing the conversation and Marcus's growing frustration, a middle-aged receptionist alongside realised who he was, and intervened. She knew his mother. She had had conversations with her about Marcus over the years. She also knew where Kitty was, and gave Marcus the address.

Back out on the road, he continued picking up fares, trying to muster the courage to head to this home. Now knowing his mother had Alzheimer's, he kept arguing with himself that she wouldn't know who he was, so what was the point? Eventually, however, he accepted that, if he didn't go, he may never get a decent night's sleep again.

Standing outside Meadow View care home late that afternoon, his heart was beating hard in his chest. He felt like the kid he had effectively been when he last saw his mother. When he had been buzzed in and entered the little office by the door, it was explained to him that he needed to take the lift up one floor, and that someone with a key would be required to summon it when he was ready to leave.

As the lift rose, he couldn't believe how nervous he felt. It was worse than any first night nerves he had ever experienced, although he had always had the booze to take the edge off those. When the lift shuddered to a stop and the doors opened, he was confronted by an elderly black man waiting to descend, who stepped aside to let him out. Marcus thanked him as he passed, then turned as the doors closed behind him. Wasn't there something familiar about that man? Unable to solve that mystery, he turned back, and set off to find someone who might be able to help him.

Passing a small office, he saw a woman in uniform sitting at a desk doing paperwork. The door was open, so he knocked on it and, when the woman eventually lifted her head to look at him, he explained who he had come to see. Waving her arm in the general direction, she suggested he try the lounge, and resumed her scribbling, clearly irritated by the interruption.

Marcus had no idea if he would even recognise his mother, but when he looked into the lounge and scanned the room, despite the ravages of time and illness, there was something unmistakable in the form of the little, grey-haired lady in the chair by the window. Quite unexpectedly, he felt the urge to cry. To run up to her, as he would once have done with a grazed knee, and fall into her lap. Resisting this urge - he was running nowhere - he slowly approached her. She seemed to be settled, with a cup of tea on a little wheeled table beside her. Other residents were looking at him, but not his mother. One old lady, noted in the home for her amorous ways and habit of trying to snog visitors, approached him with lips puckered, but suddenly changed her mind when she was close enough to clock the unprepossessing features. As he got closer, Marcus realised his mother was having a nap. He stopped, unsure if he should proceed, then made a decision, took a couple more paces forward till he was right in front of her, and uttered a word he hadn't said for forty years, save perhaps when scripted.

'Mum?'

There was a momentary twitch of the eyebrows, a flicker of distress, then her expression settled once more.

'Mum?'

Her head jerked up and her eyes opened, then were quickly overshadowed by a deep frown, as though irritated to be disturbed.

'It's me, Mum. Marcus.'

Kitty looked at him momentarily, but then looked away, as though disgusted by what she had seen. 'Get away from me. I know what you want. Why won't you all leave me alone?'

Marcus wasn't sure if she had recognised him. He hoped not, given the reaction. So he tried again.

'It's Marcus, Mum. Your son.'

Kitty looked at him again, but this time her eyes stared at him with a fire. 'Go away, I said. Touch me and I'll stick a knife in you. Is that what you want?'

Marcus was taken aback. This was not the woman he remembered. She would never have hurt a fly. Why was her language so violent?

Suddenly a voice beside him said, 'Don't take it personally.'

Marcus turned to see who had spoken. It was the same black man he'd seen getting into the lift.

'She'll have had a dream. She'll think you're some bogeyman out to get her, no doubt.'

The accent was West Indian, Marcus thought.

'It's Marcus, Kitty,' the man continued. 'Remember?' And he gently laid a hand on her arm. At first she recoiled, but something in the way the man touched her gradually soothed her, and the anger started to subside.

Who was this man? Marcus was thinking. How does he know me? How does he know Mum? He looked at him, trying to place where he'd seen him before.

The man turned to Marcus and smiled. 'You'll be wondering who I am, no doubt.'

'Well, yes. You seem somewhat familiar.'

'As you did to me. That's why I came back up, when I had realised why. But then I have seen much more of you than you have of me, over the years.'

Marcus frowned.

'On the telly,' the man clarified.

Oh, he's just a punter, Marcus thought, and tried a little smile, although he really wasn't in the mood right now.

'Seymour McKenzie,' the man said and held out a hand.

Marcus looked at it a little suspiciously, but remembered he was no longer that man, and shook the hand. Before he could withdraw his own though, Seymour gripped it tighter and leant confidentially in.

'The name means nothing to you then?'

'Should it?' Marcus was trying not to get irritated.

'We wanted to invite you to the wedding, but we couldn't find you.'

What was the man on about? What wedding? Marcus was

beginning to wonder if perhaps this was just another confused resident.

'When we tracked you down later, we let you know though. Remember?'

Marcus did not. He had no idea what the man was talking about. He looked back towards his mother, rather hoping the man might leave them alone. Then he noticed a handkerchief on the floor beside Kitty's chair, and bent to pick it up. Thinking his mother might have dropped it, he looked for anything that might identify it as hers. When he saw the name someone had written in black ink along one edge, Kitty McKenzie, slowly he began to piece it all together. So they were married. Of course, that was where he'd seen him. At the house. Where did she find him?

'When did you marry?' he asked.

'June, 1980.'

What? I was hardly out the door, Marcus thought. 'Really?' he said. The cogs were whirring rather slowly, but suddenly Marcus got it. Immediately he looked at Seymour with new eyes, scanning his features for any evidence to confirm his interpretation of what was going on here.

Reading Marcus's face, Seymour smiled. 'I bet you wonder where I was all your childhood.'

Marcus was dumbstruck. He couldn't form words at all. He simply looked at Seymour, and then at Kitty. What a week this was. What more could it throw at him? So this man was his father? The man he had never known, who had never been in his life, but who turns up again as soon as he leaves home.

'Bit of a shock, eh?' Seymour smiled again and hoped his son would not react badly.

Suddenly Kitty said, 'Stop talking about me. I am here you know.'

'I know, Kitty. I was just talking to Marcus. He's come to see you.'

'Where is Marcus?'

'He's here. Look.'

Kitty looked about vaguely, but didn't appear to see anything of note, and slipped back into her own world, where she seemed to be once again tormented by anxieties.

'Not to worry, love.' Seymour looked apologetically at Marcus. He was of course used to the fluctuations in consciousness and mood, but he realised it must all be very confusing for Marcus. 'Your mother can't always take everything in, I'm afraid. She doesn't always know me. But she is still in there. You just have to be patient.'

Marcus still had nothing to say. If his mother had known him, he might perhaps have apologised to her. For leaving. For ignoring her attempts to make contact. To try to make up for all the years when he was too up his own bottom to care about her. But now it was too late. He'd lost the chance. She didn't know who he was. He felt he was getting upset, and he didn't want to show that to this man, who may be his father, but who was a complete stranger. So he simply turned and walked out of the lounge.

Once in the corridor, he walked to the lift. There didn't appear to be a button to press. Then he remembered he needed a key to summon it. He couldn't even make a smooth exit. It was like floundering in the wings flapping your arms about trying to find a gap in the curtains to get off stage. And then he felt a hand on his shoulder. His audience was on the stage with him, just to get a good close-up on his misery.

'Let me find you a key,' he heard Seymour say, but he didn't turn to him. He remained facing the lift, stewing in his wretchedness.

He was still there when he felt the presence of Seymour again, and he saw out of the corner of his eye a key being inserted and turned. Suddenly the doors were opening and he staggered forward, then stood and waited till he heard the doors close behind him. Only then did he turn to find the buttons and press G. When the lift jerked into action, as he had so many times this week, he found he was sobbing once again.

When the lift stopped, he quickly wiped his face on his

sleeve and prepared to be seen, but no-one seemed to be about. Judging by the smell, it was meal time. He made his way along to the front door and looked for a means of opening it. On the outside he could see through the glass an old man searching through a small bunch of keys with one hand, while peering through a magnifying glass in the other. Finding the key he needed, he opened the door and came in. Marcus stood back, then grabbed the door to prevent it shutting again. Realising someone was there, the man raised his lens to scrutinize the features, then quickly dropped the glass and shuffled off.

Marcus stepped into the fresh air and marched to his car. Only once inside did he finally fully let out all the sorrow he was feeling.

24

Inspector Richard Hutchinson was at his desk, collating all the evidence he had so far. There was a knock on the door.

'Come in.'

It was Sergeant Moore.

'How's it going, boss?'

'Hi Steph. Just waiting on confirmation of dental records, but we managed to get a fingerprint off that corpse. If the teeth agree, we may have an identification.'

'And?'

'I'll not say just yet. In case it's wrong. Don't want to tempt fate.'

'Fair enough.' But Stephanie could see he was excited. He thought he had something significant.

'What about your investigations? That director?'

'Hopeless. Unfortunately.'

'Really? Nothing?'

'No complaints, no. But I have spoken to a few actresses who worked with him over the years. They all seem to think it's par for the course. That's just the way he was, and they live with it. They actually seem quite fond of him.'

'Ah well. As I said, another world.'

'You know, one of them said he came into her dressing room after a show, while she was getting dressed, and she quickly pulled on her bra, and found his hands were inside it when she got it on. She thought it was funny.'

'Maybe you spoke to the wrong ones.'

Was that it? she wondered. Should she press on?

'Anyway. What did you want?'

What did she want? 'Oh, yes. Is there anything I can offer Ellie's parents? You said I could continue to liaise, and I promised them I'd visit them in their new home. Be nice to offer them some encouragement.'

Hutchinson considered this. 'I suppose you could say we have an interesting new line of enquiry, without going into specifics.'

Sergeant Moore wasn't sure this would be enough to warrant a visit, although she had read with interest what Cynthia had written about Ellie, and it might be nice to have a chat about that, now she felt she knew the girl better. But she didn't want to upset them unnecessarily.

'Oh, and that desk. If they want it, can I get it over to them?'

'Sure. I thought they were selling it.'

'Maybe not. We'll see. Perhaps I'll pop over tomorrow then, if that's okay. See what they're thinking.'

'Sure, Steph. Thanks.' He turned his attention back to his paperwork. Suddenly he realised Stephanie was still standing there. 'You okay?'

'Sorry. Yes. How do you sleep?'

'Sleep?'

'After seeing things like in that flat? Doesn't it stay with you?'

'You get used to it. Sure you wouldn't like to talk to someone?'

'I'm fine. Not to worry. Bye.' And she left the room.

Hutchinson was thoughtful. Should he have been more honest? Did he really need to play the hard man? The truth was it was always horrible. And it did stay with you. But it was also true that you do get used to it. You get used to the nightmares.

As if to prove to himself he could cope, he picked up a photograph of the corpse and studied it. Maybe there was something he'd missed.

25

When Imogen arrived home and came into the lounge, she found her father sitting in silence in his armchair. He looked more exhausted than ever.

'You alright?' she asked.

Marcus looked up and gave her a weak smile. 'Hello. Yes, fine.' But he wasn't feeling fine. He still hadn't told his daughter he had received his DNA results, but now the reality of them had been revealed to him, he had a whole lot more to tell. And he realised that it was not just his loss that he had cut himself off from his mother; he had deprived Imogen of a grandmother and, now he knew, a grandfather too. The poor girl had only ever had him, her only family. He had been so unfair to her he now could see, and he felt real shame.

'Come and sit down. I have something to tell you.'

Imogen sat on the settee, a look of concern on her face. 'What is it?'

Slowly Marcus told her the full story, starting with the DNA results, and finally ending with Mr Seymour McKenzie. When he had finished, they both sat in silence for some time; Marcus hoping he had not permanently damaged the most important relationship in his life, Imogen simply dumbstruck.

Eventually Imogen spoke. 'Can I meet them?'

'Of course.'

Now knowing that she had had family so close all her life, and being unaware only because her father had chosen to estrange himself from his mother, Imogen should have been furious with Marcus. But she just felt sad. Everything was sad. That her mother had gone; that her father had not been there for her through those devastating early years of that loss; that there were grandparents nearby who might have provided what Marcus didn't; and that she could now never get to know her grandmother. She got up and silently took herself off to her room.

Marcus sat on, running through his head the years of stupidity and waste for which he had been responsible. His failure as a husband, as a father, as a son. His casual racism, his arrogance, his selfishness. Now he knew who the real cunt was.

He had been sitting there for some time, trying to work out what he should now do to try to make amends to everyone he had let down, when he heard the front door opening. Realising it must be Kai, and that Imogen must have given him a key, Marcus didn't feel irritated at all. He was beyond that. He felt he owed everyone. There wasn't enough he could give to put things right.

Kai stuck his head into the lounge. Marcus, who had got up, gave him a sad smile and said, 'Evening bruv.'

Kai frowned. What had he said? 'Evening. Is Immy back?'

'In her room.'

'Cheers.' Kai headed down the corridor to the bedroom. He knocked and entered. Imogen was curled up on the bed.

'You okay?' Kai asked, concerned.

Imogen sat up. Kai could see she had been crying.

'What is it?'

Imogen woke up a couple of hours later in Kai's arms. She remembered how sweet he had been to her when she had explained everything. Now she'd had a nap, she felt better; sleep is wonderful for allowing the assimilation and processing of new information. Kai stirred too, and smiled at her.

'Fancy a drink?' she asked.

Emerging from the bedroom, they realised from the aromas and noises that Marcus was preparing a meal. Wondering what he wanted this time, they stuck their heads into the kitchen.

'Smells good,' Imogen said.

'Hungry?' Marcus asked.

'Sure. Alright if we pop for a quick drink first?'

'Of course. Take your time. Where are you going?'

'The Sack? Maybe.' She looked to Kai to see if he was alright with that. He shrugged.

Marcus turned down the heat under a pot on the hob. 'That could do with a gentle simmer for a while. Mind if I join you?'

If they did, they weren't going to let on, and the three of them were soon clattering down the outside stairs.

Entering the Sack of Balls, Marcus was pleased to see Colin behind the bar.

'Evening, Col. Good to see you. I believe you've met Kai here.'

Colin was taken aback by this arrival, given he rarely saw Marcus these days, and that he had never seen him socialising with one of them. But Marcus had a point to make and, putting an arm around Kai's shoulders he asked, 'What will you have?'

'Lager please. Krugelhoffer.' This was most disconcerting; the arm thing.

'Ein grosses Krugelhoffer, bitte. Imogen?'

'White wine. Please.'

'And a soda and lime for me please, Col.'

Colin set about pouring the drinks and Marcus removed his arm from Kai's shoulders, but gave him a little slap on the back as he did so. Kai glanced at Imogen, who stifled a little giggle.

When they all had a drink, Marcus paid, then led the others over to a table. To their table, as it happened, but he didn't know that. Once they were all seated, Marcus looked across at Imogen and Kai, sitting beside each other on the banquette.

'Here's to you two,' he announced. 'You make a most attractive couple.'

Imogen squirmed.

Kai said, 'Thanks mate,' and clinked glasses with Marcus.

Imogen then recognised the signs. Marcus was preparing to make a speech. She could tell by the way he was adjusting his position on his chair and placing his palms on the table. There was also the tell-tale preparatory lip action and eye lowering. Then he raised his arms in the air.

'I've been a cunt. Okay. I recognise it.' He lowered the arms.

'I wish to offer you both my deepest apologies for my many failings. But especially to you, Imogen, for being such a crap father.' Imogen made to speak, but he shut her down. 'No. Don't disagree. I have, so let me apologise. You'll be wondering why I didn't let you meet your grandmother, and the honest answer is, I don't know. Having avoided all contact for so long, I guess I didn't know how to re-establish it. Maybe it was cowardice. Maybe I was ashamed. I don't know. All I do know is that chucking another drink down my throat stopped me thinking about it. And when I'd eventually stopped, you had already made it to that point without her, so why complicate it, I suppose was the thinking. But probably, more honestly, I wasn't thinking about you. It was me. I didn't know how to handle it myself. I couldn't face the rejection I guess, if she didn't want to see me. I hardly deserved the prodigal's welcome.'

The other two studied their drinks intently.

'Then there is this colour thing. This race thing. It turns out we are all mixed with spoonfuls of pitch, of varying capacity. You Kai, and my father, have a good tablespoon, me a dessert spoon, Imogen a teaspoon. And yes, that's a rubbish analogy. A possibly racist analogy. I need to learn what is and isn't racist. From my new perspective, perhaps my sensitivity will improve. But my point is, if I came across as racist before, and I'm sure I did, it wasn't because I felt superior to people with darker skin. It was just that I thought they were different to me. Not of my world. That I had nothing in common with them. And maybe I shared the guilt of all white people that we, that they, have been pretty shitty to black people over the years, and perhaps said black people would be justified in being a bit pissed off with them. In wanting to do them harm. Isn't that behind all racism? Fear. That they might get their comeuppance? Isn't that why white supremacists need so desperately to keep black people in their place? To ensure they have no power? So they aren't strung from trees themselves. And the Ku Klux Klan cover their faces? Fear. Well, we are the future. We are neither white nor black. We are the forerunners of a beautiful time to come in which the world no longer divides itself by race or borders or ideology or religion. A world -'

'Dad. You're getting very loud. And you're going to knock your drink over. We get the point.'

Kai couldn't conceal his smirk.

'Yes. Well. I have a lot to get off my chest. I've had to do a lot of soul-searching this last week.'

Colin had been listening intently to this sermon. Was he understanding this? Was his mate one of them?

'Yes, well we get you're sorry,' Imogen assured her father. 'And you'll be a good boy from now on. But what about your parents? When are we going to see them? Did you make an arrangement?'

Marcus hung his head. 'No. Not exactly. Not at all. It was all a bit of a shock. I'll get in touch. Maybe we could pop round. See my old house.'

'That would be nice.'

'Now. You two finish your drinks. I'll go and check on the dinner.' Marcus got up and headed towards the bar. Colin looked uncomfortable. 'Did you hear that?'

'Why?' Colin was defensive.

'Just wondered.' He placed his glass on the bar. 'Thanks, Col. See you again.'

'Sure.'

Marcus headed for the door, then turned back. 'Colin. Courage, mate. Courage.' And he heaved open the door and exited.

26

Marcus rose early on the Friday morning. To continue his rehabilitation into the human race, he needed to go and see his father. To apologise for walking off the previous day and to arrange for him to meet Imogen. He didn't know how much of his time Seymour spent with Kitty, but he thought he should get to his house early to ensure he didn't miss him.

Turning into Asquith Road again, he felt the queasiness return. It was around 8.30 and people were leaving for work. As he approached number 63, he saw there were a couple of spaces vacant, and he pulled into one across the road from the house. Turning off the engine, he sat for a while, wondering if it was too early to disturb the man. After a few minutes, the door of number 63 opened and Seymour, fully dressed, put a bin bag into a wheelie bin and moved it out on to the pavement. When he re-entered the house, Marcus got out of his car and crossed the road.

He was ridiculously nervous, and kept repeating the word 'courage' to himself. Once outside the door, he took a deep breath, rang the bell and waited. After a brief hiatus, in which Marcus could feel his heart pounding in his chest, the door opened.

'Marcus! Good morning to you. Please come in.' And Seymour turned and walked towards the back of the house.

Marcus stepped into the hallway he hadn't seen for over forty years and followed him into the kitchen.

'Would you like a cup of tea? Coffee?'

'Whichever you're having.'

'Well I am a tea man myself. You cannot get better than a nice cup of English Breakfast. The perfect way to start the day. I'll just put the kettle on. Please take a seat.'

Marcus sat at a small table against the wall. He was pretty sure the same table he'd eaten at as a child.

'I came to apologise for running off yesterday. It was all a bit overwhelming.'

'Perfectly understandable. Quite a shock, I'm sure. But I'm glad you came. I didn't know if we'd lost you again.'

'No no. Not at all.'

There were photos pinned to a cork board hanging on the wall above the table, along with various bills and tradesmen's cards. There were several of the same two children; two boys. Black boys. Seymour saw Marcus studying them.

'That's George and Theo. Our grandchildren.' Then Seymour realised. 'Your nephews.'

What? He had a sibling? Seymour could see his surprise.

'You have a sister. Rebecca. That's her.' Seymour pointed to another photo of a woman with lighter skin than her children.

Marcus thought she looked like a nice person. Someone he'd like to meet. 'Does she live in London?'

'Oh yes. Not far away.'

The surprises just keep coming, Marcus thought. He knew it was his own fault he didn't know this stuff, and he felt ashamed.

'Obviously she's a lot younger than you. Still in her thirties.' Seymour filled the teapot with boiling water and put the lid on, before placing a cosy over the top. 'Can I offer you a bite to eat?'

'Oh no. Tea's fine.' Marcus realised his mother must have had this sister rather late. He had so many questions to ask, but he didn't want to bombard the man. 'You have a granddaughter as well, you know.'

'Yes. Imogen. It would be lovely to meet her.'

Marcus realised the thing about being a celebrity was his business was everyone's, back then. Of course, there had been that magazine feature. Poor Imogen. She didn't get any say in that.

'That was one of the reasons I came. She's anxious to meet

you.'

Seymour smiled. He was glad Marcus had told her about their encounter. About his existence. 'Excellent. We must all get together. It's all been far too long.'

'I'm sorry about Mum. That can't have been easy.'

'No. I've not completely lost her though. Not yet. She has her moments.'

Marcus was wrestling with something. He wanted to ask a question, but he didn't know how to phrase it. Seymour, perhaps sensing it, saved him the trouble.

'She never stopped thinking about you, you know. Hoping you'd turn up.'

Marcus could feel himself welling up. It was what he wanted to hear, but it wasn't easy to hear it. And it certainly wasn't what he deserved. But then there is nothing surer to break down your defences than forgiveness. Not that he was having any trouble blubbing like a fool this week.

Seymour placed a cup of tea in front of him. 'There. That'll help. There's sugar there if you take it.'

Marcus couldn't speak. Why was the man being so kind to him? Shouldn't he be furious? He stirred in a spoonful of sugar, and sipped the tea. A tear dropped into it. Seymour brought his cup over and sat down at the table.

'It's sure been a long time, son. A long, long time. But you're here. In my house while I'm still in it. Who knows how long I've got.'

Marcus nodded and sniffed. What a foolish man he was, and had always been. What a different life he might have had with this father in it.

'You said yesterday that you expected I was wondering where you had been all my childhood. What happened?' Marcus asked.

'Ah, well. It's all rather sad. Something of a misunderstanding. We were misled. Your mother's parents were against our marriage. Lies were told. I blame myself for accepting them. I should have known better.'

'You didn't choose to be absent.'

'I did not.'

Marcus was reeling. It was one blow after another. Seymour put a hand on his shoulder. Marcus bit his lip.

To move the conversation on, Seymour asked, 'So. How's Fleur?' He didn't know if she was still in Marcus's life, but he knew she'd disappeared from his television screen, and he wondered where she was.

Marcus looked at his father, wondering what he knew of Fleur, beyond her career. He cleared his throat. 'Fleur? She left. I'm afraid I don't know where.' Should he mention the police?

'Oh dear. That's sad. How recently?'

'Years ago. Imogen was four.'

Oh, dear dear dear. That is sad. I'm very sorry. For both of you.'

'Yes. Well. I'm sure *I* deserved it, at least.' He sipped his tea. He didn't really want to think about Fleur. It made him feel so bad. Not knowing what had happened to her. If she was still alive. God, he hoped she was. He really wanted to see her.

'I shall be going back to see Kitty soon. I go every day. Do you want to come?'

Marcus considered this. 'You don't think I'd just upset her?'

'*I* upset her. That's just the nature of the cursed disease. But she appreciates me being there too. I'm sure of it. I wouldn't go otherwise. If you just sit with her, she might enjoy that too.'

'Okay then. If you think so.'

When they had finished their teas, they got up to head out. As they passed the front room, Seymour turned to Marcus.

'Come here. Let me show you something.'

He led Marcus into the room and over to the fireplace, where he stood to one side indicating a 10' by 8' framed photograph of Marcus, aged about eleven, in his school uniform, taking pride of place in the centre of the mantelpiece.

'In case you doubted what I said.'

Feeling another deluge imminent, Marcus turned away and headed for the front door, lest his father should think him a complete snivelling idiot. He crossed the road to his car, dangerously blinded by salt water. He felt he was about to actually sob loudly, and tried to cover it with coughs. He quickly got into the car and attempted to suppress the overwhelming emotions before Seymour got in, which he did to some extent, as it took his father a little while to ensure he had everything he needed and to get across the road. As soon as Seymour was belted in, Marcus started up and drove off in the direction of Meadow View.

By the time they got there, Marcus had regained his composure, and he jumped out of the car and came round to the passenger side to offer any assistance his father might need.

When they stepped out of the lift on the first floor, they spotted Kitty marching away down the corridor, apparently on an urgent mission. Marcus looked at Seymour.

'She'll be back in a minute,' Seymour said. 'It's a dead end.' And they set off after her, ready to greet her when she headed back towards them. Sure enough, as they approached a corner, Kitty appeared and turned towards them. She seemed quite distressed and was muttering to herself. Suddenly she spotted Seymour, and tears filled her eyes. She threw herself against him and sobbed into his chest. Marcus thought, I see where I get it.

Seymour stroked her hair and offered soothing words, and gradually Kitty calmed down.

'Shall we go into the lounge? Get you a cup of tea?' he asked, trying to make it sound like the most delightful thing they could possibly do.

'Nice cup of tea,' Kitty said, and allowed herself to be carried along by Seymour's arm around her shoulders.

Marcus followed on behind, noting how thin his mother was. How frail.

When Seymour had got her settled in an armchair, he went to see if he could persuade a member of staff to make them all a cup of tea, and Marcus found a couple of upright chairs and placed one either side of Kitty. Sitting on one of them, Marcus immediately felt out of his depth. What should he do? His mother was fussing with her clothing, running her hands along the hem of her skirt and then smoothing the material over her knees. Did she even know he was there? Maybe he should speak, but it didn't go well the last time he tried that.

Suddenly Kitty said, 'I wonder what happened to Marcus?'

Marcus was taken aback. But she wasn't looking at him. Was she addressing him?

'It's me, Mum. I'm Marcus,' he felt he had to say.

Kitty looked at him briefly, then turned her attention back to her skirt.

Seymour reappeared and came and sat the other side of Kitty.

'Tea's on the way,' he said. 'How are you two getting along? Did you see Marcus has come to see you, Kitty?'

She carried on smoothing her skirt. Marcus looked helplessly at his father.

'Take her hand?' Seymour said. 'Make contact.'

Marcus wasn't sure this was such a good idea. She clearly didn't recognise him. She might kick off. But Seymour smiled reassuringly, so he reached out a hand and placed it over one of his mother's, and when she didn't object, he gently lifted it and held it palm to palm. Kitty seemed calm, but unresponsive. The effect on Marcus though was profound. To be holding his mother's hand after all these years, to have a physical connection with her, to feel her warmth and life, made him feel like a child again. He wouldn't have done this since he *was* a child. As a teenager, he wouldn't have allowed it. He turned his head away to hide the effect it was having and looked out of the window. The view was blurring once again. Suddenly he felt another hand on the back of his. He froze. The hand started patting his soothingly. Slowly he turned back to see what was happening. Through his tears he could see it was his mother's other hand at work. She had a contented expression on her face. Marcus quickly turned back towards the window, but his father must have seen the way his body was twitching as he tried to keep it together.

At that moment Marcus's mobile started ringing. He eased his hand from out of his mother's grasp, and pulled the phone from his pocket. He wiped his eyes as surreptitiously as he could with his fingers so he could read the screen. It was a number he didn't know. Normally he wouldn't have answered it, but it provided him with the excuse he needed.

'Sorry. Better get this.' And he slipped out of the lounge into the corridor, where he answered the call.

It was Inspector Richard Hutchinson. He needed to speak with him, but he didn't want to do it over the phone. Could he pop round to Marcus's flat, or would Marcus be able to come to the police station? The one in Peel Avenue. He sounded very serious, but not as inquisitorial as Marcus had previously found him. This reinforced his hope that he was no longer a suspect.

Marcus explained that he was not at home and, if it was urgent, it would be quicker if he came to the police station. The Inspector told him to ask for him at the front desk and he would come down.

Ending the call, Marcus re-entered the lounge. Seymour now had Kitty's hands in his and was gently talking to her. Without going into any detail, Marcus explained he had to go and meet someone. He was sorry to be dashing off when his mother was calm, but he was afraid it was important. Seymour thanked him for coming.

'Come back whenever you want. Bring Imogen.'

'I will. And we'll sort out some sort of get together. I promise.'

Seymour took a pen from his pocket, and wrote a number on the back of a till receipt he found in his wallet. He handed it to Marcus. 'Call me.'

'I will.' Marcus put the receipt into his own wallet, then raised a hand in farewell, and was about to leave when he remembered he needed a key.

'Ask a member of the staff. Several have them,' Seymour told him, and Marcus went in search of one.

As he pushed open the front door of Peel Avenue police station, Marcus reflected on the fact that he had never had cause to enter this place before, despite his colourful history of rowdy nights and disreputable behaviour. Somehow, even at the height of his drinking, he had charmed his way out of difficult situations, and this building had only ever been one he had seen from the outside.

When the desk Sergeant had called the Inspector, Marcus went and sat on a chair and waited. He was starting to feel nervous. What could this be about?

'Good morning, Mr Thorn,' Hutchinson said as he emerged from the stairwell. 'Let's go in here.' And he led Marcus into a room with couches and a coffee machine. 'Would you like something to drink,' he asked, indicating the machine.

Marcus remembered he was about to get a cup of tea at Meadow View until he left so abruptly, but he declined.

'What did you want, Inspector? Have you arrested Poot?'

Hutchinson looked very serious. 'No, Mr Thorn. Shall we sit?'

When they were settled on adjacent couches, the policeman took a breath and announced, 'Mr Thorn, I am afraid I have some bad news. We have found a body in Mr Poot's flat.'

No shit, Marcus was thinking. How is that bad news? If Poot's been up to no good, that is very good news for me.

'We have made an identification of the corpse. Of the woman. I am afraid there is no doubt whatsoever that what we have found in that flat is the body of your wife, Fleur Hardy.'

27

At first Marcus's instinct was to laugh. He'd seen the corpse. How could that have been Fleur? But when Hutchinson reiterated that there could be no doubt, there was both fingerprint and dental evidence to confirm it, he sat in shock. He hadn't seen her for twenty years. He supposed she would have changed. Even without the ravages of death. And looking at the Inspector, and seeing his total conviction that it had indeed been Fleur, he slumped forward and buried his head in his hands. It would have been devastating enough had he not been in Poot's flat and experienced his subsequent sea change with regard to Fleur, but now that he had, the acceptance of this identification ripped him apart.

Any suspicions Inspector Hutchinson still had about Marcus's potential involvement in his wife's disappearance or death, evaporated. This was the rawest grief. Sure, the man was an actor, but no actor is this good.

'Is there anyone you'd like me to call?'

Marcus was incapable of hearing the question, let alone responding, and eventually the Inspector felt it would be the decent thing to do to leave him alone for a while, and he quietly left the room.

When he returned a good twenty minutes later, with Sergeant Moore at his side, Marcus was curled in the foetal position on the floor. Hutchinson looked to his Sergeant helplessly and she knelt beside Marcus and gently asked if he was okay. At first Marcus remained motionless, but when the policewoman asked a second time, he eventually stirred and looked towards her with tormented eyes. Meanwhile Inspector Hutchinson persuaded the machine to produce a cup of tea, which he pumped a good few shots of sugar into and carried over towards Marcus. Once Stephanie Moore had managed to get Marcus back on to the couch, Hutchinson handed him the tea.

When he had eventually had a couple of sips of the sweet brew, Marcus looked towards the Inspector and, in a hoarse voice, started to fire off questions.

'Why was she there? Where had she been all these years? Had Poot imprisoned her? How did she die?'

'I'm afraid we don't yet have the answers to most of those questions,' Hutchinson replied. 'But it would appear she had taken a drug overdose. Diamorphine. Heroin.'

Marcus was incredulous. He couldn't reconcile such a fate with the Fleur he knew. He was the one with an addiction, not her. She wouldn't have. Then he remembered the painkillers she used to pop in the last years before she vanished. Had she developed a dependence on them and eventually moved on to the hard stuff? It just didn't ring true, although he realised he didn't even know why she had started on the medication. He had just put it down to lady troubles. One of the hazards of the female anatomy. Had he asked? He suspected probably not. What a truly crap husband he had been.

When Marcus had finished the tea, he said, 'Should I go now?'

'If you'd like to. We'll keep you informed with developments.' Inspector Hutchinson took the empty cup. 'Are you sure you're okay to drive?'

'I think so.'

Then the Inspector remembered himself. 'Oh, before you go, and I know this may seem a bit of an imposition given this terrible news, but it would really help in our investigation of your wife's death.'

Marcus looked at the policeman. What was he being asked?

'Sorry,' Hutchinson continued, 'but because you used to live in that flat, if we could identify any remaining fingerprints you might have left there, we could eliminate them and concentrate on the rest.'

'After all this time?'

'They can persist. Especially on some surfaces, and in less disturbed places. It would just require a quick scan. Shouldn't take long.'

Marcus shrugged, then followed the Inspector to another room and co-operated with the instructions he was given, and once he had provided all the prints requested, he was escorted back out to the front desk.

'Thank you, Mr Thorn,' Hutchinson said, and shook his hand. 'I am truly sorry for your loss.'

Marcus said, 'Thanks,' and went out through the door on to the street.

When he had gone, the Inspector turned to his Sergeant. 'Thanks for your help there, Steph. Never been good at that. Poor sod.'

'Is there anyone else we need to tell?'

'Well, we'll let Thorn tell the daughter. Apart from that, she doesn't seem to have anyone. Parents gone. There was a brother, but he's gone too. Bit of a dysfunctional family. Booze and drugs. Remarkable she turned out as she did, and made something of herself, even if she went the same way eventually.'

'All a bit odd though, isn't it? She's missing for twenty years, and when we find her, she's only just died.'

'Very odd. But then so is that Poot. God knows what he's been up to. We still haven't come up with anything related to Ellie Nelson, though. Did you go and see the parents?'

'Yes. First thing.'

'How are they settling in?'

'Mrs Nelson is having a great time. She's already made loads of friends. I got the impression Mr Nelson is finding it a bit harder though. Keeps going off for walks. Don't think he likes crowds.'

'No insights that could help us? Didn't you get more detail on the girl?'

'Yeah. I feel I know her better, but that's all. I hope I didn't put them through it all for nothing. Oh, by the way, they're going to keep the... the desk. I'm getting it dropped off this afternoon.'

'Fair enough.'

'Mr Nelson says he's going to hide his valuables in it. Don't think he trusts his fellow residents.'

Richard Hutchinson smiled. 'Don't think he trusts me either. With good cause if I don't come up with something soon.' This thought spurred him on. 'Right. I'm going to see if I can match up any of Thorn's dabs, and see what we're left with.' And he headed back into the fingerprint room.

Stephanie Moore was frustrated she couldn't get stuck into the investigation herself, and reluctantly headed to the stairs. She had plenty of other less interesting stuff on her desk she had better address.

28

Marcus had said he was okay to drive, but he really wasn't. He didn't even know in which direction to point the car. Where was he going? What was he going to do? Eventually, having narrowly avoided a collision, he pulled over and sat staring into space. How was he going to tell Imogen? All her life she had held out the hope that her mother would return. Now all she could do was bury her. And what if it *was* his fault she'd gone? According to the note it was. She needed to get away from him. What had he done to his daughter? What had he caused his wife to do?

A loud horn startled him. Glancing in his rear-view mirror, he saw it filled with the red front of a bus. Realising he was at its stop, he pulled away. He needed to get home. Willing himself to concentrate on that one task, he worked out where he was and, with some considerable effort, managed to get himself back to his flat. Switching off the engine, the reality of his situation overwhelmed him again, and it was beyond him to do anything other than sit once more in trancelike stupefaction.

It was the persistent nagging of his bladder that eventually cut through, and he hauled himself from the car and up the stairs to his flat.

Bladder drained, he sat down in his lounge determined to process and make sense of everything that had happened to him during the most traumatic week of his life. What did he know that he hadn't known a week earlier? Well, first, he was the product of two loving parents. That he certainly hadn't known. He really didn't understand why his mother had never talked about his father. Second, a girl he had once known had disappeared the night she was expecting to meet him, and, while he was pretty certain he had not met her that night, he suspected his old flat-mate Howard Poot might know something. Which led him to the third fact; Poot was still living locally, albeit under the care of the NHS and while labouring under the delusion that he was the leader of the Western world, and being consequently too barking to provide any answers. Fourth, when his wife took off, she may not have intended it to be a permanent parting of the ways, and again Poot was in some way involved, because, fifth, that same beautiful wife had turned up dead in the fucker's flat.

This last fact, of course, trumped the rest. This was the one he couldn't make sense of, and which was going to torture him. Had Fleur been just down the road all these years? With that man? How could he have kept her there? Surely she couldn't have been there willingly? If not, why hadn't she left when Poot had been detained? She didn't appear to be tied up or restrained in any other way. None of it made sense.

Throughout the afternoon Marcus agonised over it all. When Imogen came in from work, she found him asleep on the settee.

'Hard day?' she asked him.

Marcus opened his eyes, and it all came flooding back, re-placing a beautiful dream, in which he and Fleur were making love under a starry sky, with the horrendous reality from which he had eventually found some respite. Imogen could see at once that all was not well.

'What is it?

How could he begin? How could he destroy her dreams?

'You're going to have to tell me. Is it your parents?' Imogen sat beside him.

'Oh Imogen. I'm so sorry. That body I found. It *was* your mother.'

By the time Kai arrived, Imogen was once again curled up in her bedroom, and Marcus catatonic in the lounge. When he even-tually realised Kai was speaking to him, Marcus could merely point in the direction of his daughter's room, and Kai went to investigate.

It took a lot longer than the previous evening before Imogen stopped sobbing in Kai's arms, at which point she announced, 'Let's get pissed.'

It was Friday night and neither of them had to work the following day. Indeed Imogen had a completely free weekend for once, so there was no need to be sensible. She was certainly not in the mood to rein herself in. Kai was aware that she was in a delicate state and, though he wasn't going to stop her, he realised he was going to have to be watchful.

The first glass of wine was empty before Kai was half way through his pint, and he jumped up to get Imogen another, but he suggested perhaps she should take a little longer over this one when he placed it in front of her. The look she then gave him was one he had not yet seen, and one he hoped to see rarely in future. They had defaulted to the Sack, and Colin too was looking across anxiously.

By the time Imogen had finished her third glass, Kai proposed they get something to eat. Of course, he was being prudent, but he was also ravenous. Imogen said she wasn't hungry, but eventually she was persuaded by Kai's professed need.

Wondering if the Parrot Café might cheer her up, Kai led Imogen in its direction. She was already quite unsteady on her feet - three large glasses of white wine drunk quickly on an empty stomach have that effect - so he kept his arm around her all the way.

Once they were seated in the café, Kai looked for the dish on the menu most likely to soak up the wine, and presumed to order it for both of them when the waitress came over. Imogen was going to protest, but ordered another glass of wine instead.

Kai wondered which was the wisest way to proceed: to talk through the cause of Imogen's upset; or to talk of anything but it, and hope it took her mind off it. Reasoning that the latter strategy would merely delay matters, he gently asked how she was feeling. Imogen looked sharply up at him, her eyes struggling to focus.

'I've felt better.'

'I know. Would you like to talk about it?'

'It?'

'Her.'

Imogen looked at the table. The waitress placed a glass of wine in front of her and she thanked her, then took a large sip from it.

'It's over,' she said, and tears flowed freely once more.

Kai put his arm round her. 'I guess you're going to continue feeling like this until you get some sort of explanation.'

'Are you trying to cheer me up?'

'Sorry. I was, but... Sorry.'

'She was just down the road. Possibly the whole time. How will that ever feel okay?'

'Well, you don't know that.'

'I don't know anything. It seems I was the last consideration. Both my parents seem to have had other priorities.'

'Well. Maybe. If it's any comfort, you are *my* priority.'

Imogen looked up at him again. Her instinct was to laugh bitterly in his face, but, notwithstanding the booze and her emotional state, the sincerity in his puppy dog eyes quelled the urge, and she dropped her head again.

When the waitress placed the food in front of them, Imogen looked at it queasily.

'Try to eat,' Kai urged her. 'You'll feel better for it.'

Imogen wasn't convinced, but she picked up a fork and had a go. Kai then felt able to tuck into his. When he had cleared his plate, he turned to Imogen. She was nodding off, a forkful of food hovering in front of her face. He gently took the fork and placed it on the plate, then took out his phone and called a taxi.

When he had got her home and she was safely tucked up in bed, he went to the kitchen and came back with a plastic bowl, just in case, and then settled down beside her. She was fast asleep. He kissed her tenderly on the forehead, then lay looking at her until he fell asleep himself.

29

When Marcus, still rooted to the spot fighting off internal demons, heard the front door shut, he threw his head back against the settee and stared at the ceiling. So he was alone? God was he alone. He had never felt more alone in his life. Dark thoughts started tormenting him. When he could bear them no longer, he got up and walked straight out of the flat and down the stairs. He set off down the lane, drawn by an invisible force, towards a destination he was not consciously picturing or aiming for. It was only when he arrived that he recognised it. Pushing open the door he tumbled into the pub. Colin looked up.

'Marcus! You've just missed them.'

'Is that so?' He plodded on towards the bar and grabbed its edge when he reached it, his arms splayed and thumbs uppermost. He ran an eye over the pumps. 'What would you recommend?'

Colin frowned. Was he talking about the beers?

'What's a nice hoppy one? Don't know any of these.' Marcus peered at the badges.

'Marcus? You're not serious?'

'What do you mean? Don't I look serious?'

'It's been years, mate. You've done so well.'

'Are you refusing a sale? What kind of businessman are you? Is it because I is black?'

Colin shifted uncomfortably. 'People seem to like the Monumental.'

'A pint of the Monumental then. Let's hope it lives up to its name.'

Colin reluctantly took a glass from the shelf and started

drawing up the blonde ale, a healthy and creamy head growing with each pull.

'Looks in fine fettle, old boy. Still keeping a good cellar, I see.'

When he'd tamed the lively brew enough to minimize the head, Colin placed the pint in front of Marcus on the bar. Marcus stood watching the liquid gradually start to clear from the bottom up.

'Always worth waiting for, eh Col?'

'Are you really sure you want to do this, mate?'

'It's just an ale, Col. What do you want for it?'

'Five.'

'Are we talking pounds?'

'Yeah.'

'Hah. Only a couple the last time.' He pulled out his wallet and handed over a five pound note. 'You might want to wash your hands after you've put that in the till.'

Colin didn't follow, and chose to ignore the comment.

Marcus stood staring at the pint until the ale had finally fully cleared. Then he spread his hands out on the bar and lowered his face till his nose was an inch or two above the foam. He drew in a deep breath and straightened up.

'Certainly smells good, Col.'

He theatrically took hold of the straight glass, placing each finger individually around it, then slowly raised it to his mouth.

'Marcus. Mate. You don't have to do this.'

Ignoring him, he put the rim of the glass to his lips and sucked in a mouthful. There was a tantalising pause as he held it there for a few seconds, then he swallowed and closed his eyes. He kept them closed as he felt the liquid flowing down his oesophagus and spreading out in his stomach. Then the familiar warmth spread through him, and the corners of his mouth curled into a smile.

'Hello, old friend. Welcome back.'

Opening his eyes again, he looked at Colin. 'Don't look so worried. That's a damned fine ale, mate.' And he proceeded to quaff down several more gulps. 'Damned fine indeed,' he announced when he had done so.

Colin knew this was only the beginning, and soon stopped questioning him, as Marcus placed each empty glass in front of him and demanded it be refilled. After the fifth, Marcus announced, 'Time to break the seal,' and headed off to the toilet. Colin watched him go, wondering if there was anything he could do to stop this, other than simply refusing to serve him.

When Marcus re-emerged and headed back towards the bar, a slight unsteadiness in his gait, Colin was hoping he might call it a day, but Marcus announced, 'Monumental though it indeed is, methinks 'tis time for something less voluminous. What malts are you keeping these days?'

Colin's heart sank. He knew this was only heading one way.

As the large whiskies started to go down, Marcus became louder and friendlier, till every customer arriving at the bar was his new best mate and deserved to be regaled with the full repertoire of hilarious anecdotes at his disposal.

By around ten o'clock, the mood had moved on to the argumentative, and when Marcus squared up to a kindly older gentleman, who merely asked if perhaps he might not bellow so forcefully into his ear, Colin knew he couldn't let it go on any longer. Coming out from behind the bar, he put an arm round Marcus's shoulders.

'Mate. I don't know what has brought this on, but you need to go home now.'

'Home? What are you talking about? The night is only just getting going?'

'Not here. You'll need to do it somewhere else.'

Marcus looked at Colin in disbelief. 'Et tu? Would you kick a man when he's down?'

'It's for your own good.' And he gripped the shoulders tightly and propelled Marcus towards the door. Marcus tried to resist, but Colin was bigger and more sober, and irresistible.

Once out on the street, Marcus stood swaying, as Colin re-entered his pub. He thought about going back in himself to protest, but decided it was Colin's loss and set off down the pavement. Without his audience, his mood darkened once more, and he decided the job was clearly not yet done. He staggered into an off licence and bought a half bottle of whisky, then carried on along the street, swigging on the bottle every few yards. Where he was heading was not even a consideration, he just couldn't stay still while these inner voices were bedevilling him.

Heading deeper into the residential streets, his ever more unsteady legs eventually brought him to a bridge. As he tottered over it, he was shaken from his stupor by the sudden noisy clatter of a train passing underneath. Stopping in his tracks, he lurched to one side and peered over the brick wall which formed the barrier. Straightening up again, he pulled out the bottle and finished off its contents. Leaning over the wall once more, he held out the bottle and let it fall, watching it smash to pieces on a sleeper. That would do it, he thought.

Pulling back from the wall he looked for some foothold, and found part of a brick was missing half way up. Thrusting a foot into the cavity, he heaved himself up, then managed to turn himself enough to sit on the top of the wall with his back to the drop. He swayed. It was approaching eleven o'clock by now, and the road was quiet. The image of Fleur's rotting body came back to him suddenly, along with the smell. How did that beautiful woman end up like that? It was more than he could bear. Recklessly he swung his legs up onto the wall and flopped backwards so he was lying on his back staring up at those stars that could outshine the city's lights. He lay like that for a while, reviewing his life's achievements. His worth. He was unable to find any value in himself. All he had done was hurt people. Abandon them or drive them away. Let it end.

Hearing the tell-tale squealing of the rails that indicated another train was approaching, he turned his head to the left to see its headlights coming towards him. Time this right and there would be no danger of failure. As the noise grew louder, he waited till the headlights were a couple of metres from the bridge, then closed his eyes and rolled to his left.

Almost immediately, he was violently jerked back in the opposite direction, and came crashing down on to the pavement on the bridge, as the train clattered beneath him, then faded off into the distance. He was stunned and shaken, but too drunk to feel much pain. Rolling on to his back, he tried to catch his breath. He had been badly winded.

He became aware of a form, silhouetted against a streetlight, hovering over him. He tried to get his vision to clear. When it did, he could suddenly see a large eye studying him. What the hell was it? He rolled away in alarm and struggled to his feet. This new viewpoint revealed an old man clutching a magnifying glass.

'What happened?' Marcus asked breathlessly.

The old man was also puffing. That was quite a force he had produced to tug Marcus back towards himself.

'You were about to make a bit of a mess. I thought perhaps you might want to reconsider.'

Marcus suddenly remembered where he'd seen this man before. At his mother's care home.

'What are you doing here? Shouldn't you be tucked up in bed?'

'I like a little stroll before I turn in. It's a nice night. Good job I do.'

Marcus didn't share this point of view. The pain should have stopped. He'd found the courage to act, and this old fool had prevented him.

'You have no idea.' Marcus shook his head pathetically and staggered back against the wall.

'Perhaps you should get off the bridge. Go and sleep this off, and see how you feel in the morning. It might not seem so bad. There must be someone who would miss you.'

It was only at this point that Marcus thought of Imogen. Yet again he was overlooking her feelings. Maybe she did care whether he lived or died.

The old man was studying him again through his lens. 'There is, isn't there?'

Ashamed, Marcus nodded. 'My daughter.'

'If you have a daughter, hold her close. Do you know where she is?'

Marcus shook his head.

'Maybe you should go and find out. If you don't know where she went, how are you going to find her?'

Marcus wasn't sure what the man meant by this, and he was too drunk to engage further with him, so he turned and staggered off the bridge and down the road.

Edward Nelson shook his head, and carried on in the direction of Meadow View care home, trying to work out why the puffy features seemed familiar.

30

Richard Hutchinson closed the door behind him and strode across to his desk. The bastard. The evil fucking feigning bastard. He had just come from a Saturday morning team meeting, and everyone agreed that such clear, intact fingerprints could not possibly have remained undisturbed on a light switch for thirty-five years. Thorn had been in that flat recently. And he had actually had him feeling sorry for him. What a performance. So he *was* in league with Poot. What awful operation were they running? Drugs. Kidnapping. Murder? What had they done with Ellie Nelson? Why could they find no trace?

Whatever Thorn had been up to, Hutchinson realised he still didn't have any evidence that he had committed a crime. He did have questions to answer though, and the Inspector was looking forward to hearing the answers. He had just decided he would pay the man another visit, when his phone rang.

'Hutchinson ... Where? ... Coming down.' And he went to find DCI Shah.

Once he was in the car, Shah filled him in.

'Looks like human remains, apparently.'

Let it be her, Hutchinson thought.

When they turned into the familiar leafy street where this had all started for Hutchinson, he could see a skip outside the house. The new owners were obviously gutting it. Rather than parking at the front, which wouldn't have been easy given the density of parked cars, they turned down a side road, then into the lane which ran behind the houses, and drove along to the garage with the old-fashioned double doors. A young man was standing outside, waiting. He looked pale and shaken.

An incident van drew up behind them, and when everyone was out, DCI Shah started issuing instructions. When they had their kit on, Shah and Hutchinson were first to enter.

Ducking under the section of railway that crossed in front of the door, they could see immediately it was indeed human remains, but not a recent death. There were only bones, hair, teeth and some clothing. After an initial assessment, there was no obvious cause of death, and the two officers went outside again. The lane had already been secured and a tent was being erected in front of the garage. Shah had a word with the team and the process of investigation was started.

The young man was standing to one side in a daze. Inspector Hutchinson went up to him.

'Hello. Inspector Richard Hutchinson.'

'Jack Willis.'

Hutchinson pulled off a glove and they shook hands.

'You bought this house from the Nelsons?'

'That's right. Moved in a couple of days ago. I was looking for somewhere to store some stuff and...'

'I see. Bit of a shock?'

'Um.'

'Well, obviously we are going to be busy here for a while. Why don't you go back into the house and carry on with your preparations? We'll let you know if we need you for anything.'

'Oh. Okay.'

'And thank you for the call.'

'No problem.' And the young man headed over to the back gate and up the garden to the house.

Hutchinson pulled on the glove again, ducked into the tent and re-entered the garage. It was an impressive train set, that was for sure. Covered in dust and cobwebs, but impressive nonetheless. On another scale to the one he had himself as a child.

Now the lights were up, everything was much clearer. There were a couple of chairs in the middle of the circuit. The remains were on the ground in front of one of them. There was an old Calor gas heater. He could also see a small holdall. He waited till everything had been marked up and photographed, then moved in on the bag. This was the most likely source of an identification, he reasoned. Unzipping it, he revealed an array of items of women's clothing and a bag of toiletries, but nothing to identify its owner. No purse, no paperwork, no ID.

Zipping up the bag again, he looked around the concrete floor. A notebook and pen were also lying there, the notebook actually beneath the hand bones. Sliding it out, he picked it up and opened it hopefully, but it contained only blank pages. There was, however, evidence that a sheet had been pulled out, a few shreds of paper still clinging to the spiral binding. Glancing around again, he suddenly spotted something in front of the heater. Crossing to it, he bent down and inspected what he'd seen. As he'd thought, charred fragments of paper. Whatever the person had been writing, had come into contact with the heater and gone up in flames.

This triggered another thought, and Hutchinson took a look at the heater in more detail. He discovered that the tap was open. No gas was leaking, but that was clearly because the cylinder was empty. Had it burned until the gas ran out? Had the person died before it did?

His mind racing, the Inspector tried to put together a theory as to what might have happened here. Had the person been writing a note when they died, and fallen from the chair, dropping the notebook and pen and causing the note to flutter towards the heater and ignite? Perfectly possible, he supposed, but what would have caused the death?

Looking around the garage, he noticed an air vent on the rear wall. No light was passing through it from outside. Leaving the rest of the team to continue their work, he went outside again.

'Is there a ladder in the van?' he asked a constable, who trotted off and returned with one.

Hutchinson was doing this himself, and he took the ladder and extended it enough to reach the top of the garages, positioned it in front of the adjacent garage, got the constable to hold the bottom, and climbed. As soon as he stepped on to the roof, his suspicion was confirmed. Behind the Nelson's garage, at the end of a garden, someone had built a large shed. In order to minimise the proportion of garden it took, they had constructed it directly against the back of the garage, completely blocking the air vent. If someone had been sitting in that garage with a burning Calor gas heater, there was no chance of any fumes dispersing, and every chance that carbon monoxide might accumulate.

Well, that was a good working theory, he just needed the boffins to come up with a date for the death, and any evidence to support the theory. And, of course, an identification.

Climbing down the ladder again, he went to share his theory with DCI Shah, then he wandered off to pay a visit to the house with the dangerously inconsiderate shed builder, to find out when it was erected.

It turned out the owners had lived there for many years, and the man of the house sheepishly admitted he had put the shed up himself, sometime in the nineteen nineties. But he offered in mitigation that he didn't believe anyone used the garage. Hutchinson gave him a dark look, took his details, and returned to his team.

DCI Shah met him as he came back down the lane.

'Something to show you, Dick. Very curious and potentially significant.' And she led Inspector Hutchinson back into the garage.

31

Imogen woke late, her head fogged and her tongue sticking to the roof of her mouth. She wasn't really a drinker, and what she'd had the previous night was more than she'd had in a long time. She knew only too well the nasty side of alcohol, and rarely strayed there. Getting up, she grabbed her dressing gown, and headed to the kitchen for a glass of water. She found Kai rustling up an omelette and with a pot of coffee steaming on the worktop.

'Morning gorgeous. How do you feel?' he asked when he saw her standing in the doorway.

'Rubbish.' And she shuffled to the sink, taking a glass from a cupboard, and filling it. When she had drunk half of it, she turned back towards Kai and leant against the edge of the sink. 'No Dad?'

'Not seen him.'

Imogen had a momentary feeling of panic, placed the glass on the worktop, went out into the corridor and peered out of the window. Her father's car was there. She went round to his bedroom and knocked on the door. When there was no reply, she opened the door. The bed was empty. Returning to the kitchen, she asked Kai if he'd seen Marcus the previous night. He hadn't.

'But his car's there. He's not working.' She remembered how distressed he had been. What could his absence mean? She went and got her phone and rang him, but it went straight to voicemail.

'I really wouldn't worry, Immy. He's probably just gone for a walk. Or off on some more hare-brained investigations.' And he persuaded her to sit at the table, then served her coffee and omelette.

When they had finished their breakfast, Kai was wondering if Imogen might be feeling up to returning to bed, but he soon realised this was far from her mind. Distracted and clearly still worrying, she quickly showered and got ready for the day, then announced she was going to see if she could find her dad. Asking her to wait for him, Kai quickly got dressed, and they left together.

Although not a drinker, Imogen's instinct on receiving her father's news had been to drink. He was a drinker. Or had been. Once an alcoholic... Trying to put herself into her father's mind, she headed to the Sack of Balls. It hadn't long opened, and she found Colin cleaning pipes when she entered. He looked up, saw her expression, and looked away almost shamefaced.

'He was here,' he said. 'Last night.'

'Drinking?'

'Afraid so.'

'Why did you let him?' She was very upset.

'He was determined. Maybe I thought it would be better if he did it here where I could keep an eye on him, than somewhere else I couldn't. He was obviously going to do it anyway.'

'So where is he then?'

Colin looked down. 'I don't know.'

'Then how is that keeping an eye on him? When did he leave?'

'Around ten.'

'And you've no idea where he went?'

'No.' He didn't mention he'd slung him out.

Imogen turned and left the pub. Kai gave Colin one of those looks he was used to receiving from him, and followed her out.

Imogen was standing on the pavement hopelessly looking up and down the street, tears running down her cheeks.

'He'll turn up, Immy.'

She couldn't answer, and set off up the road.

Meanwhile, in a small park, a mile or so from where his daughter was searching for him, Marcus was lying on the grass feeling truly awful. He had been woken by the cold, wet nose of an Alsatian sniffing his face, and now dog walkers and children were giving him a wide berth as they went about their Saturday morning business.

His eyes closed and his face pressed into the grass, he reviewed the events of the previous night. How had he thought alcohol could solve his problems? When had it ever? He thought his hangover days were over, but this was a humdinger he was experiencing once again. Then he remembered the bridge, and shuddered. He wouldn't now be suffering such misery had it not been for that myopic wrinkly. But Imogen would. And, despite the viciousness of his headache and the queasiness of his stomach, he was glad the man had intervened.

Realising Imogen might be wondering where he was, he went to pull out his phone. It wasn't there. He checked for his wallet. Also gone. Someone had clearly taken advantage of his condition. Bastard.

He struggled to his feet, and immediately recognised the salty taste in his mouth that presaged a major evacuation. He staggered over to a nearby tree, and, with one hand against the bark, he vomited forth the liquid contents of his stomach, which, being inconsiderable, soon meant he was dry retching down to the bile. When the last spasm was over, sweat dripping from his forehead and dribble from his mouth, he rounded the tree away from the rancid discharge, and leant against the trunk breathing heavily. Wiping his mouth on his sleeve, he pushed himself away from the tree and headed out of the park.

Progress was slow and wretched, and he didn't even have the money to buy something sweet and fizzy to help counteract his thirst and headache, so he pushed on relentlessly homeward, dreaming of the can of Coke in his fridge, and his bed.

After what seemed an eternity, he rounded the corner into the back lane and staggered the last few steps to his outside stairs. As he lifted a leg to start the climb, he heard a voice calling behind him, and he turned to see Imogen and Kai approaching. Imogen ran up and hugged him.

'You scared the life out of me. Where have you been? Why didn't you answer your phone?'

'I do apologise. I have somewhat disgraced myself, and I am profoundly sorry to have caused you any distress. Suffice it to say, I spent the night alfresco, and am now most desperately in need of rest and recuperation, not to mention hosing down. I have also been the victim of a perfidious pilferage, and amongst the items removed from my defenceless and prostrate self, was my phone. There must now follow an episode of card cancelling, although I fear that horse is already over the horizon.'

Well at least he's putting on a show again, Imogen thought, and helped him up the stairs to the flat.

32

Richard Hutchinson was sitting at his desk staring at an array of paperwork and photographs spread across it. What was he to make of it all? Identifying the remains in the garage had proved to be remarkably simple. It had been the Nelson's garage, their daughter was missing, so they needed to eliminate her first, and of course they already had her dental record on file. The fact that it matched the teeth in the garage brought an end to the search, but by no means to the end of the questions. Naturally, Hutchinson was relieved he had finally tracked down the missing woman after all these years, but it didn't resolve the matter. Where had she been? She certainly wasn't there in 1985. He didn't yet have a time of death, that was going to take the lab a little while yet, but, given that he was fairly confident she had died of carbon monoxide poisoning, surely it couldn't have happened prior to the erection of that shed. He had been back in touch with its owner, and got him to narrow down the date of construction. He had remembered he had had a party in the garden soon after he'd put it up, both to christen it - he'd used it as his bar - and to celebrate the Labour victory of 1997. Therefore, Ellie Nelson had died subsequent to May of that year. So where had she been since 1985, and why was she in the shed? And indeed, what might the connection be with Thorn and Poot?

He realised he needed to ask the Nelsons some questions, although he really couldn't believe they knew anything about it. But first he would have to break the news.

Sergeant Moore was not on duty over the weekend, but Hutchinson called her anyway. He couldn't leave it till Monday, and he thought she would want to be involved. She definitely would want to know they had found Ellie. And he could certainly use her support. His instinct was correct, and, late on the Saturday afternoon, he picked her up on his way to Meadow View care home, and updated her with the developments as they drove.

The manager had allowed them to use her office, and Cynthia Nelson made the slow journey along from the lounge, Edward by her side, and they sat down with the two police officers to hear what they had to say.

'We have some news,' Inspector Hutchinson began.

'About Ellie?' Cynthia immediately asked.

'Yes, Mrs Nelson. I'm afraid we have found her remains.'

Cynthia took a sharp intake of breath and Edward said, 'Where?'

'That's the thing, Mr Nelson. We found her in your garage.'

'What?' Edward was astounded.

Cynthia looked as though she might pass out, and Stephanie Moore jumped up and knelt in front of her.

'Are you okay, Mrs Nelson?'

Cynthia placed a hand on her chest and tried to catch her breath. 'I think so.'

'I'm very sorry to bring you this news,' Hutchinson continued, 'and I realise you may always have held out some hope, but this will bring an end to your uncertainty, and you can finally lay her to rest.'

'How can she have been in the garage?' Edward Nelson was getting distressed.

'We don't know yet, Mr Nelson.' The Inspector was well aware they needed answers, and he was sorry he couldn't supply them. 'We don't think she passed away for at least twelve years after she went missing. We can't be sure when exactly yet, and we really don't have any explanation for where she had been or why she came back and ended up there.'

The Nelsons tried to absorb this devastating information. Their daughter was still alive for many years after she left them, and she never came back or even got in touch to let them know she was okay? This was unbelievable and so upsetting. And then she did come back, but instead of coming to their door, she goes into the garage and somehow loses her life? It was too much.

'This isn't right,' Edward complained. 'You must have it all wrong.' But he remembered the missing key. Could she really have been in his kitchen to get it? 'Did you find a key?'

Inspector Hutchinson nodded. 'In her pocket, yes. Along with the house keys.'

Well, that much made sense. 'How did she die?'

'Well, we don't know for sure yet, but it looks like she may have been overcome by fumes. Carbon monoxide. From a Calor gas heater.'

Edward looked horrified.

Hutchinson continued, 'The neighbour who lived behind you built a shed against the ventilation.'

Again, this made sense to Edward. If this was some cruel trick, they were certainly giving it verisimilitude.

'Look, I'm so sorry to give you all this on top of the terrible news,' Hutchinson said. 'But that's where we are, and I thought you would want to know rather than me waiting till we had the full story. If there is anything you can think of to help us piece the rest together, please let us know.'

Sergeant Moore whispered in her boss's ear.

'Yes.' Hutchinson took the prompt. 'Yes, it looks like she was writing a note. Maybe to you.'

'What did it say?' Edward immediately demanded.

Hutchinson realised at once he had told it in the wrong order. 'I'm sorry. I should have said first. The note seems to have got set on fire. We only found ashes. But she had a notebook and pen. It does look like she was writing at the time she was overcome.'

She was always writing. Again with the plausible details. But the rest...? Edward and Cynthia were bewildered.

'Look, you are going to need some time to digest all this.' Hutchinson got up. 'And we obviously need to get you more answers. We'll leave you for now. And again, I'm so sorry.'

'Me too,' Sergeant Moore added.

Hutchinson went to find the manager to let her know to be attentive to the Nelsons. Stephanie Moore helped Cynthia up.

'This is all so horrible and confusing, I know. But as I said before, the Inspector will get to the bottom of it.'

When she had settled the Nelsons in the lounge, Sergeant Moore found Hutchinson, and they made their way out to the car.

'Thanks for coming, Steph. I do appreciate your help.'

'No problem, boss. Why didn't you tell them everything?'

The Inspector considered his answer. Then he said, 'I thought it might be too much. Wasn't that enough to lay on them for one day?'

'I suppose.'

'Let's get you home.' And he started the car and drove away.

33

Imogen and Kai were curled up on the settee watching an old romantic film. It was early evening and Imogen was feeling a lot better. She was enjoying the film and Kai's embrace, and trying not to dwell on her mother's fate and the many unanswered questions surrounding it.

Marcus had headed straight for the fridge when he had entered the flat and downed a can of Coke. Then he borrowed Imogen's mobile and called the bank and his phone company. It turned out the bank had been trying to get in touch with him to query a large purchase that had been attempted. For a car. Fortunately, it was a total idiot who had robbed him. So bank balance intact and SIM deactivated, he went to his room. Imogen now heard him in the shower, and hoped he was feeling better, though his ablutions were punctuated by little yelps.

When the film finished, Imogen wiped a tear from her eye. She didn't mind tears like that. They were actually rather nice. Warm, romantic, happy tears. There had been too many of the other sort this week.

Marcus came into the lounge as the credits rolled.

'Good film?'

'Yes, thank you.' Imogen sat up. 'How are you feeling? Oh my God! What happened to your arm?'

Marcus was wearing a T-shirt, and his left arm was pretty comprehensively blackened with bruises.

'Oh that? Had a little tumble. My own stupid fault. But otherwise, I am feeling better. I'm sorry any of that happened. It won't again. A one-off aberration.' He sat in the armchair. 'I was lying in bed there, and I suddenly realised it's your birthday tomorrow.'

Kai looked at Imogen, surprised. She seemed surprised herself, but after some thought she said, 'Oh yeah. Last thing on my mind.'

'What do you want to do?' Marcus asked her.

'Nothing. Don't worry about it?'

'You've got to mark it, Immy.' Kai wished he had known. He had nothing for her.

'It's your quarter century, my dear. You can't leave that uncelebrated.'

'Do you really feel like celebrating?' she asked her father.

'Something low key, perhaps. Look, I know it's been a horrible shock for both of us, and believe me, I wish I could make sense of it, but we have to keep going. Maybe it will all become clear eventually. Let me take you both out for a meal, at least.'

Kai was thinking he'd rather take her on his own. 'Oh, thanks. Cool.'

Imogen shrugged. 'Whatever.' Then she remembered. 'How would you pay for it?'

'Ah.' Marcus realised she was making a valid point. 'I'll transfer some money into your bank. You can sort it.'

'Maybe.' She would see how she felt tomorrow. 'By the way, did you go and see your dad?'

That seemed an age ago. 'Yes.'

'How was it?'

'He seems like a decent sort.'

'And?'

'He was very nice to me. Maybe too nice. Seems you have an auntie too. And cousins.'

'Really?' Imogen was conflicted. She was hurting so much from the finality of the loss of her mother. To suddenly have new relations... 'What sort of cousins?'

'Two little boys. I've only seen pictures.'

This was exciting news. She was suddenly acquiring a family. 'When can we meet them?'

'I just need to make an arrangement. Events took over yesterday. I didn't get chance.' Then he remembered the number Seymour had given him was in his wallet. His stolen wallet. 'My father' - that was a weird thing to hear himself saying - 'Dad' - even weirder - 'gave me his phone number. But it was in my wallet. Maybe we should all go and see Mum tomorrow. He's always there too.'

'Okay. That would be nice. Best birthday present, grandparents.' She became thoughtful.

After a pause, Marcus rubbed his hands together enthusiastically. 'So, what shall we do tonight?'

Imogen was shaken back to the room. 'A quiet night in would seem the sensible option, don't you think?'

'Really?' Marcus knew she was right. He was still feeling delicate. 'Fair enough. Shall we get some nosh delivered?' He couldn't actually remember when he last ate. While he could afford to shed a few pounds, he was in danger of organ failure if he didn't input some nutrition soon.

When they had placed an order, and Imogen had paid for it, they had to decide what the three of them would actually do with the evening. While Marcus and Kai were starting to get used to each other's company, their proximity was not yet what you might call relaxed. Given that Marcus and Imogen were both never far from, and usually actively engaged in, thoughts of Fleur, Marcus wondered if he could find any more reruns of *Primary Care* episodes, so they could see her once more, alive and gorgeous. He picked up the remote control and started channel hopping. Wasn't it around this time of day he'd found it last time?

Imogen and Kai watched him, wondering what new madness had beset him. When he eventually came upon the opening credit sequence of the show and the familiar theme tune, Marcus turned to them and said, 'Shall we watch a bit of Mum?'

It wasn't long before Millie Moffat strolled into reception, preceded by her chest, and announced to the jolly and kooky receptionist - not a species frequently encountered in real life, Marcus thought - that she was popping over to the pharmacy to ask Matthew Hope if he could order her in some dressings. Said kooky receptionist, Poppy Lane - a neurotic and poisonous blatherskite in life, Marcus recalled - followed her seductive progress across to the pharmacy. Marcus watched wistfully. Fleur's fundament had been her crowning glory. How he missed it.

Kai was beginning to appreciate from where Imogen had inherited some of her finer features, and also wondering how Marcus could have snaffled such a stunner. But the editor suddenly cut to the pharmacy, and Matthew Hope, in white coat, holding a measuring cylinder to his eye and assessing some orange liquid, and Kai was amazed. It was clearly the person sitting feet from him, but, even as a straight man, he could appreciate that Marcus had been an Adonis. The dark curls, the brooding eyes, the chiselled features. How he had squandered his assets.

Marcus too felt his loss. Mirrors were his friend back then. And as Millie Moffat arrived at the counter and smiled at Matthew, Marcus felt it deeply. Her smile, her beauty, her voice, her eyes. His mind then cruelly thrust before him the image of her maggot infested corpse. The contrast was brutal and heartbreaking, and he violently, but briefly, shook his head to throw it off.

Imogen missed this. She was watching the screen in awe. These were her parents. Yes, they were acting, but the chemistry between them was plain to see. As the two of them held each other's gaze, and their attraction to each other was made manifest, the editor cut to the waiting room and the hilarious Mrs Bootle, the regular, hypochondriacal patient, whose frequent attendance at the health centre was a staple of the show's light relief. It seemed on this occasion it was her eye that was troubling her, as she was holding a bag of frozen peas over one of them.

Marcus turned to the settee. 'Never thought she was funny,' he said, and got up to see if there was any sign of the delivery person. He was fading.

Kai turned to Imogen to see how she was bearing up. She

looked at him briefly and gave him a quick smile, then turned her attention back to the television, eager for her mother to reappear. Soon enough she did. This time it was Matthew who was being treated to the rear view, as she headed back to reception and shared her delight with Poppy at her latest encounter with the dreamy druggist. As she bent to whisper in the receptionist's ear, Marcus, who had gone into the kitchen to warm some plates, glanced through the hatch and noticed the scar across Fleur's throat, the legacy of a thyroid operation he recalled. Didn't ever detract from her looks though, he thought.

The doorbell rang, and he pulled back from the hatch and went to get the life-saving sustenance.

'Do you want it at the table or on your laps?' he called out as he returned to the kitchen with the bulging carrier bag.

'Probably easier at the table,' Imogen called back, not taking her eyes off the screen.

So Marcus plated up the food, yet another curry, and brought two plates round and placed them on the table. 'There you go. What do you want to drink?'

'Water,' Imogen said.

'Yeah, water's fine,' Kai agreed.

So Marcus poured three glasses from the tap and placed them in the hatch.

When the screen cut away from Millie Moffat again, Imogen and Kai got up, took the glasses and went to sit at the table, where Marcus joined them with his plate and some cutlery.

They adjusted their chairs so they could still watch the screen as they ate, then tucked into the food.

Marcus was trying to recall this episode. He was wondering if this was the one where they first kissed, and when, later on, he saw Millie walking to her car, he realised it was. Yes, it was the end of the day and here he came after her. That's right, she had to open her boot and rummage around aimlessly in it as he approached, admiring the view. Then she turned and found him standing there, his dark eyes twinkling and a smile on his face. She was pinned against the car; how could she resist?

When he moved in, and it became obvious what was about to happen, Imogen turned her attention to her plate, but she couldn't help glancing up from time to time as the prolonged lip contact proceeded. Marcus could still feel it. It had, after all, been their first kiss in reality too. He remembered in the brief rehearsal they had stopped short of making contact. And one take was sufficient. It couldn't be improved upon, and no technical issues necessitated a repetition. Marcus remembered this, because he would very much have liked to repeat the scene. As many times as they wanted. But he had to wait until the script allowed another opportunity. Actually, he wasn't sure that was the case. Hadn't he managed to sneak one off camera not long after this? Anyway, what was certain was that this was the beginning of a beautiful relationship, which had been cut short within a decade.

As they pulled out of the embrace and held each other's eyes intensely, the theme tune cut in and the credits started to roll.

Marcus turned to Imogen. 'You okay?'

'Yeah.'

'Well it looks like you can spend a little time with her this way. If you want. Note the channel.'

'I will.' And she went and picked up the remote control, selected the guide and set up a series link to record all episodes.

When she sat back at the table she said, 'Is that how you were in real life?'

'Pretty much. At first anyway.'

'I don't remember that.'

'You were very young. We had our moments. Even then.'

Imogen was looking very sad again. Marcus wasn't sure he had done the right thing by putting that show on, but Imogen suddenly turned to him and said, 'Thank you for that.'

'My pleasure,' and he put his hand on hers.

When they had finished the meal, Imogen and Kai took the plates into the kitchen. Imogen decided it would be better for the planet if she just washed them up in the sink. There were only the three of them, plus the glasses and the cutlery. She called through the hatch to her father, still sitting thoughtfully at the table. 'What did you do with those rubber gloves?'

Marcus considered the question. What rubber gloves? Oh, of course, and he got up and went into the hall. 'They'll be in that bag still. I think it's out here.' He found the canvas shoulder bag he'd taken to Poot's flat hanging from a coat hook by the door, and thrust in a hand and pulled out the yellow gloves. As he did so, he saw a metallic glint, and something fell at his feet. Looking down, he saw a gold chain lying on the floor. It was coiled, but he could see it was long. He bent down and picked it up. Why was it familiar? And what was it doing in that bag?

'Have you got them?' Imogen called from the kitchen to the accompaniment of a filling washing bowl.

Marcus studied the little clasp at one end, and suddenly his stomach turned over. It was shaped like a crab, the pincers on one side attached to one end of the chain, and those on the other side able to be opened to attach to the other end. He had seen it round Ellie Nelson's waist all those years ago, during his drunken, loveless encounter. It was the evidence he had been looking for in Poot's flat, and he didn't even know he had found it. It must have been in that drawer with the postcards, and got picked up with his clumsy, rubber-clad fingers. So Poot had her in his flat. When? His mind started racing. What did this mean? He was in the flat himself the night she disappeared. Knowing Hutchinson, he'd get the blame. If he knew. But he couldn't show it to him now. He was no longer a suspect. It would do more harm than good. And how could he explain how he'd got it anyway? His whole plan had been ridiculous. Had he left himself with any functioning brain cells? He shoved the chain in his pocket, and took the gloves into the kitchen.

Once the washing up was done, they all settled in front of the television again, and Marcus flicked channels once more away from some dreadful ancient costume drama, involving wigs and ridiculous French accents. Quite unexpectedly, he came across the face of Ellie Nelson again, and immediately put down the remote.

When the news item had finished, Marcus looked at Imogen. This must definitely mean he was in the clear. In her own parents' garage? Probably them then. All the news channel seemed to have was that her body had been found, not how she had died or when.

'Poor girl,' Marcus said. Any lingering doubts he had regarding his own involvement in her disappearance were now removed. He had certainly never been to her house. Or her garage. It didn't explain how the chain had ended up in Poot's flat though. Maybe that was to do with himself. Maybe she'd left it behind the night he'd taken her back. It didn't really matter now. She didn't die in the flat, so it wasn't him. He sighed. His mind turned to Inspector Hutchinson. Both his bodies had now turned up. He must be very pleased with himself.

He flicked on till he saw Steve McQueen throwing a ball against a wall. He smiled.

'Shall we?'

'Whatever.' Imogen really didn't mind what they watched, so long as it was distracting, and Kai was certainly not going to argue.

So they settled down to follow the exploits of the allied airmen in Stalag Luft III.

34

Inspector Hutchinson was back at his desk. Another Sunday morning and he was at work, rather than reading the papers with his feet up. But he would have plenty of time for that soon enough, when his retirement arrived. Now he had a mystery to solve.

All his theories were crumbling, however. Two missing women, whom he suspected had come to sticky ends at the hands of one or both of two degenerate actors, had now turned up. While both were unquestionably dead, neither appeared to have reached that state by another's hand. But that did not mean there wasn't the possibility of foul play at some point in their stories. So, while he was waiting for all the forensics to come back in the case of Ellie Nelson, he must turn his attentions back to the other body. And Marcus Thorn's involvement.

Deciding he needed to invite Thorn in for a little chat, he pulled out his mobile and called him. When Thorn's phone failed to ring and an automated voice told him that the person he had called was unavailable, the Inspector felt his anger rising. The man had better not be trying to avoid him. He'd just have to go round and confront him then.

As he was approaching his car, his phone rang. It was Stephanie Moore.

'Haven't you got anything better to do with your Sunday, Steph?'

She couldn't stop thinking about the Ellie Nelson case, ever since Hutchinson had shared the details of the grim discovery in the garage. She had come up with a theory she wanted to run by him.

'Steph. You're not on the case. Enjoy your day off and don't worry about it. I need to speak to Thorn. Bye.' He ended the call, got into the car, and drove off.

For a Sunday, the Thorn household was up pretty early. Imogen was actually rather excited at the prospect of meeting her grandparents, and was first up, making coffee and getting together breakfast for them all. Marcus and Kai were both feeling bad that they didn't have anything to give her for her birthday, and each promised they would rectify that as soon as they could. Imogen claimed not to want anything. A family was more than enough.

By ten o'clock they were drawing up in the street outside Meadow View care home, Marcus having driven despite the distance being short and the weather lovely, because his body was even more stiff and painful than the previous morning. As they approached the front door, it opened, and Marcus immediately recognised the old man coming through it. His instinct was to hide, but he quickly realised it was too late for that, and he took hold of the door and stood to one side, hoping the man would not notice him. He would not have, had he not raised his magnifying glass when he sensed their presence, and, when he recognised Marcus, he swung it round and took in the other two as well. Turning back to Marcus he said, 'Glad you found her.' And, despite the lens through which it was conveyed, Marcus received the full meaning of the look he was given. Edward Nelson then shuffled off, seemingly with the weight of the world on his shoulders.

When the old man was out of earshot, Imogen asked her father what that had been about.

'No idea, I'm afraid. This place is full of bewildered folk.' And he signed them all into the visitor's book, and led them to the lift.

As they emerged on to the first floor, Marcus headed for the lounge, and Imogen and Kai followed behind, taking everything in. Marcus poked his head around the door frame and surveyed the room. There was no sign of his parents. He spotted a member of staff through in the adjoining dining room, and went to have a word with them.

Imogen and Kai stood waiting, smiling at anyone who looked at them. Some looked suspiciously, others smiled back, but most were oblivious to them, trapped in their own troubled worlds.

Kai turned to see an old lady, still in her nightdress, entering from the corridor. When the woman spotted him, she stopped in her tracks. A lascivious grin then formed on her face, and she sidled forward, puckering her wrinkled lips as she approached him, then went in for the snog. Kai didn't know what to do. He didn't want to swat her away, but neither did he want to let her have her way with him. Noticing what was happening, Imogen tried to distract the woman by asking her who she was. But the woman was unstoppable, and Kai was only rescued when a member of staff answered Imogen's question by calling across, 'Doris. Please leave the poor boy alone.' Doris dropped her shoulders sulkily, and turned away from Kai, laying a regretful hand on his shoulder, then gently trailing her fingers down his arm as she moved away, and winking back at him.

Marcus came back towards them with a young woman in uniform. 'They're in the garden apparently. We have to go back down in the lift.' And the care assistant led them back to it and inserted and turned a key.

As Marcus led the way into the garden, having received directions, he spotted Seymour and Kitty sitting together on a little bench. Seymour got up when he saw Marcus approaching and looked to see who he had with him.

'Good morning,' Marcus said. 'Sorry I didn't call. I lost your number. This is Imogen, and this is Kai. Her...friend.'

Seymour was delighted and shook their hands enthusiastically, 'I am so pleased to meet you at last, Imogen. And very pleased to meet you too, young man.' Then he turned to his wife. 'Look Kitty. This is Imogen. Our granddaughter.'

Kitty looked at the strange faces. She smiled at the prettier ones, then immediately appeared troubled when she saw Marcus. Imogen knelt down in front of her.

'Hello Grandma. It's so lovely to finally meet you.'

A smile reformed on Kitty's face. 'They said you were coming, but I wasn't sure why they wanted me to stay. I told them I didn't want it, but... Why do they keep doing that?' She was starting to become distressed.

Imogen kept smiling, realising her grandmother's thoughts were confused. 'Don't worry about them. We've come to see you. How are you today?'

'Oh, you know. I only came back the other day. I was making the lunch and it all fell down and they wouldn't listen to me.'

'Oh dear. Well, I will. It's nice out here in the garden, isn't it? Such a nice day.'

'Oh, yes. I always bring them here. I built that wall and then they stopped it growing, but I wasn't even there.'

'That's right. I'm glad you're here now.'

Seymour smiled at Imogen, delighted she knew at once how to talk to Kitty. 'Let me find you something to sit on.'

'I'll help you,' Kai said. They soon returned, Seymour with one chair and Kai two.

They all sat in a circle. Seymour let Imogen sit on the bench with Kitty. It wasn't long before the two of them were holding hands, both delighted with each other, and continuing a conversation with little meaning, but great warmth.

Marcus looked on, enjoying seeing his mother animated and apparently happy, but with a terrible underlying regret that he had not allowed this conversation to take place at a time when it would have made sense.

Meanwhile Seymour struck up a conversation with Kai, and had soon learned that his grandparents started life in Jamaica and had come to Britain separately in the nineteen sixties, where they had met, married and brought Kai's father into the world.

Stephanie Moore was angry. Why wouldn't Hutchinson listen to her? She had made getting into the head of Ellie Nelson her mission, and what she had come up with was consistent with the woman she felt she now knew. It may not be what happened, but surely it was worth exploring. Well, if he wouldn't take her seriously, she wasn't going to just sit at home and forget about it. She couldn't. Anyway, she was feeling awful about Ellie's parents. She and the Inspector had turned up yesterday and delivered this devastating news, and then just left them. She felt she had to check in on them and see how they were coping, now they had had a night to absorb it all.

As she approached Meadow View on foot, she thought she recognised one of the cars in the street. Wasn't it Thorn's? It was certainly a licensed taxi of the same model and colour.

Once inside the home, she looked into the ground floor lounge and saw Cynthia sitting in a corner by herself. The last time the Sergeant had called round, she had been chatting away with other residents. Stephanie smiled as she approached and Cynthia looked up and gave her a rather sad smile in return.

'How are you, Mrs Nelson?'

'Oh, you know. Been better.'

'I know. I'm sorry to have laid all that on you. It's a lot to take in. Especially as it doesn't make much sense. How's Mr Nelson?'

'Not too good. He's gone off on another of his walks. Don't think this place is really for him.'

'Oh dear.' Stephanie Moore was feeling bad. She wanted to share her theory with Cynthia, but she knew she couldn't, not least because it would be so upsetting. She glanced out through the lounge windows into the garden. She could only see the back of his head, but she was pretty sure that large mop of grey curls belonged to Marcus Thorn. 'Would you excuse me a minute.' And she made her way through the lounge to the open door to the garden. From this angle she could see his profile and knew she had not been mistaken. Pulling back to avoid being seen, she went out into the corridor, pulled out her phone and tapped on Inspector Hutchinson's name.

'Boss. You're looking for Thorn, aren't you? ... That's because he's here. ... Meadow View. ... Don't know. ... Okay.' She ended the call. As she headed back into the lounge, she suddenly realised that Cynthia wouldn't know that the man whom her daughter had been going to meet on the night she disappeared was sitting within her sight. And she couldn't tell her. She was quite upset enough.

'Sorry about that. Just had to check in with the Inspector.'

'That's alright, my dear. How's he getting on?'

'He's hard at it, don't worry about that. Don't think he'll be taking any time off till this is all sorted out.'

Out in the garden everyone was continuing to get to know each other. Imogen was now talking to her grandfather, and finding it a far more rewarding experience than she had with her grand- mother. He was so interested in her and what she had to say that, had she not been so happy to have found him, she might have been feeling rather sad that she had missed out on this all her childhood. Kai listened in, enjoying Imogen's happiness after all the recent sorrow.

Marcus was trying to have a conversation with his mother, but she didn't appear as delighted to speak with him as she had with Imogen. He could see the others were caught up in their chat and he had her to himself. But how could he let her know how sorry he was for leaving her? She didn't even know who he was. Then there was the other thing. The thing he had only thought of again as he was lying on that bridge. The other reason he had walked out and never come back. Auntie Fi. The supposedly God-fearing lodger, who had started coming into his bedroom, ostensibly to wish him goodnight, when he was about thirteen. Who had taken it upon herself to educate him in the subject of the female body. Why had his mother let her do that? Why had she not stopped her? That was the reason why he was so angry with her at the time. The reason behind so much of his subsequent behaviour, perhaps. And none of it, he now realised, was Kitty's fault. If she had known, of course she would have stopped it. But now she never would. At least she was spared that unhappiness.

He reached forward and took her hand. She looked down at his.

'I'm sorry, Mum. For everything.' He surprised himself that he had said that.

Kitty was still looking at their entwined hands. Marcus wasn't expecting a response. Certainly not one that made any sense. First, she patted his hand with her free hand, as she had the last time he'd come to see her, then she looked up at him, and, for the first time, she seemed to see him. She frowned. Then an expression of profound sadness crossed her face. When she spoke, it was as if a clear-thinking Kitty, trapped inside this fading shell, was making herself heard.

'My boy. Is it you? Where have you been? I've missed you so much.'

Marcus was overwhelmed. 'I'm so sorry,' was all he could say before he let go of her hand, fell to his knees and lay his head in her lap. She placed her hand on his head and patted his curls.

The others looked across. For Kai this was really awkward, but Imogen and Seymour were equally moved, and when Marcus eventually pulled away and struggled back on to his chair, Imogen got up and came and gave her father a hug. Then she turned to Kitty, who was sitting staring into the distance.

'Are you okay, Grandma?'

But Kitty seemed lost again. Her brief grasp on reality gone. No-one but Marcus had heard what she had said. Realising she was no longer looking at him, he got up, and without saying anything to the others, headed back into the building. Imogen was going to follow him, but Seymour suggested she give him a moment.

When Sergeant Moore caught sight of the movement outside and saw Marcus heading her way, she jumped up, anxious he didn't get away before Inspector Hutchinson arrived. Marcus came through the door into the lounge and headed out into the corridor before the Sergeant could intercept him, but as she caught up with him at the front door, she saw Hutchinson approaching from outside.

'I think Inspector Hutchinson would like a word with you, Mr Thorn,' she said to Marcus's back.

Marcus swung round, trying to control his emotions, and surprised to see the policewoman again. 'What? Why?'

'He'll explain.' She pressed a button high on the wall and the door clicked open.

'Good morning, Mr Thorn. And where are you heading?' the Inspector asked, pushing the door open, but blocking Marcus's exit.

'Nowhere. Just needed some air.'

'You've just come from the garden,' Stephanie Moore said, a hint of mockery in her voice.

Marcus was not going to explain himself further to these two.

'I would be very grateful if you would accompany me to the station, Mr Thorn,' the Inspector continued. 'I have a few questions I need to ask you.'

'Do I have any choice?'

'You do, but I would recommend you co-operate. It is really not in your interest to hinder my investigations.'

'Well, I'd need to let my family know.'

'I'll do that,' the Sergeant said.

Marcus was too exhausted to fight them, and reluctantly went with the Inspector to his car.

35

Edward Nelson had eventually returned from his walk to get his lunch, and then had spent some time in the garden with his paper. But two little boys were visiting one of the residents from upstairs and, while he knew they were only playing, he had found their games a little too irritating, and withdrawn into the lounge. Now, while he could still hear the odd shout or scream from them, he was more annoyed by the television which some of his fellow residents insisted was on most of the time, regardless of what was on it, especially as he couldn't see the screen without going right up to it with his lens. Cynthia had gone to their room for a post-lunch siesta, and Edward was wondering if he should have joined her. But he wasn't sleepy, just rattled. He was still struggling to make sense of what the police had told him the day before, and the implications. While he had already had to accept that he didn't know his daughter as well as he thought, he was finding it a step too far to believe that she willingly stayed away and chose not to contact them.

In the garden, Imogen was getting to know her Auntie Rebecca and Uncle Stephen, and her two cousins, George and Theo. They often came to see Kitty on Sunday afternoons, and when Marcus had had to leave, Seymour had let Imogen know that they would be there. So she and Kai had come back after lunch to meet them. In the back of her mind the whole time were thoughts of her father. What did the police want with him? He hadn't had chance to sort out a new phone, so she knew she couldn't contact him.

Rebecca was delighted to meet Imogen, but was disappointed not to be seeing her brother. She had grown up with his picture in her front room, looking over her, and watching him on her television, so actually meeting him had become something of an obsession for her. But her niece seemed lovely, and it was going to be so nice for the boys to have a new cousin in their lives. Especially such an excellent role model.

Kai was trying to entertain the boys, but he was struggling not to get them too excited. He was well aware the residents would be wanting a quiet Sunday afternoon, and when that man with the paper had got up and gone in, he had tried to find a more static game with which to amuse them. But he didn't want to stop playing with them as it was allowing Imogen to have a good chat with her newly-discovered family.

In an interview room in Peel Avenue police station, Marcus was flagging. The stupid policeman was going round in circles. How many times did he have to say he was just looking for some evidence to get himself off the hook? Why did the man seem convinced there was more to it? Everything he had told him had been the truth. He still had keys, he'd entered the flat, for the first time in thirty-five years, and discovered the body. Then he'd made sure that the police were made aware of it. Would he have done that if he had anything to hide? Naturally he was furious with himself that he had touched the light switch when he had taken off the glove - all this could have been avoided if he had used the other hand - but it was an emergency situation and an understandable mistake.

'Why was your wife there, Mr Thorn? What were you doing with her?' Hutchinson was now using his quiet, weary tone.

'I don't know why she was there. I hadn't seen her for twenty years. How many times do I have to say it?'

'The truth, Mr Thorn. I'm only interested in the truth.'

'Clearly not.'

'What were you and Poot involved in?'

'Nothing. I haven't seen him since 1985.' This was an unfortunate thing to say, given that the Inspector knew he had visited his old flatmate in hospital, and only reinforced Hutchinson's conviction that he was being fed a pack of lies. Which in turn allowed him to justify what he did next. Opening a folder he had in front of him on the table, he rummaged through the paperwork and found, among several photographs, one of the corpse in Poot's flat. He yanked it out, spilling out other photos, and slapped it onto the table in front of Marcus.

'Look, Mr Thorn. That is your wife. How does that make you feel seeing her like that?'

Marcus flinched and tried not to look at it. 'Bloody awful. What do you think?'

'Really?'

'For fuck-' Marcus was getting to the end of his tether, but he suddenly saw a picture of Fleur sticking out from underneath other spilt photos, and cut short what may well not have helped his cause. The thing that arrested his attention was the hair. He'd never seen her before without the peroxide glamour wave. Wondering where Hutchinson had found the picture, he asked if he could have a look at it.

'Which one?'

Marcus reached across and tapped a finger on the one he wanted. The Inspector frowned and picked it up. He studied the face, and then looked at Marcus quizzically. 'This one?' He turned it round towards Marcus. When he saw the whole face, and not just the top of the head that had been sticking out from beneath the other photos, Marcus's stomach lurched, and he stared at the face in horror.

Edward Nelson was realising the move to Meadow View had been a terrible mistake. For him, at least. The bloody television alone was going to drive him mad. Now there was some drama on. From what he could make out, it involved a doctor and a hysterical patient seeking assurances that she would make it till the end of the day. Edward wondered if he would himself. He decided he couldn't bear any more of it and would take his chances in the garden again. Getting up, he was heading back to the garden door, when he heard a different voice coming from the television. A familiar voice. He stopped in his tracks, and listened intently. There was no mistaking it. He'd have recognised a single word. Swinging round, he headed towards the screen, raising his magnifying glass to his face as he did so. Once in front of the television, he studied the image in search of the source of the voice. As he did so, a couple of the other residents asked if he wouldn't mind moving, as he was blocking their view.

'Ted. What are you doing?' It was Cynthia. She was mortified her husband was being so inconsiderate.

Edward turned to his wife, leaning on her walking frame, and beckoned to her. 'Look Cynth. It's her.'

'What are you talking about? Come away from the telly. No-one can see.'

'Look!'

Cynthia inched her frame forward, apologising to her fellow residents as she did so, and slowly approached the television, peering at the screen now Edward had stood to one side. She couldn't see anyone she recognised on it.

'What are you talking about, Ted? Who is it?'

'I can't see her, but I can hear her. Can't you see her?'

'Who Ted? See who?'

'Ellie. I can hear Ellie.'

Marcus was trying to make sense of what he was looking at. Inspector Hutchinson was holding up a picture of Ellie Nelson. Marcus could see it was her; the same mousey hair, the same nose, the same chin as in the graduation photo. But unlike in that photograph, she was not squinting into the sun, and he could see her eyes. They were Fleur's eyes. He couldn't mistake the eyes of the woman he loved. What could it mean?

Cynthia stared at the screen. All she could see was a blonde woman, not unlike Marilyn Monroe, and an exotic-looking dark-haired man, engaged in an intimate exchange. But suddenly the woman's face was in close up, and Cynthia could see her eyes. Edward too could now make them out through his lens. The woman had Ellie's eyes and Ellie's voice, but someone else's face. Edward and Cynthia looked at each other, horrified.

Just then, Imogen bounded into the lounge from the garden on her way to find a toilet, and saw an old couple framing Millie Moffat on the screen. 'That's my Mum,' she announced, and everyone turned to look at her.

'What is it?' Inspector Hutchinson asked, seeing the look on Marcus's face. 'Is there something you would like to tell me at last? What did you do with her? Ellie Nelson? Where did she go?'

Marcus glanced up at the policeman, aware that he had spoken, but not taking in his words. He looked back at the photo. Hadn't he gone to bed with this woman? How had he no memory of those eyes? How would he not have recognised them when he met Fleur? What on earth was going on here? Once again, he tried to dredge up memories of his encounter with the girl. He hadn't been attracted to her. Why did he end up in bed with her?

It was the chain, the memory of the gold chain with the crab clasp round her waist, that suddenly let the light in. And not over her belly. From behind. And once he could picture her from that angle, he knew the why and the how and, with a sudden jolt of pure horror, the who.

He looked up at the Inspector, who was himself taken aback by the look on Marcus's face. Marcus reached across and picked up a handful of the photographs on the desk and shuffled through them till he found one of Fleur. An old publicity shot. Hutchinson didn't stop him. Marcus placed it beside the one of Ellie Nelson and looked back and forth between them. Then he turned them round for the Inspector to see, and covered the lower halves of each with a sheet of paper from the folder. Hutchinson frowned. What was the man up to? But eventually, after looking between the images several times, even he could see it. The two pictures were of the same woman.

36

Richard Hutchinson was depressed. After he had let Thorn go, he had sat on trying to piece together what it all meant, and now it was clear to him he had not covered himself in glory. But it wasn't his fault there was no picture of Julie Christie with her fingerprints. That was someone else's administrative cock-up. He had just wanted it to be something it wasn't. To make a name for himself. That was where his blame lay. Now he would retire into obscurity, his only consolation that he had, at least, found his missing person, after so many years.

He was going to have to accept that he may never know everything. Only Poot could answer how the Christie woman ended up in his flat, and maybe how Ellie Nelson came to assume her identity. But his sanity may never return. What he did know was that the woman was badly malnourished when she died, and had given herself a hefty dose of heroin. It was only conjecture, but he imagined Poot may have been keeping her for favours in exchange for narcotics, and, when he was detained, she gradually used up any remaining food and drugs, keeping one final fatal dose to bring her sad life to a close. After all, she had no identity any more. And no-one had missed her. She had not been on the missing persons register. Not until he, himself, had started looking into Fleur. The theory did fit with the little he had managed to get out of Poot. If he weren't inured to the tragedy of the lives of so many who end up as drugs death victims, he might have felt a little pity for her.

Of course, he already knew that Ellie Nelson had had work done. That was evident from her remains: the two silicone-filled sacs; the metalwork in the jaw and cheeks. But why had he not made the connection? Was this what Steph had been trying to tell him? He had some grovelling to do.

Marcus had made his way home in a daze. So, the terrifying girl who had sent him all those postcards, whom he didn't fancy and whom he had avoided, had got him in the end. Was he really so shallow that a bit of cosmetic surgery was all it took? And how had he never realised? But then he only had her 'thyroid' operation scar to go on. And the boob job, of course. Nevertheless, he had fallen in love with her. And he really had. With *her*, not just her looks.

He knew Fleur Hardy was an invention, but he had thought his wife's real name was Julie Christie. He had no reason to doubt what she'd told him. Julie Christie, it would seem, was some poor, unfortunate, red-haired drug addict, living in squalor in Poot's flat. Who'd presumably been there for years. Lured in and kept there by her addiction, to service Poot's needs. And, abandoned by Poot, eventually dying there alone. How did he ever believe that grotesque body he'd found in his old bedroom had been his wife's? But *Hardy*? Really? Ellie Nelson to Fleur *Hardy*? That was his little joke; kiss me Hardy, he used to say to her in better days. He hadn't realised she was a fan of British naval history.

Well, none of this changed the fact that she was dead. It may not have been a recent death, it may not have involved drugs, but she wasn't coming back. Hutchinson had explained about the Calor gas heater. Marcus guessed that would not be a traumatic death; she wouldn't have suffered, and he took some comfort from that.

As he reached the stairs to his flat, he looked at his empty parking space and remembered his car was still outside Meadow View. He'd have to go and get it. Then he remembered his mother. And Imogen. And the fact it was her birthday. The poor girl. He still had nothing to give her but yet more shocking news.

As he opened the flat door, he noticed an envelope on the

mat, and picked it up. Hand delivered. Addressed to Imogen. A birthday card, presumably. No-one appeared to be home, so he laid the envelope on the dining table and collapsed on to the settee.

Meanwhile, back at Meadow View, there was quite a kerfuffle in progress. The McKenzie clan had been drawn in from the garden, at first to retrieve the boys, who had followed Imogen. But then they had got caught up in events, and all were now in the lounge trying to make sense of quite extraordinary assertions and implications. Imogen had told the old couple, whom she now knew to be Mr and Mrs Nelson, that not only was the blonde woman on the television her mother, but the dark-haired man with her was her father, Marcus Thorn. This name had naturally provoked some consternation in the Nelsons, only exacerbated when Imogen then told them that he had been sitting out in the garden that very morning.

It was all very difficult to take in for everyone. Imogen suddenly realised that, if the Nelsons were right that her mother was really their daughter Ellie, then she was their granddaughter, and she was now standing in a room with all four of her grandparents. She turned to look at Kitty, now not the only bewildered person in the room. Kitty gave her a big smile, which Imogen returned. Turning back to the Nelsons, Imogen looked at them through new eyes.

'We clearly all need some answers here, and my Mum is not around to provide them. But it would seem that you might be my grandparents, and that fact alone is very exciting for me. So, could we perhaps all sit down and talk this through?'

'I think that might be a very good idea,' Cynthia said.

'Good. Thank you. Let's do it then. But first, I am bursting for the loo.' And Imogen dashed off to find a toilet.

Edward was still in shock. There were now adverts on the telly, so he raised his lens, found the power button, and switched it off. No-one objected, but Kai was slightly disappointed, as the commercial in progress was one his team had worked on, and, in different circumstances, he could have bragged of the fact.

Imogen soon returned, and everyone tried to find something to sit on. Cynthia found herself next to Seymour, and looked up at the kindly man she'd found so enchanting when they'd first met. She tried to absorb the fact that she might actually be related to him.

Before long there was a large circle of assorted furniture, supporting a wide age range of people, many of whom shared DNA, and all of whom needed answers, even if George and Theo's involved promised ice creams, rather than family history.

Marcus was awoken by the front door opening, and got to his feet, unsure how long he had been asleep, but quickly remembering the news he had to impart. Imogen burst into the lounge, followed by Kai, delighted to see her father home, and spewed forth her own news at a rate of knots before Marcus could get a word in. As her news chimed so well with his own, Marcus was glad he didn't now need to be the one to lay it on his daughter. And as there seemed to be quite an element of excitement in the telling, he realised what she had learnt had not all been bad for her.

When Imogen had finally got it all out, and Marcus had provided his supporting evidence, they all sat in silence for a while reviewing what they knew, and wondering about the gaps in the story. And what sort of woman could have done such things and never told the ones she supposedly loved.

Suddenly Marcus said, 'Oh, there was a card for you. On the table.' And Imogen got up to get it, remembering it was her birthday and surprised to be receiving anything as old-fashioned as an actual card, having not, until now, had any older relatives to send them.

Sitting back on the settee, she opened the envelope and looked at the picture on the front of the card; a pretty young woman in a floral dress, with dark hair, playing with a kitten in a lavish Victorian parlour. Painted in oils, she supposed. Intrigued who might have sent it, she opened it, and her face lost all its colour.

Marcus was alarmed. 'What is it?'

Imogen couldn't speak. Her eyes were devouring whatever was written in the card. When she had finished, she allowed Marcus to take it from her, while she sat with tears streaming down her face.

This is what Marcus read:

Happy birthday darling.

I'm sure you must be surprised to be receiving a birthday card from me. Obviously, I don't know how long it is since my life ended, but the fact that you have received this, must mean it has, and before I could attempt the explanation I obviously didn't get to give you.

I instructed my solicitor to deliver this to you on your 25th birthday, if he hadn't heard from me otherwise, because I thought, by this age, you might be old enough to understand, and have fallen in love yourself, and know how powerful an emotion it can be. So I've written you a full explanation. This is where my plan may fall down, because, while the solicitor was under instruction to be sure he was delivering the card to your current address, at the time I am writing this, with you having a little nap in your bedroom, I obviously don't know where that might be. My hope is that you still have access to the large oak cupboard that I am looking at in the lounge of our flat. I realise your father might, by now, have drunk himself into an early grave, so I am really hoping you still have it. Assuming you do, if you completely pull out the middle of the five drawers that run across the top under the shelf, you'll find a cord at the back. Pull it, and all will become clear.

I'm sorry that it has to be this way, and I hope you won't judge me too harshly. Just know I loved you more than anyone on the planet, and I'm sorry I couldn't tell you this sooner. I couldn't lose you or your father, and I feared I would.

I hope to see you again wherever I now am, and always re-

member how much you were loved.
Mum xxx

Imogen was already up opening the doors to the cupboard. Marcus dropped the card and came to assist. Kai, completely confused, now picked up the card.

When Imogen pulled the cord, out popped a drawer. Her stomach fluttering like crazy, she lifted out the manilla envelope with her name on, and opened it. Inside she found several sheets of paper, held together by a staple in the corner, and filled with the familiar curly letters.

'Shall we do this together?' She took it over to the settee and sat down in the middle. 'Sit either side of me.' And Marcus and Kai did as they were told. Then they read.

Darling Imogen.

What follows is a complicated story, and one I should have given you face to face, but it obviously hasn't been possible. What you need to know is that I am not Fleur Hardy, nor Julie Christie. My real name is Ellie Nelson.

I was brought up by two loving parents, Edward and Cynthia Nelson, and the fact that you are reading this means I never found the courage to tell them this story either. Had I done so, I would have told you sooner too, and you would never have received these pages.

What I need you to understand is that I adored your father. I had seen him on stage as Mercutio in 'Romeo and Juliet', and he was so mesmerising I was completely overwhelmed by my feelings for him. I got to meet him offstage and it was as though he couldn't even see me. He showed no interest in me whatsoever. I couldn't bear this. But I kept coming to see him perform, and kept going to the bar afterwards, hoping desperately that he might eventually take an interest in me. He didn't. Until, that is, I noticed him looking at me from behind. The theatre and the bar were small, and they had put mirrors all round the bar walls to make it less claustrophobic. I was surreptitiously watching him in a mirror, when I saw his eyes on my backside. He was clearly interested in that. I needed to capitalise on this, so, I am ashamed to admit to you, I started taking every opportunity to let him get a good look. I was brazen.

This eventually paid dividends, and one night he took me home with him. I was so happy. I gladly gave myself to him. After this I convinced myself I had won him over. My parents took me away for a holiday, and I used to write to him every day. I was so excited to get back and see him. I'd told him I'd come to his local pub as soon as I was back.

When I arrived at the pub, however, his flatmate was hanging around outside. A man called Howard Poot. An American. I'd met him briefly the morning after my night in the flat. He told me Marcus wasn't coming, and that he was off to Belgium the following day, so, if I wanted to see him, why didn't I come back with him to the flat. Of course I went with him. But when we got there, Marcus wasn't there. Howie said he'd probably just popped out. Why didn't we have a drink while we waited for him.

I woke up in Howie's bed. I don't know how I got there, or what happened to me, but it was daytime, my head hurt, and Marcus had gone. I was distraught. Howie denied any foul play, but he was a very odd person and I couldn't trust him. I tried to get out of the flat, but the door was locked with a mortise. I couldn't. I started to panic. What was he going to do with me?

He kept me there for several days. I wouldn't eat anything he tried to feed me. I was terrified he would drug me again. I only drank water I poured from the tap myself. All the time he was trying to convince me his intentions were good.

Something happens to you after a while of this treatment. The lack of food. The disorientation. The dependence on the whims of this man for your survival. You start trying to convince him you're on his side. Trying to keep him from harming you or raping you.

He used to brag to me how rich he was. What a good catch he was. He seemed to think this treatment, this imprisonment, was a way to win me over. So I played along. Made him think he had a chance, but that I wasn't good enough for him. As I was. Still thinking, even in this situation, that this might be an opportunity to improve my chances with your father. I knew I wasn't the prettiest girl in the world, but I had nice eyes, good skin, and apparently my figure had its attractions. Maybe Howie could arrange to improve my less appealing features. Then he'd have a woman who deserved his attentions.

Amazingly he went for it. He seemed to have so much money at his disposal that he persuaded one of the best surgeons out there to do the work, off the record. It seems anything is possible if the right inducements are offered.

So, over the course of several months and a few clandestine weekends, I was transformed. It was painful and slow, and all the time I kept Howie away from me with promises I was his as soon as the work was over. Throughout it all I stayed in Marcus's room. Surrounded by his stuff. His clothes, with his smell on them. This kept me going through the more painful days. Obviously, I was eating now, but I took charge of that. I think he was convinced by this point I wouldn't flee. And he was right. I was seeing this through.

I had tunnel vision by this stage, just concentrating on my goal to become the woman your father would love. So I went along with the new identity Howie found me. I didn't ask who this Julie Christie was, or how he had all her details, I just became the woman, for the sake of seeing the process through. I couldn't be Ellie Nelson any more, after this, I had to be someone new. Someone Marcus would go for. Of course, there would be the risk he would recognise me anyway, but he never did. He really hadn't studied my face in any detail. Then there was the booze. He wouldn't have had the sharpest focus.

By the time the transformation was complete, I had to get away. Howie's parents were starting to question his expenditure, and one day, when he was engaged in a heated phone conversation with them, I quickly packed up a bag I found with the few clothes I had persuaded him to buy me, ones which accen-

tuated my new figure, gathered up Julie Christie's paperwork, grabbed a handful of notes from a stash he kept for paying his drug dealer, and slipped out. Howie had stopped locking the mortise by this time.

Then I was on my own, a new woman, on a mission to find and win your father. And the best way to do that, I decided, was to become the sort of person he usually seemed to go for, from my observations – an actress. I'd certainly honed my craft in that flat. The new look made this remarkably easy to achieve.

I can see this may paint an unattractive picture of your mother. I suppose I was always single-minded. But your father and I were very happy, and we made you, the most beautiful little child in the world. It all seemed worth it.

Living with the guilt of this deception hasn't been easy, believe me. I would dearly have loved not to be constantly living a lie, but there was just too much to lose.

Now, unfortunately, I'm starting to pay the price. The pain is unbearable at times. Some sort of neuralgia in my face. The boobs are aching. And I can't go to a doctor with it. None of this is on my medical record. On Julie Christie's medical record. I just have to live with it. And take what pain relief I can buy over the counter. This is why I've written you this explanation. I have this foreboding that something will happen to me. Something bad. Maybe that the pain will get so great, I won't be able to take it any more.

I hope you can see in this account a woman you can still love. I will never stop loving you. And if your Dad is still around, let him know I never stopped loving him either. He was the man of my dreams, flawed though he was, and I never regretted making him mine.

May you have a wonderful life, with a wonderful partner, and, if I left you early, never feel undermined I wasn't there. I'll have been sending you my love all along, wherever I am.

Bye bye, darling.

Mum xxxxxxxxxxxxxxxxxxxxxxxxxxx

The trio on the settee were in pieces, even Kai, and held on to each other.

37

Marcus took it upon himself to let Inspector Hutchinson see Ellie's letter, and he, in turn, determined to see if there was any possibility of bringing charges against Howard Poot. Maybe he would get someone banged up after all, even if it was just in a more secure hospital.

When all the forensics were back, confirming time of death, DNA, et cetera, among them was a fragmented account, deciphered from indentations on the cover of the notebook on which Ellie had been resting her notepaper, that confirmed she was attempting to reconnect with her parents, in the hope they would forgive her. While nothing was going to remove the hurt Edward and Cynthia were feeling that she had thought it better to let them believe her to be dead, than come clean with them and risk losing her man, they did draw some comfort that she had finally come back to them. Even if she had decided to write the note first, rather than just coming to their door, and so lose her life so tragically. But there was comfort for Edward too that she had chosen to be in the garage. It was their shared happy place, and he presumed she was glad to be there.

There was also, of course, the consolation that was Imogen, the granddaughter they would come to adore over the final years of their lives, who, in turn, produced great-grandchildren with her new husband, Kai, the first couple of whom they lived long enough to meet.

After the long, lonely childhood Imogen had endured, she was finally getting her rewards for never resorting to the self-pity to which she might have felt entitled. Among these was the whopping inheritance she had received from her maternal grandparents, while they were still alive, as they had the proceeds of their house sale sitting in the bank, which they were never going to need, save for the capped sum required for their care. The rest all went to Imogen, and she and Kai were able to get their own place to start their married life together.

The McKenzies too became a regular part of Imogen's life, and when first Kitty, with Seymour at her side, then Seymour himself, with the whole family at his bedside, passed on, all the rest of the family stayed very close.

As for Marcus, all alone now, even for him life suddenly got better. Once the press had got hold of the story, and his face had been seen on every screen and tabloid front page in the country once more, he received a phone call from his agent. An agent he assumed dead, and certainly not one he thought was still representing him, given that he had heard nothing from her in years. She'd had a call from the Rattigan Theatre. Was he interested in giving his Abanazar this Christmas?

And so he tentatively resumed his acting career, discovering how very much more enjoyable it was to perform without the booze sloshing around. And given that Ellie hadn't overestimated his gifts – within his battered body still lurked a formidable talent – the offers kept coming, albeit no longer for hunks and lovers.

As for Ellie, she lived on in her daughter's drive and determination, as she worked her way up in her chosen profession, becoming both expert and innovator in old age medicine, with a particular focus on Alzheimer's. And though she didn't live to see the woman she had created with the man she had fought so hard to win, Imogen had forgiven her, and occasionally put the chain with the crab clasp, which her father had one day handed to her, around her waist, and felt it like her mother's embrace.

Printed in Great Britain
by Amazon